HOPE

Also by Linda Calvey

FICTION

The Locksmith
The Game
Faith

NON-FICTION

The Black Widow
Life Inside

HOPE

Linda Calvey

МЛ Р

Copyright © Linda Calvey 2025

The right of Linda Calvey to be identified as the Author of the Work has been asserted by her in accordance with the Copyright, Designs and Patents Act 1988.

First published in 2025 by Mountain Leopard Press
An imprint of Headline Publishing Group Limited

1

Apart from any use permitted under UK copyright law, this publication may only be reproduced, stored, or transmitted, in any form, or by any means, with prior permission in writing of the publishers or, in the case of reprographic production, in accordance with the terms of licences issued by the Copyright Licensing Agency.

All characters in this publication are fictitious and any resemblance to real persons, living or dead, is purely coincidental.

Cataloguing in Publication Data is available from the British Library

Hardback ISBN 978 1 8027 9506 6
eBook ISBN 978 1 8027 9508 0

Typeset in 13/19pt Adobe Caslon Pro by Six Red Marbles UK, Thetford, Norfolk

Printed and bound in Great Britain by Clays Ltd, Elcograf S.p.A.

Headline's policy is to use papers that are natural, renewable and recyclable products and made from wood grown in well-managed forests and other controlled sources. The logging and manufacturing processes are expected to conform to the environmental regulations of the country of origin.

Headline Publishing Group Limited
An Hachette UK Company
Carmelite House
50 Victoria Embankment
London EC4Y 0DZ

The authorised representative in the EEA is Hachette Ireland, 8 Castlecourt Centre, Dublin 15, D15 XTP3, Ireland (email: info@hbgi.ie)

www.headline.co.uk
www.hachette.co.uk

To all my friends who stood by me in the darkest of times, especially Sue and Laura, Tracy Mackness, Mo, Julian Hardy, and last but not least, Ash.

I love you all. True friendship is a gift worth more than gold xx

PROLOGUE
1994

'Will the foreman of the jury please stand?' asked the clerk of the court, presiding over a criminal case in one of London's busy crown court rooms.

The jury of twelve hadn't been deliberating for very long, and now they seemed reluctant to catch anybody's eye. This might not bode well for the defendant.

A frisson of tension swept through the high-ceilinged courtroom, and there was a collective intake of breath and a brief shuffle of behinds on the wooden benches from almost everyone present.

Sisters Faith, the oldest, and Charity, the youngest of the three Wills sisters, glanced nervously at each other, and then at their mother, Maria, who was sitting between them.

Maria's face – aside from the livid scar with plum-coloured, puckered skin on one side – was otherwise pale and tense, with a vein clearly fluttering above her eye nearest to Charity. Maria gripped the wooden balustrade before them all, perched high up in the public gallery, her knuckles showing white, and Charity heard the click of her mother's swallow as she laid a hand on Maria's thigh in comfort.

Faith looked then at the judge, a man with an unappealing jowly face, the tiniest wetly-purple mouth she thought she had ever seen, and what could only be described as a victorious glint in piggy eyes that glistened beneath the white horsehair of his full-bottomed wig. There was a red sash over his violet outer robe with its lilac facings.

Faith knew the sash was called a tippet and the fact it was scarlet indicated he was presiding over a criminal trial. But then she felt bad for thinking about this rather than what the jury's foreman was about to say, which either way would be life-changing. She realised she hadn't even heard the charge being read out to the jury by the clerk, a charge to which her sister Hope had pleaded not guilty.

'Guilty,' declared the foreman in a downbeat, deliberately serious voice, and Maria gave the tiniest squeak as she snatched a hand to her mouth.

The family knew they must keep quiet, otherwise the judge would insist they be escorted from the courtroom. He had explained this to them early on in the proceedings, in an extremely patronising way, which had rankled considering how well the Wills family knew their way around a courtroom.

Hope

Hope, the accused, and the middle Wills sister, stood defiantly in the dock, keeping her head high, eyes straight ahead and her expression deadpan. She was so still it was almost scary.

Her hair shone gunmetal black in its sharply angular bob that contrasted so vividly with her pale skin and blood-dark lipstick. She wore a tight-fitting suit. The jacket, with its bulky and extravagant shoulder pads and nipped-in waist above a flared peplum, accentuated the painfully snug fit of the pencil skirt. It was a striking look, even if the skirt was so tight it meant Hope had to go sideways to get either up or down any steps. Although Faith couldn't see her sister's shoes, she knew Hope would be wearing the highest and sharpest stilettos possible, most likely in a shiny patent, making her feet look minute.

Still, the raised dock looked very large and ominous for just Hope, even proud and erect as she was standing. Two prison officers were either side of her, but standing back in each far corner of the dock and looking more alert now than at any time previously in the proceedings. If Hope was going to kick off, now would be the time; this they knew from experience.

Hope's barrister was on the courtroom floor far below her, closer to the judge, who was also raised aloft on his own dais, the barrister readjusting his black robe with a flounce as he tried and mostly failed to give an impression of confidence that he could argue his client's sentence downwards, while the frown beneath the judge's wig above him promised precisely the opposite.

Maria, Faith and Charity tried to send Hope messages of love and support with imploring eyes, but Hope continued to stare at the judge through narrowed and unblinking lashes, her eyebrows a straight line beneath her blunt fringe.

'You may sit,' the judge told her, and Hope made sure that she took her time lowering herself onto the seat, her stony expression unfaltering as she made the whole court wait for her to be ready to hear what the judge had to say.

The judge seemed unnerved by Hope's unbowed demeanour, if the small wobble to his voice was anything to go by. After he cleared his throat he then announced, 'I will hear mitigating circumstances from counsel, and I believe reports are ready for me today.'

He turned then to the side of the court, and said, 'You, the jury, are excused – thank you. The case before you was full of shocking behaviour for you to examine, and I am sorry about that, but I am glad you followed my guidance and interpretation of the law that it was an open-and-shut case.'

The Wills family exchanged pained glances. In their opinion the judge's summing up and instruction to the jury had been biased against Hope and most unfair, and they were convinced he had stretched the letter of the law shamefully in the prosecution's favour. Innocent until proven guilty hadn't seemed to enter his thoughts.

After the jury had been escorted out of court through their own side door, Hope's barrister did what he could in outlining various points of mitigation, but the judge's expression made it clear to all that he wasn't going to be deterred from his initial thoughts, with the expectation clear that sentencing was going to be hefty.

But before he got to this, the reports from social services and a psychological evaluation that had been prepared prior to trial were handed to the judge. He read them meticulously, and painfully slowly.

'Stand up,' he demanded at last, pulling his tortoiseshell reading spectacles from his large nose as Hope and her barrister got once more to their feet. Hope's unblinking gaze had never wavered from the judge since she had sat down.

'You have been found guilty by a jury taken from your peers of one of the most heinous crimes, that of . . .' he paused dramatically '. . . conspiracy. To. Murder,' the judge told Hope, emphasising the word 'murder'.

Most pantomime dames would have baulked at the judge's weighting of his words in this way, thought more than one person watching the proceedings.

Hope made very sure she responded to the judge with

as bored an expression as she could muster, and she jutted out a hip as she adjusted her weight on her needle-sharp heels.

The judge paused and reordered the papers before him, and then he declared, 'And as a result of your actions that have now been proven in this court, a person lost their life. That is a tragedy, a matter of the utmost seriousness.

'Therefore, as a lesson to others that they should under no circumstances behave as you have, I have no choice but to sentence you to a prison term of eight years, with the recommendation that you serve the full sentence.

'I would remind you that in the case of poor behaviour in prison by yourself in any criminal sense, it is possible you could be brought back to court on subsequent charges and your sentence further extended. So it is to your advantage to accept with good grace this lengthy prison sentence and to tell yourself you will keep to yourself and demonstrate exemplary behaviour while you are inside. And I recommend that you should spend your time considering your poor conduct and deeds, and the bad choices you have made in life. You have not been the sort of person who right-minded members—' Hope allowed a small, sly smile to lift one side of her mouth at the judge's use of the word 'members', his rapid double-blink in answer, showing that he regretted this unintended double entendre '—of society want around them.'

Hope

Maria and her two daughters in the public seats thought they heard Hope exhale a snort of defiance. Certainly, she didn't look the least ashamed or embarrassed over the judge's deliberate attempt to shame her so publicly. That wasn't to say that Hope didn't think murder was a serious business, as after what had happened to her grandmother, she knew this wasn't the case. It was more that Hope thought the case brought against her was ridiculous.

'Take her down,' the judge snapped.

And as Hope was escorted down the steps to the underground holding cells, she held the judge's eye until the very last moment as he frowned threateningly back at her.

As the taut tension in the courtroom relaxed once Hope was out of sight, the clerk said, 'Court rise,' and then everyone got to their feet. The self-important judge huffed as, laboriously, he rose upright and then bowed in the direction of the barristers, before he left through a door in the wall behind his grand seat that looked a bit like a throne.

As people began to make their way out of the courtroom, Lisa, Maria's good friend, leaned around Charity and said what they were all thinking. 'Appeal!' Lisa's own family was so close in all senses to the Wills family these days, as they had split a huge house in Cadogan Terrace in Hackney into flats, and they were all now heavily intertwined with one another.

And then Big Danny, Lisa's husband and something of a gangland kingpin in east London, poked his head forward from where he stood on the far side of Lisa, dwarfing everyone by his bulk, as he added, 'Credit where credit's due. Our Hope acquitted herself well through that, not a chink in her armour. She's got some nerve, Maria, and she does you and the rest of us proud. She can hold her head up high.'

With an exhausted sigh, Maria gave a small nod.

Big Danny was right, she supposed. But Hope should never have been convicted. Hope wasn't an angel, but then the rest of them weren't either, except maybe Faith. In any case, none of them deserved to be linked to murder.

Not if they hadn't pulled the trigger, or plunged in the knife.

Murder was a despicable crime, Maria whole-heartedly believed, still raw after what had happened close to the arches on the Isle of Dogs.

But murder should never be weaponised against an innocent party.

And none of the Wills party believed for a moment – not a single instant even – that Hope had had anything to do with what she had just been sent to prison for.

It was all so wrong.

Very, very wrong indeed.

CHAPTER ONE
One year and a bit earlier . . .

Annie Wills' funeral wasn't going to be forgotten easily by anyone who was there. It was the first funeral Faith, Hope and Charity – and Maria too – had been to, and the horse-drawn hearse, with the black feathered plumes aquiver at each horse's poll, had sent the girls' grandmother off in style, with many people standing with their heads bowed on the Stepney streets as the funeral procession passed by.

To nobody's surprise, Maria went through it all in something of a daze.

But then she had held her mother's body as Annie's lifeblood pulsed to the fading beat of her heart onto Maria's lap and then sluiced into the gutter in a seedy street close to the arches on the Isle of Dogs. The stab wound Maria's punter had made with the knife when her mother Annie tried to protect Maria from his vicious assault looked so disconcertingly small.

But Maria had understood immediately that Annie was dying as her blood felt thick and warm – too thick and too warm for any inconsequential injury – as it saturated Maria's skirt and stickily dripped over her legs to the dusty tarmac.

Faith, Hope and Charity knew how traumatised their mother was, as for days Maria had barely been able to eat or drink, and then she had howled uncontrollably when Joyce – Maria and Annie's saviour when they'd fled Wakefield for London in the Swinging Sixties all those years earlier – quickly became terminally ill after Annie's death, having hid her lung cancer for as long as she could. But Joyce running to help had damaged her fragile lungs beyond repair, and so Maria's attacker had in effect killed two women in their sixties that same day, as Joyce was laid to rest a fortnight after Annie's death.

But it was at Annie's funeral, that a distinguished grey-haired man in an expensive suit stood solemnly to one side of the church. He didn't seem to know anyone there. Other than Maria, Faith noticed.

Seeing their mother allow him to stand close by and talk quietly into her ear, with his hand laid on her back in comfort, and Maria not seeming tense or standoffish as she always was with any man who seemed to be taking liberties felt, in Faith's opinion, extraordinary.

Of course, Maria knew thousands of men from over twenty-five years of streetwalking life, but she always took care they understood at all times that the deal was they remained punters and she was simply a prostitute who temporarily serviced their sexual needs, and nothing more or less than that on either side. Indeed Maria was known in the sex worker community for always making it crystal clear that a few minutes of vanilla sex was as far as it was ever going to go, and never once deviating from that. Her daughters had always found this firm stance somehow reassuring.

The Wills sisters glanced at each other in puzzlement when the grey-haired man's words seemed to comfort Maria, and after a few moments, she seemed relatively eager to speak with him.

Faith, especially, couldn't stop watching, and when Maria said something to him that made him look penetratingly towards Faith, she felt her heart bump in some sort of recognition, although she couldn't have explained quite why this was.

After the funeral, as they waited back at their house in Senrab Street for Annie's wake to begin, Faith stared at herself in the mirror above the living-room fireplace. And then she realised deep within her, perhaps as far inside as her bones, something she was absolutely sure of.

It was that this grey-haired man – who had a strong sense of authority about him – and she were connected in a way that didn't apply to Hope and Charity. The longer

Faith gazed at her reflection, the more she could see the face of this man looking back at her.

Maria saw what Faith was doing, and the answering expression in her mother's eyes as the first guests arrived at the wake told Faith her instincts were correct. If this man wasn't her father, he must be her grandfather, and then Maria confirmed he was indeed Faith's grandfather.

A slew of questions ambushed Faith, but the worn-out expression on her mother's face made Faith bite them back. And she heard herself say to Maria that for now Annie's wake was paramount, and they owed it to Granny to give her a good send-off. Maria's grateful smile in answer stayed in Faith's mind for a very long time.

For none of Maria's daughters knew who their fathers were.

Faith had worked out a long time ago that her own father was something to do with when Annie and Maria lived in Wakefield. Faith knew too that Wakefield was where Maria had received her dreadful injuries to her face in an attack so severe it was a miracle she hadn't been blinded.

But it had never quite added up – Maria would have been sixteen when she birthed Faith, and Faith knew that Annie, although a sex worker herself, would never have countenanced Maria selling her body at such a tender age.

Hope

Annie had mentioned on a couple of occasions that she and Maria had had to run away from Wakefield, and if a kindly doctor hadn't given them forty pounds on the night Maria's face was slashed, they would have arrived in London with nothing other than the clothes they stood up in. Joyce had taken them in and, with the help of her church and the kindly Father O'Reilly, had guided them to a new life. Both Annie and Maria had claimed that their biggest bit of luck was being housed by the council right next door to Lisa and Big Danny, Big Danny letting it be known that the Wills family was under his protection now. And nobody messed with Big Danny.

Growing up, the three girls hardly noticed the still-jagged, dark and obscene scars that puckered the whole of one side of Maria's face and made her eye grotesque as it watered constantly below a gnarly scar that puckered her eyebrow wildly.

At secondary school things altered. It wasn't easy being the girls with a mother so badly disfigured facially that she was known far and wide in the local community, to the point that people occasionally shouted at Maria in the street, or made fun of her as she walked by.

But as time passed and Maria got used to how she looked, although she never stopped hating each whorl and flare of her scars, she began to make sure to hold her head up high and never look away when anyone stared rudely.

The days of her hiding or downplaying her injuries slowly became a thing of the past. And as for earning a living as a whore, shame on anybody who looked down on her, her square shoulders screamed silently. Indeed, it was never far from anybody's thoughts that the chances were the husbands of those snooty women who thought her no good were probably regular buyers of Maria's time.

And gradually the three girls learned not to feel ashamed of their mother, nor how she earned a living as a streetwalker serving grubby, needy men.

The reality was that Maria's scars proved popular with a very particular sort of man, she was disgusted to find, but she learned to tune out their groans of excitement as they ran their rancid fingers or rough tongues over the bulbous scar tissue on her cheek, always dampened by a salty tear from her injured eye as they pounded away.

Street prostitutes had a long history of enduring immense dangers, unprotected by the police and the authorities, let alone the criminal underclass on the streets in which they plied their trade, and so Annie and Maria tried to look out for and protect each other as best they could.

Their luck had finally run out, that balmy summer afternoon a client of Maria's viciously stabbed Annie to

Hope

death when she tried to pull him away from hurting Maria.

Faith, Hope and Charity were horrified at what had happened.

But none of them had been surprised.

In fact they'd always half expected this outcome. They'd never known if it would be their granny or their mother who'd pay the price of being in the wrong place at the wrong time with the wrong man.

Still, before Maria and Faith could have the discussion Faith longed for about her birth father, first Charity and then Hope threw spanners in the works that immediately diverted everybody's attention.

And nobody had been expecting either of those crises.

But that was sisters, wasn't it? Always ready to surprise and grab the spotlight for themselves.

CHAPTER TWO

It was as they sat round the lavish dining table at Christmas six months after Annie's funeral when Charity broke down, nearby Christmas tree lights giving her tears a jewelled quality that would have made them pretty, had Charity clearly not been so obviously desperately sad and upset.

But their Christmas Day had started out so differently.

Now that his business interests (although the Wills family liked to joke about his empire) – 'many fingers in many pies', was how Big Danny liked to describe the ways he made his money, or 'a bit of this, a bit of that, anything as long as it's under the table' – were doing well and he had a bit of cash to flash, Big Danny had insisted he was treating them all to a fancy Christmas lunch.

Gone these days were Big Danny's old, obvious gang affiliations, as he was focused on seeming as legitimate as possible. But he wasn't above calling in the odd favour or two if he felt like it, and so he'd had a quiet word with a limousine firm who owed him for something illicit he'd done to help them out. The result was two matching white limos turned up to the new large house they all shared in Cadogan Terrace in east London's Hackney at noon, ready to ferry everyone in style to a posh private members club out in the countryside up Epping Forest way, with the promise of champers on tap and so much festive food they'd all be in comas afterwards. This was a public sign to the local community that Big Danny had the prestige to ask, and be given, cars from a rival firm; he thought it prudent to send out, just now and again, the message that respect was still due to him.

For the irony was that Big Danny had his own limo firm that was more upmarket than the Christmas Day limos, and much more upmarket than his large fleet of Transits constantly driving to Dover for the ferry to France, where ridiculous amounts of alcohol and cigarettes would be bought for knock-down prices, and quickly passed on to corner shops across the south-east of England. Back at the fag-end of the 1970s, Big Danny had laundered some money for a gang and had gone half-shares in buying a sizeable amount of some derelict land on the Isle of Dogs, purely as he needed somewhere to park the Transits; nobody had seen coming the explosion of land prices when the City firms began relocating there in the 1980s, and Big Danny had had the sense to buy his partners out the moment he could. He was now realising that all his shady business

Hope

interests aside, he was sitting on a gold mine because of the sky-rocketing value of the real estate he owned.

The three Wills sisters, all young women now, had been told to dress ready for a party for their Christmas lunch. They hadn't needed asking twice.

Maria admired them in their finery, and she wished Annie were still alive to share their normal joke about how the trio's glad rags seemed always to be an oddly exaggerated extension of their personalities. Faith, Hope and Charity might be as close emotionally as sisters could be, but they were all very, very different from one another personality-wise, and their clothes, make-up and hair made sure that this was evident for all to see.

Earlier that morning, Faith walked over from her own flat to get ready with her sisters, with her clothes, make-up and presents all primly stowed in a neat carry-on travel case that had two wheels and an extending handle so that it could be easily wheeled around. The rest of the family had heard Faith coming down the street well before they saw her as the small wheels of the case bumped noisily over the concrete slabs in the pavement.

This didn't stop both Hope and Charity eyeing the case with envy – it was quite a new type of luggage they'd not seen up close before, and as they investigated its internal fixings, they could see how useful it was.

Hope turned to Charity and said, 'Up west tomorrow?'

She didn't need to say that the Boxing Day sales on Oxford Street would be perfect for buying their own wheeled cabin luggage.

'You bet,' Charity replied.

'Oof. If only I'd have known, that would have sorted your Christmas presents with a lot less strife,' muttered Faith, thinking she needn't have invested quite so much time in carefully choosing perfumes she thought her sisters would like (Thierry Mugler's Angel for Hope, and Eternity by Calvin Klein for Charity), as well as the two Hermès silk scarves she had picked out just as carefully for each sister.

Faith had decided scent and a scarf wouldn't be right for her mother, and so for Maria she had found a beautiful luxe cashmere sweater in Maria's favourite colour, although she was betting already that after her mother admired it when they came to open their presents, she'd say that she was going to keep it 'for best' and consequently there was a high chance the sweater would never again see the light of day. But that wasn't really the point of the gift; all Faith wanted was to let Maria know that she was very loved.

The twins laughed at Faith's frustrated expression over the time spent on their presents. Both loved the bustling crowds all eager to take advantage of the sales at this time of year, although of course Charity preferred not to pay for hers.

In fact, Charity, now nearly twenty-seven, had never

had any sort of proper job, as she had got married when just seventeen to Lisa and Big Danny's only child, Little Danny, who had always treated her like a princess who shouldn't need to go out to work. But Charity had craved a bit of excitement, and so her mother-in-law Lisa carefully tutored her in the art of shoplifting and selling on the goods.

Back when Little Danny was a nipper and Big Danny had stints in prison, Lisa kept the family afloat with her hoisting skills. And although there had been close calls over the years, Charity had only ever had the one appearance in court, despite her many years of shoplifting at Lisa's side from high-end West End stores.

Charity frowned then as she studied Faith's case carefully, realising that no matter how she squared it, a piece of luggage that size was always going to be too big and too obvious for her to be able to lift.

Hope realised exactly what her twin was thinking and she elbowed Faith a bit too hard in the ribs as she announced in Charity's direction, 'Newsflash – Charity has to pay for something, shocker. Women and police officers faint in London street. And ninety-nine store detectives given the day off.'

'Newsflash,' replied Charity demurely, and without missing a beat slapped back by referring to Hope's own livelihood, which was working as a dominatrix in a

Stepney establishment, 'East London men expecting slap, tickle and Boxing Day bondage face severe shortage. Run on banks expected as they know they'll have to pay double when Scarlet is back cracking the whip in the new year.' Scarlet was the name that Hope worked under.

The twins raised their glasses of Buck's Fizz to each other with a grin – they always knew how to make the other laugh, especially when they poked fun at how each other spent their time.

Faith sighed loudly to make a point, and then said, 'I see Father Christmas didn't bring either of you any maturity.' Faith was only two years older than her sisters, but she'd always acted as if they were decades younger than she.

Of course this only made the twins' determination to keep thinking of newsflashes about each other all the more necessary as far as they were concerned, and the newsflashes quickly got very raucous.

By the time Faith had taken her wrapped presents through to the living room to put under the tree to be opened when they got back from lunch, and then returned to her case and pulled out a dress that she arranged with great care on a hanger she then placed on the outside top of the wardrobe door, before leaning down to retrieve a neat pair of court shoes, the twins found themselves almost crying with laughter.

Hope

'What?' There was no mistaking that Faith was getting grumpy.

Hope hiccupped and then answered, 'Don't you see it, Faith? That is a very smart dress. If you were forty-five and a member of the WI, that is. Even Mummy would think it too old for herself. And if she were still with us, Granny would have rejected those hideous shoes as way too frumpy for *her*. Honestly, Faith, you need to act your age, rather than as someone fifteen or twenty years older—'

'Shut it, Hope,' said Faith, the East End accent she'd tried so hard over the years to smooth away popping unbidden to the fore. 'At least I'm not still stuck in my goth listening-to-Sisters-of-Mercy phase.'

Hope glanced down at her black drainpipe jeans and battered suede pixie boots that she'd had for years (the scruffier and more faded they were, the more she loved them). She was wearing a baggy T-shirt she had got years ago at a Sisters of Mercy concert that advertised their upcoming tour. She liked the T-shirt very much, and so right in front of Faith she smoothed it back down over her hips, just to be irritating, and said, 'You'd be a lot happier if you listened to the goth in you.'

And sure enough, Faith rolled her eyes, exactly as Hope knew she would. Those months of working as a dom had done wonders for her being able to read and manipulate people, usually without them ever realising.

She and Faith both turned towards Charity who was now virtually suffocating them all with an obscene amount of hairspray and then backcombing and fluffing out her steaked blonde hair, a routine she was now doing on repeat.

'No outing without Day-Glo,' said Hope conspiratorially to Faith, with a toss of her head in the direction of Charity's back, who had gone large on neon accents for her outfit, with nuclear-lime shoes, clunky bangles and big earrings chosen to contrast with a tight and shiny turquoise dress that showed off her deep tan and washboard-flat stomach. Charity and Little Danny spent every moment they could at Big Danny's timeshare on the Costa del Sol.

Even Faith had to laugh, and Charity turned to blow her a kiss from her shocking-pink glossed lips and then lifted up the can of hairspray again, this time in a way that showed she really meant business.

'Better not get too close to any candles, Charity,' advised Faith.

'See, I knew you wanted to embrace the darkness, Faith,' said Hope. And this time all three sisters laughed.

And so the three young women finished getting ready, before they glugged the dregs of their Buck's Fizz and went to show off their glad rags to Maria, who thought they all looked remarkably similar to how they had when Charity had got engaged to Little Danny at age sixteen,

Hope

a whole decade earlier, back when the 1980s was embracing New Romantics and big hair and synthesisers.

As a family, thought Maria, they might all talk a little posher now they were older and living in the large and actually spectacularly grand house in Cadogan Terrace, overlooking Victoria Park in Hackney, which had been divided into homes for Big Danny's family and for Maria's, with everyone now happily living adjacent to one another under the same roof, other than Faith who had taken out a mortgage on a flat within walking distance.

But they had all remained true to themselves, thought Maria, despite the hard balls life had thrown at them. And this made Maria feel good. It had been tough along the way for them all, but they were survivors and, best of all, they all believed still that 'family' was key to a happy life.

It wasn't long before Big Danny was guiding Maria into the back seat of one of the limos, and then doing the same for Lisa, who wriggled across the leather to the middle seat beside Maria.

Secretly, Maria was dreading the lunch. Even though she had been reluctantly persuaded a few weeks back to go to Knightsbridge with Lisa to choose a dress, shoes and a handbag, all legally paid for – Maria had been very firm about that – and Lisa had even insisted on treating her to an eye-wateringly expensive coat, since Annie's murder, Maria had gone back to hating being out in public, especially in a location she didn't know well nor feel comfortable in.

It was horrible having the sort of face everyone stared at; since she was a teenager, she had never had a single day when somebody hadn't done this. And if there was one thing Maria longed for, it was anonymity and to sink into the background in a way that nobody would ever notice her.

But Lisa and Big Danny obviously wanted to make a fuss and push the boat out this first Christmas without Annie and Joyce, and as the girls had seemed keen as well on the idea of a bumper outing, Maria hadn't had the heart when it came down to it to stand in the way of the planned festivities.

Big Danny made sure Little Danny was escorting the three girls in the other limo with old-fashioned good manners, before he clambered into the first vehicle and sat beside Lisa. 'Our twenty-ninth Christmas, girl. Not too shabby, eh?' he said in his wife's direction.

Lisa smiled and then nodded. 'We'll have to push the boat out for our thirtieth.'

'Sure thing, Leese. Whatever you want, princess. It'll be Little Danny and Charity's ten-year anniversary too. What is—'

'Tin,' Lisa interrupted.

'Ah,' said Big Danny.

Maria gave a quick smile over how attuned to each

Hope

other they were, which neither Lisa nor Big Danny noticed as they were too busy staring at each other.

As their driver braked for a corner, Maria turned to gaze out of the limo's window as it made its way through the grey streets of London that were almost empty of cars this one day of the year, as so many people were concentrating on spending holiday time with their families inside their homes. There would be a surfeit of potatoes roasting, and mountains of veg being prepared in the houses they drove past.

Maria thought to herself that she couldn't imagine what it would be like to be as close to somebody as Lisa and Big Danny had been for very nearly three decades now. They clearly had the sort of marriage she could only wonder about.

For a moment she felt a pang so vicious it hurt almost as much as a real-life punch would have, right below her ribcage, and Maria breathed sharply in and then had to hurriedly blink away some threatening tears. She'd known she might feel a bit wobbly without her mother by her side this first Christmas but, having already visited the church first thing to light a candle for Annie, and one for Joyce, now she was determined not to quell the party mood and so she told herself to get a grip. Being mournful about not having her own relationship when this was something she'd never wanted really was a bit daft, no?

Then, as the limo picked up speed as it had reached a bigger thoroughfare, Maria realised there had once been a time when she had assumed that was her due. It was way back when she was a teenager, a period she believed she too would find a loving husband and they would go on to form a caring and supportive partnership, and produce a veritable football team of sons who would make every Christmas Day a time of jokes and japes.

Once, Maria had believed that she would cook lovely meals for the family and enjoy ironing everyone's clothes, and that she would also work in a job that made good use of her intelligence. Maria had been a very able pupil, had always been top of her class at school, and it hurt that she had never been allowed to use her brain in any meaningful way.

Although she no longer walked the streets following Annie's death, too many years of punters wanting Maria stupid and incapable of having any opinions had left an indelible scar on her psyche. And her father Gary's treatment of Annie had been a terrible example of marriage, and Maria knew she had very often turned a blind eye; it had been easier, and safer, for her and her mother that way.

But that was before she had had dealings with Fred Walton and, well, after that, the rest was history.

Things had moved so quickly with Fred that, as Maria's drifting thoughts were interrupted when she heard and then felt Big Danny put his arm around his wife's shoulder and affectionately pull her tight to him, that she'd never even had a chance to fall in love or even actually enjoy any particularly positive interactions with men during her life, aside from with Big Danny and Little Danny, and Father O'Reilly. And all of those had been strictly platonic, thank goodness. What she had felt for Fred might at the time have seemed like love, but she knew it never had been.

Funnily enough, she'd never thought of how she had missed out in not having ever been properly in love, Maria realised.

It was because life had taught her very quickly that men could be terrifying. Because of Fred, she'd been forced into prostitution at sixteen, and as soon as that had happened, all of Maria's attentions had subsequently been focused on *not* thinking about men at all if she could help it, never for a second believing that with her face so mutilated anyone could ever find her in the least attractive, or if they did, that there wouldn't be something seriously wrong with them that Maria would be wise to avoid.

And over the years the punters she serviced demonstrated again and again how perverse men could be, being all stiff pricks at the mere sight of her scars, to be followed nearly always by just a few thrusts and then an anguished moan. A proportion of the clients had been nicer to her than others, of course, and in fact several had been rather sweet on her, sometimes bringing her a small gift if they were a regular.

But the truth of it was that Maria always found it hard to think with anything like respect concerning any man who chose to visit a prostitute, especially a whore who showed the world so clearly by the marks on her cheek just how low a man could stoop. And while she had frequently sold her body, she'd never sold her mind.

Still, what Lisa and Big Danny had, and which seemed to Maria's relief to be repeating itself in the next generation, with Charity still as in love with Little Danny, and he with her, as they had been the moment they clapped eyes on each other as toddlers, looked to be very, very special.

As Big Danny had promised, there was lots of champagne, which they enjoyed alongside some small nibbles to get their palates going, sitting on deep leather Chesterfield sofas in a snug in the country club's library, where a large log fire crackled before them in the grate.

And then they were escorted across carpet with a pile so deep that their feet sunk into it, to the dining room and towards a large oval table with an array of crystal glassware, silver cutlery and monogrammed plates that had been set aside just for them.

The centre of the table had large candles and decorations

made from pine evergreens with cones, and brightly berried branches of holly, with silver and white 'snow' dusted lightly over the top of the display; the smell of the pine near the candles was deep and intoxicating.

Charity was the first to sit down, with a waiter gently pushing her chair under her, and then he shook out a heavily starched napkin and placed it on her lap.

But Maria noticed immediately that something was wrong as Charity, who would normally have at least thanked him or, more usually, said something amusing as a waiter spoilt her, kept her eyes down and her mouth resolutely closed without any hint of a smile.

Whatever could be the matter? Maria wondered. For, just a few moments previously in the library, Charity had seemed to be her normal sunny self. And Little Danny and Faith and Hope had been cheerful and relaxed too, and it didn't seem likely therefore that there had been any arguing as they had travelled to the lunch in the other limo. Maria looked around but she couldn't see anything or anyone untoward that merited Charity's glum face.

Then suddenly Charity jumped up, brusquely pushing the waiter out of her way and she went to sit right at the opposite end of the table. Little Danny had just sat down beside Charity's first seat, and he kept his napkin clutched in his hand as he sprang up with a startled look on his face as clearly he hadn't been expecting Charity to do this.

Hope and Maria looked at each other, and Hope frowned in a way that Maria took to mean she didn't know what was going on either with her twin.

Everyone's attention was turned towards Charity, but her expression remained stern and her shoulders set in a way that discouraged discussion, and so they all pretended nothing was untoward. But her good mood of when she and her sisters had been getting ready was dead and buried, as the tears glistening in her eyes seemed to say.

Still, uncertain how to proceed as this was all very aberrant, everyone else took their seats cautiously and then continued to act in a way as if nothing peculiar was going on, just in case the difficult moment could be smoothed out without too much fuss, each one of them manfully stepping in to make sure the conversation never flagged and there were never any awkward pauses. Everyone, that is, other than Charity who sat silently looking at her lap, and later with a paper hat from a Christmas cracker sadly creeping to one side of her head.

But it wasn't until after they'd had their prawn cocktail starter, and finished their roast turkey main course, and were taking a much-needed breather before the flaming Christmas pudding was served, and they'd just raised a glass to absent friends, knowing that Annie and Joyce would be the top of everybody's lists, that a baby in the group on the table next to them let out a wail.

Hope

It was being jiggled in its mother's arms and she was sitting right behind Big Danny, who had taken Charity's first seat, and he gave a start as he hadn't noticed there was a little one quite so close to him.

Big Danny looked around, and when the baby caught sight of his pink-cheeked face, the wine he'd consumed with his meal giving him a rosy glow, its face crumpled as the howls began in earnest.

'Good pair of lungs,' Big Danny joked to the mother.

Lisa said to the baby, who now had puce cheeks and eyes tightly closed as if to holler with full concentration, 'I feel like that when I see his face too,' clearly poking gentle fun at her husband in a way that would show the adjacent table that they were used to babies and a few bellows weren't a big deal, and Big Danny responded with a bark of laughter.

Lisa grinned, and then she looked towards Little Danny, and said, 'You were louder than that when you were a nipper. We used to say we needed ear plugs as you sure let us know if you were hungry or needed a snooze or a new nappy.'

The baby took a deep breath, and then notched up the noise.

'I'm so sorry,' said the mother in the general direction of Big Danny's table as she stood up and one-handedly hastily gathered a few things together before she transferred the baby to her other arm and went to make her way out of the dining room.

'Really, please, sit down, it's no problem, we—' Maria was saying to her, when she was jolted in her chair by Charity pushing past as she hurried out of the dining room, her paper hat softly dancing in her wake as it slipped off.

Maria knew she had heard a sob escape as Charity went by.

She looked towards Little Danny, who was now staring out of the window with his shoulders slumped, appearing very defeated, and apparently determined not to explain what was going on or risk catching anybody's eye.

Nobody else seemed at all sure of what to do, and so Maria said, 'Everybody wait here, and I mean you too, Little Danny. I think it best that I go. Just for a little while. And then you find us if we've not come back quite soon.'

Everyone stayed where they were, but Charity's hasty exit had killed the Christmas mood.

Ten minutes later neither Charity nor Maria had returned.

'Gawd,' said Hope in a frustrated voice. 'And just when I was going to tell you all something I've decided. Typical of Charity to make it all about her. I could strangle her sometimes.'

Hope

'Oh for Christ's sake, shut up, Hope,' snapped Little Danny. 'You don't know what you're talking about.'

And this was so sharp and strange coming from Little Danny that Hope looked towards Faith for reassurance. It was all very peculiar as he was normally the epitome of 'cheeky chappie', always ready with a one-liner or an awful pun.

Faith turned towards Big Danny and Lisa, but their puzzled expressions suggested they had no more idea what was going on than she did.

'What were you going to say, Hope?' asked Big Danny a little wearily after a lengthy pause when everyone fiddled with their napkins, during which Lisa laid a comforting hand on Little Danny's forearm.

'Ach. I hadn't wanted it to come out quite like this,' said Hope, ignoring Faith's look of warning that Hope wasn't to say anything controversial. 'But I suppose it can't hurt now. I just wanted to say that in the new year I've decided to auction my virginity to the highest bidder. It's going to be a great way of generating interest at Chantal's, and it will be good for my pocket too.'

There was a silence that was so shocked the air around them seemed as if it was alive with a crackle of electricity. In an instant the atmosphere at the table felt quite different to when they had all been subdued after Little Danny's blunt retort to Hope.

A waiter who had just arrived with a very small dustpan and brush that he was about to use to get rid of any crumbs on the tablecloth quickly made himself scarce the moment he heard Hope's declaration, his eyes round with surprise.

Faith thought he'd be telling the other waiters within seconds what Hope had said, and for a second she closed her eyes in resignation at this thought.

Naturally they all knew Hope was a BDSM mistress called Scarlet. It was one of those situations nobody approved of. But Hope was and always had been headstrong, and since Hope had joined Chantal's, if they dared mention anything negative, she always replied, 'Those in glass houses shouldn't throw stones, should they?'

And because everyone, other than Faith, made their living doing things the other side of the law, up until now this comeback had been enough to quell further discussion.

Once Faith had risked saying, 'Hope, you don't need to do this, you know. You aced your accountancy exams, and Big Danny's had you doing the upper tier of his books for years, and some of his mates have asked about using you too. There's nothing wrong with being an accountant, you know, and I can't help thinking you are worth more than this in every sense.'

'Spoken like someone who hasn't actually had to tot up

a non-tallying profit and loss account, and prepare books for the Inland Revenue. Talk about practising for being dead . . .' Hope retorted.

'OK, I hear you,' Faith said. 'But to do *this* . . .'

'Oh, fuck off, Faith. Stop being so high and mighty, miss fancy-pants fuckwit lawyer. What's wrong with being Scarlet? I make my clients very happy, and I earn more than you per hour just for making somebody lick my shoes – it's easy work and I'm good at it, although there's much more to it than simply whacking an arse now and then with a paddle. I've told you before that I don't have to do anything actually *with* them, you know. It's not like what Mummy or Granny had to do down those alleys, as my rule is they can't ask anything of me in the physical sense, and I will never touch them, other than to put them in a dog collar or a truss or something like that,' said Hope. 'Anyway, if you can't say anything nice, don't say anything at all.'

Faith had told everyone about this exchange, and since then it had been rare for anyone at the table to comment overtly on Hope's extremely specialist work. She worked out of a house managed by a madam who called herself Chantal, although really Chantal had been born as plain Alice Smith, but the services of 'Chantal's' yielded a much higher price tag than anybody would ever have paid for 'Alice' to perform the very same deeds.

Chantal's was purely a house where men went to be dominated. Penetrative sex didn't come into it.

And any man who made the mistake of suggesting this was quickly disabused of the notion. If he dared to suggest it again, it was a case of 'two strikes and you're out' and he would be unceremoniously escorted off the premises by one of the giant bouncers and immediately barred for life.

Instead, Chantal's was all about pain and subjugation in various ways, the unifying factor being that none of the mistresses ever had to touch their clients in a sexual way, or let the punters do anything to them in the physical sense.

What the mistresses did instead was to humiliate the men before them. And these men came in eagerly for precisely this sort of degrading experience. In fact Chantal's was so busy that Chantal had to have a waiting list for its services.

Hope knew that she was the very best mistress at Chantal's. She'd invested heavily in specialist leather and latex clothing, and a variety of whips and equipment, the horse-wear such as bridles and saddles for the clients proving incredibly popular. Even as a child, she'd always had the knack of standing back a little from what was happening around her, and of the three sisters she was the one who'd always felt the least conflicted about Maria and Annie's line of work.

Hope

As Charity claimed from schooldays, Hope was naturally bossy. The only difference was now that she was bossy while holding a whip.

Hope saw her kink skills a little differently.

Sure, she'd grown up trying to tell her sisters what to do, but really she was a pragmatic person – working at Chantal's suited her perfectly as she got well paid for little physical effort, her special skill lying in her ability of working out precisely what it was that would give each of her clients ultimately the biggest kick. And because she refused to make herself too available for when she would allow clients to see her, this meant that when she did work, she could charge a premium rate that made the other mistresses jealous.

Hope's reasoning was that she'd tried the sensible office routine and it had suffocated her, and she acknowledged that Faith was right as she'd never had any problems passing any sort of exams with distinction. But as she actually found the idea of sex repugnant, and she already had contacts in the sex-work trade, she'd be a mug if she didn't exploit her own unique combination of natural talents. And one had to be smart to keep adding twists to the services she sold, Hope firmly believed. Indeed she was certain that it was her street smarts that had led to her devoted clientele.

She'd chosen her name Scarlet, as when working this

was the colour of her heavily lipsticked mouth. Her eyes were always made up with smoky dark eyeshadow, but few clients ever saw this, as usually she favoured sunglasses so that her clientele couldn't gauge what she thought of them as she slowly buckled some spurs around her heels within inches of their eyes while their cheeks were pressed into the ground. Her glossy black hair was trimmed once a week to make sure the severe lines of her bob with its intense angles and corners would hold and fall back into shape no matter how much she cracked a whip or tightened a gimp harness.

The windows to Chantal's were covered inside so that not a chink of light could escape, and nobody on the street outside could look through them. The rooms were soundproofed, although the basement was reserved for the more extreme demands of selected customers – cages, dog kennels, wooden racks, and so on – just to make doubly sure any passers-by didn't think criminal acts were going on inside because of the cries. There was even a wet room if anybody wanted to experience waterboarding or other explicit forms of torture with water.

The front door looked ordinary from the outside but was really a special security door, as the establishment could have very large amounts of cash on site by the end of the day. All that anyone could see from the outside was a very discreet and small plaque that said 'Chantal's'.

Hope

Chantal never needed to advertise what went on or have a public phone number. Instead customers came from far and wide through personal recommendation only, and if they didn't follow all the exacting rules that Chantal set out for them, that was it – game over, with no chance of redemption. Unsurprisingly, everybody abided by the rules. If there was one thing that governed the kink world, it was rules and boundaries.

Maria refused to talk about what went on at Chantal's, after Hope once went into far too much detail about a man who wanted to soil himself into an adult nappy as a baby would as Hope looked on, and then, still wearing his now heavy and dangerously squishy nappy, Hope gave him a baby's bottle of warm milk that he sipped through an old-fashioned rubber teat, after which she was required to hose him off with a powerful jet of ice-cold water as he screeched when periodically she ran the stream over his testicles.

She had trebled her fees for this, and had taken a working practice tip from a client of hers who was a pathologist, who told her when she asked him about dealing with the bad smells of decaying bodies, 'You have to decide if you want to sniff them, or not – quite often I have to as a part of an autopsy, but I would suggest that you always say no to this as there are some odours that *really* stay with you, for hours sometimes – but beforehand, or else the moment

I can, a good dollop of Vicks pushed up into the nose can work wonders.'

Hope was eternally grateful for this advice.

Another client paid her handsomely to dress up as a dog in a faux-fur suit he'd commissioned, complete with a collar and lead, and to be instructed by Hope to eat – no knife and fork for this – smelly tinned pet food from a brown heavy ceramic bowl with a blue inner lining and a bone emblazoned on the bowl's front, from the floor as Hope teased him by threatening to stand on one of his hands in her sharp stilettos.

If he was very 'good', Hope might be persuaded late at night when she was sure that the local children would be in bed to take him for a 'walk' in Victoria Park while he wore his furry suit, during which Hope would yank periodically on the lead attached to his collar as he gambolled alongside her on all fours, occasionally stopping to lift a leg or sniff a dog turd. If he'd been 'a very, very bad dog' on the walk, Hope would reach for a muzzle, and he always quivered with excitement as she did it up as tight as she could.

He had given her a tip of one hundred pounds on top of her extortionate charges the night she refused to let him stand up and walk home normally on two legs when he complained of aching legs and arms after she made him chase after a tennis ball she lobbed as far as she could into the distance.

Hope

Chantal and Hope had clutched each other with laughter when later they imagined what he had said to whoever it was that he had commissioned the adult-sized doggy suit from.

Maria forced herself to take some small comfort that although Hope had followed Annie and her own path into being a sex worker, the fact that Hope never had to perform any sort of actual sex with any of her punters in the physical sense as, for them, humiliation, pain and degradation were much more satisfying than mere sex. And because of the rules and the bouncers at Chantal's, Maria thought that what Hope was doing was probably safer in the physical sense than even many normal heterosexual romantic relationships out in the real world that were well away from sex work.

But after hearing about what those two men had wanted from Hope, Maria had begged Hope never to tell her about any of her other customers as she found it too upsetting.

Now, for those still sat around the Christmas lunch table at the country club, what Hope had said about auctioning her virginity hardly computed.

They all knew Hope had never had even so much as a kiss from a boy (or a girl, as Maria had occasionally asked herself if this was where Hope's natural inclinations lay, or in fact anyone in between), let alone had Hope experienced any of the sort of amateur fumblings that most teenage girls and young women experience, and so everyone was having difficulty believing Hope had actually said what they thought they had heard. Losing her virginity seemed simply beyond the pale, let alone the fact that the whole point of Chantal's was no intercourse.

And so the shocked silence swirled around the table. As a little choir organised by the country club began to sing carols in the library, the sound softly filtering through, and waiters hovered indecisively nearby as they couldn't tell if they should serve the pudding course with two of the party absent, making what was going on at the dining table seem all the more incongruous, Hope looked challengingly from face to face across the table.

Faith suspected the waiters were lurking close enough to hear, should Hope have any more bombshells to drop.

Hope didn't disappoint.

'Yes, I said exactly what you are doubting I actually said,' she announced, and then added in a deliberate attempt to shock, her voice ringing clear as she milked the tension for all she was worth: 'Someone will pay through the nose to pop my cherry, I just know it. I'm pretty certain it will never actually come to an act of sex as the money probably lies bigger in the imagining of it, rather than the deed. But I'll go along with it all the way, and make up my mind whether to have sex or not when it comes down to it.

Hope

I'll have a small whip with me just in case somebody doesn't want to listen. And Chantal is on board, just this once, as business is always quieter in the new year as everybody will have spent up for Christmas, so we're thinking a virginity auction like this will pull in the pounds.'

A set of serving spoons bounced on the carpet behind them, confirming, yes, the waiters were close enough to listen in.

There was a lot of information, and implications too, packed into what Hope had just said, and those at the table were stunned into silence once more as various imaginings flashed across their minds.

'Blimey, Hope,' exclaimed Faith at last, 'you sure know how to kill a mood. So, whatever Mummy is talking about with Charity right now, it's not going to be anything like this – you're going to rattle the bejesus out of her when she gets wind. What on earth has got into you, Hope? Today is not the day to break this sort of thing. In fact, no day is.'

Hope couldn't resist saying naughtily, 'I thought we needed a Christmas lunch to remember, now that Granny isn't here to keep a lid on things.'

'Poor Granny, right now, is spinning in her grave in horror at what you've just broadcast to all and sundry,' declared Faith, and a couple of the nearby waiters looked a tad shamefaced to have been rumbled.

And Faith's expression was so forbidding that it made

Hope laugh, and one by one the others joined in, even Faith, although Little Danny could only manage a wan smile or two, and then he pushed himself back from the table to stand up, saying he had to go and speak to Charity.

CHAPTER THREE

Maria had followed Charity out through the big double doors to the club, then watched her stop at the bottom of the steps up to the front door as she looked around, before she made her way to a bench towards the side of the building, where she slumped down with her head in her hands. She ignored the dramatic view over the carefully husbanded lawn and the manicured flower beds that had been put to bed for the winter. Everything about the way Charity was sitting telegraphed despair and unhappiness.

Maria allowed her youngest daughter a minute or two to herself, and then Maria slowly headed to the bench where she gingerly perched on the wooden slats, making sure to leave quite a lot of space between them. She didn't want to have Charity unnerved and jumping up and scampering away again.

A waiter headed over unobtrusively, bearing an armful of blankets, a small box of tissues and a glass of water, and Maria nodded a thank you as she took hold of everything and then placed the blanket pile between herself and Charity, before reaching for the top tartan wool rug to wrap around her own shoulders, as it was close to dusk now and the temperature was plummeting, suggesting there would be a sharp frost later that night.

Charity seemed oblivious to everything, and although Maria wanted, as any mother would, to make sure Charity didn't get cold by wrapping the thickest one around her daughter's shoulders, she forced herself not to say or to do anything, telling herself that Charity would take a blanket or two if and when she was ready.

The waiter was now almost all the way back inside, but his face had been so calm and blank when Maria caught his eye that she told herself Big Danny must be paying a heck of a lot for their lunch, to the point just about any behaviour from the guests this afternoon was going to be something the country club's staff had seen and wordlessly dealt with before, and they certainly weren't going to make any unnecessary song and dance about it, or come over unnecessarily dramatic. If she had known what Hope was about to unleash at the lunch table, she might have thought differently.

Even so, it was all such a far cry from everything Maria had been used to in her own past, that it felt disconcerting.

She couldn't quite get over the fact that once she and the girls, and Annie too, had lived next door to Lisa, Big Danny, and Little Danny in a small terraced house in

Hope

Stepney's Senrab Street, a place where drama seemed a built-in part of everyday life.

Yet now Big Danny's business interests had grown to the point that having enough money to splurge on anything he wanted appeared to be no object at all. He seemed very happy that Maria and the girls were part of his good fortune as well, although Maria suspected a lot of that had to do with Little Danny and Charity having got married.

Maria and Charity sat quietly, each deep in their own thoughts.

Then Charity sniffed and wiped her hands over her tear-stained cheeks. 'You don't have a hanky with you, do you?' she mumbled.

'No, but I have these.' Maria passed her daughter the tissues.

After noisily blowing her nose, and then having a drink of water, Charity turned to look at Maria. Her eye make-up, so carefully applied earlier, had run and given her panda eyes, and even the bounce in her hair looked wretched.

'If you're ready to tell me what's wrong, I'm here, Charity,' said Maria. 'I hope you know you can say anything to me. Anything at all. But if you'd rather not confide in me, and keep it between you and Little Danny, then I do understand.'

Charity smoothed a hand across her flat stomach and then slapped herself hard in the belly, so hard in fact that it made Maria wince. 'See that, Mummy. That's the stomach of a woman who can't get pregnant. The womb of a wife who doesn't conceive. And having our baby is the one thing that me and Little Danny long for. We've tried everything. And each month, I think this is it, and every month I'm wrong. Little Danny doesn't know what to say to me any more, and I never thought that would happen between us, and I don't know what to do or what to say to him. And we'll never stay together if we don't have a baby. He'll leave me and have the family he wants with another woman. And I'll have to watch that. When that baby cried just now, I couldn't bear it . . .'

Maria swapped places with the blankets. She arranged one around Charity, and pulled her close, kissing her on the top of her head. Charity was crying once more, scaring her mother with the violence of the sobs.

'That must be very difficult for you both,' said Maria, and she felt Charity nod her head in agreement. Now Maria could understand Charity not wanting to sit near the baby in the dining room. It all made much more sense. The young couple had hidden the problem so well that it hadn't been obvious, and Maria added, 'I didn't know you were trying, dear. But perhaps the most important thing for you and Little Danny is to remember that you are both healthy, and sometimes it can take a little time. You are both only twenty-six, remember.'

Hope

'Well, it didn't take much for you to fall. Or Granny. Did it? And me and Little Danny have been trying for *years*.'

'Charity, my love, please don't ever compare yourself to me or Granny as we were never in control of anything that happened, and neither of us could welcome a child into a safe and caring marriage, although we loved you all. Every day was a struggle and at the back of my mind was always the thought that social services would knock at the door one day and just take you all away. It was horrible and I wouldn't wish it on anyone,' said Maria. 'You have been lucky enough to find a *wonderful* person to be your husband, a man who loves you as much as you love him, and that is what you need to think about. Little Danny is probably as emotional about the situation as you are, and so now you need to love and support each other.'

Charity began to cry again. 'But our love can't survive if it goes on like this. And neither will our marriage . . .'

Maria couldn't think of what to say and so she just pulled Charity close and let her cry herself out.

She'd always assumed that any one of her daughters would be able to have a baby if that was what they wanted, but now it seemed maybe it wasn't going to play out like this.

She saw the white of Little Danny's shirt in the gloam heading across the grass towards them.

Maria kissed Charity again, and said, 'Little Danny's come to find you.'

And as she relinquished her seat for Charity's husband, Maria squeezed his arm as she passed to let him know she understood what was wrong.

Neither Charity nor Little Danny said anything as Maria left, and as she went back inside, she couldn't work out if that was a good thing or not.

CHAPTER FOUR

Two days later Maria was ringing the bell to Father O'Reilly's presbytery early in the morning, hoping that he might be in and have a few minutes to spare for her.

His housekeeper opened the door and then ushered Maria into the reception room that was kept for the father to deal with members of his congregation.

Maria looked around – it was clean and tidy, and a newly lit fire was in the grate behind a three-panel fire screen, but the furniture and carpet were definitely showing more signs of wear than she remembered, and there were no central-heating radiators, so even with the coal fire, it felt chilly. The large table in the middle of the room and the chairs around it bore witness to heavy use.

Clearly, Father O'Reilly wasn't one of those priests who liked to live in comfort while many of his flock struggled to feed themselves at the end of each week. Stepney was one of the more run-down areas of London and it had a lot of social problems, and he and his church were actively involved in the community, with many people visiting the presbytery for a host of reasons each year.

Maria thought back to when she had first been in this room, which had to be getting on for thirty years ago now, the very day after Annie and she arrived in London from Wakefield. Furniture-wise, it looked remarkably similar then and now.

They had spent their first night in the smoke at the home of Annie's friend Joyce. Annie had met her when they were both prostitutes in Wakefield, offering extra services at the men's gambling and drinking club Ted Walton ran. Maria had been a teenager at the time, and Annie had been determined to give her daughter a better start in life than she herself had had. When Joyce left to set up on her own in London, with Ted's blessing as Joyce was a favourite of his and he felt she had earned the right to move on, Joyce made sure to give Annie her address down in the smoke where she'd be living, saying if there was ever anything Joyce could do to help, Annie only had to ask. This was a blessing, as things turned out.

Annie had told Maria that the assumption between them was that there could come a day when Annie's fist-happy husband Gary might do something really daft that would upset the Waltons, and then he'd threaten to turn on Annie in fury, ensuring that Annie had to leave the town where she had grown up. Gary had history of this sort of

Hope

behaviour, and Maria had long known her father to be a confrontational, violent drunk, and she had always gone out of her way at home to avoid him when he was pissed.

Neither of the friends expected Annie would need to take up Joyce's kind offer quite so soon as had happened, or that it wouldn't be Gary who was to blame for their swift exit from the streets of Wakefield, but Ted Walton's son Fred and his vicious fists, and his ring with the nub of a razor blade embedded in it designed to do maximum damage to the soft skin of a face.

On that first morning in London after Annie and Maria had fled on the overnight postal train a sympathetic guard had sneaked them onto, Joyce had been visibly shocked when she opened the door for them and caught sight of Maria's bandaged face, blood pockmarking the white of the dressings, although Joyce had tried hard (and mostly failed) to hide from Maria how bad the injuries were.

In fact, Maria had been in such a severe state of shock at the time that all these years later she could hardly recall anything about her first twenty-four hours in the capital, other than she had found Joyce to be extraordinarily kind.

When Joyce died of lung cancer mere weeks after Annie's death, it had felt very hard as Joyce had, since that very first day, virtually never left their side, and she had come to feel to the whole family as close as any blood relation, a much-loved aunt who spoilt and cared for them all.

But it seemed that without Annie around, a light had been extinguished in Joyce too, and she had quickly faded.

Maria knew Father O'Reilly had taken Joyce's passing just as hard as all the Willses had, as she had been a staunch member of his church who could be relied upon to help out in useful ways at the many community events the church was involved in.

But as she'd fallen asleep that first night, Maria overheard Joyce reassuring Annie that while Joyce would love to keep Annie and Maria staying with her, for the good of the baby Maria was carrying – the baby that was now Faith, a grown woman successful in her legal career – the best thing would be for Joyce to take Annie and Maria over to Father O'Reilly the next morning. The father would know what to do.

And he had.

Father O'Reilly came up with a cover story for the council housing department that he had found Annie and Maria in his church but they had been too traumatised to give him a full account of what had happened to lead to Maria's severe injuries, although he was in no doubt they were an emergency case and that the council needed to take responsibility for them, as they had nowhere to go.

He'd said already to Annie and Maria that they mustn't mention Joyce at all, as if the council thought there was an option that meant the housing services department didn't

Hope

need to step in, the pair would be bumped right to the bottom of the council housing wait list.

When doing good, Father O'Reilly hadn't been averse to white lies, clearly, and this had very much endeared Annie and Maria to him.

And sure enough, with Father O'Reilly insisting to the officials that this mother and daughter didn't have any friends in London or anywhere else they could go, and they were too scared to return to where they had come from (all of which was in fact true), social services noted Maria's pregnancy, the severe facial injuries she'd sustained and her young age.

The result was that they had promptly moved her and Annie into temporary accommodation in a hostel. Their shared room had been grim – *really* grim – but they were determined to stick it out without complaint.

After all, with what they'd been through, how could a few mice and families that shouted at each other at all hours of the night be worse? The best things were to make sure there were no crumbs in their shared room, and that a kitchen chair was firmly wedged under the door handle at all times, and those problems were pretty much solved.

Ultimately, that room in the run-down boarding house proved to be the most welcome stepping stone to them being allocated a council flat a few months later.

The flat itself, although spacious by comparison with

their single hostel room, was far from ideal, as it was on the fifth floor of a run-down old-fashioned red-brick block of flats and there hadn't been a lift. That had proved a real challenge when Maria got pregnant a second time to an unknown punter out on the streets, before she learned how to take care of herself in that way, and it had led to the birth of Hope and Charity.

Lots of stairs and three little ones proved a thorough workout on good days, and a nightmare on bad ones.

But Annie and Maria remained far from complaining. To them the flat, and every single one of the many steps up to its door, felt a palace.

A mistimed visit from a horrified housing officer who'd had to help manhandle the unwieldy pram and heavy bags of groceries up the many staircases had led to them all being rehoused after that in Senrab Street, Father O'Reilly calling in help with the move from some strong men who were over from Ireland and were helping out at the church.

Maria smiled as she remembered how Hope and Charity as toddlers had embraced their new-found feet and how they could run almost as quickly as Faith when the front door to their new home was opened, and all three girls careered without stopping down the hall and through the kitchen and out to the small backyard, their little sandals slapping noisily on the bare wooden floorboards.

In Senrab Street Annie and Maria had a rocky start at

Hope

first, Annie defending her daughter in a furious row with new neighbours Big Danny and Lisa, who'd immediately taken umbrage at the very first sight of them, making everyone very aware that they didn't appreciate having two whores move in next door.

But apologies were quickly made and the argument all but forgotten, and so it had all come good in the end, with that small terraced house growing into a place of happiness and sanctuary as Big Danny made sure they were safe, right up until the day Annie was murdered.

And one of the influential constants through those long years had been Father O'Reilly, with Joyce never far away.

What had especially endeared Father O'Reilly to Maria over the years was that while he was a good Catholic priest, he never once gave the slightest hint that he looked down on her or Annie, or commented negatively about how they supported their children, and nor had he ever tried to push his views on the sanctity of marriage forward in any uncomfortable way.

She and Annie thought of themselves as faithful Catholics, but also as women with very limited choices, and when push came to shove, putting food on the table was always going to trump propriety. They'd known that wives and mothers in the father's congregation would be horrified by the realities of both how they lived and also the way Father O'Reilly steadfastly refused to criticise their whoring. But he never breathed a word and somehow they were able to hold their heads high, making sure to ignore their punters as if they were strangers, any time they ran into them.

Instead the father concentrated on offering practical support and kindness, and on encouraging Annie and Maria to be as safe as possible and look out for each other when they were working. They loved him for this.

None of the good things the Wills family had experienced since those very first days would have happened without Father O'Reilly, Maria believed. Unfailingly, he had been at their side every step of the way, always on hand to offer wise counsel with a smile.

Maria knew she could never find the perfect words to express to him how much she felt in his debt, but she hoped very much that Father O'Reilly understood how important he was to her.

She lived outside his parish now, but she hadn't been able to think of who else to turn to for some sound but unbiased advice, and so she hoped he wouldn't mind her turning up out of the blue like this, arriving like a bad penny, in the belief that he could help her unravel her problems one more time.

The door opened and Father O'Reilly came in, his eyes twinkling and his cassock having the faint whiff, as it

Hope

always did, of a combination of men's cologne and a slight trace of sweat. The father had to be at least seventy now, and maybe even older, but he wore his years well, thought Maria as she smiled a hello.

He clasped both of her hands in his as he said warmly, 'How very good to have you here, Maria. I had been planning on coming around tomorrow to see how you all are and to wish you season's greetings and to thank you for the card and the socks, but you've beaten me to it. The first Christmas after the loss of a loved one is difficult, and I know you will all have been thinking of our Annie. And there was the passing of dear Joyce too. It's been a most difficult year for us all.'

'Thank you, Father,' said Maria. 'Yes, we lit candles for them both first thing on Christmas morning, and at lunch we raised a glass or two in Annie's memory, and Joyce's too. I really wished they could both have been with us as Big Danny treated us to a slap-up lunch on Christmas Day, out near Epping Forest at a grand place he found for us – they would really have enjoyed it, as we were all treated like royalty, and I would have loved seeing my mother being spoilt so, just the once. I still turn to say something to her, you know, and then I remember she's gone. I don't think I'm ever going to get used to her not being here . . .'

Maria's voice had cracked, and so to give her a breather, the father said, 'That is the sign of what a wonderful woman Annie was, you know, Maria. And the girls all OK? I know they're too big now to be called girls, but to me they'll always be those little nippers charging around Senrab Street.'

'Oh, Father . . .'

As the note of torment in Maria's voice showed he'd hit a nerve, Father O'Reilly put his hand up to stop her saying anything else, and he poked his head out of the door to call, 'Shamus! Shamus? Are you near the kitchen?' There was a muffled rumble from somewhere near the back of the presbytery, and then the father answered, 'Ah good, yes, a pot of tea for two would be just the ticket.'

He turned towards Maria and he indicated that she should wait with what she had to say until they had their tea in front of them, and then opening the door again, he added, 'And some of those biscuits Mrs Mortimer made for us too please, Shamus.'

The father turned and sat down at the table and they made small talk for a while.

Then a man roughly Maria's age shuffled in, and she assumed this was Shamus. He had the rumpled and defeated look about him of a man who had lost at the lottery of life, and he made sure to keep his eyes averted, but Maria believed that if anyone could help him, it would be Father O'Reilly. She'd have liked to say this to him, but she didn't think it her place to draw attention to his

Hope

hang-dog demeanour. Shamus added a log to the fire after he'd placed the tea tray on the table, and then he left them to it.

'I'll be mother, and you can tell me what's upsetting you so,' said Father O'Reilly as he reached for the teapot.

Maria sighed. 'I hardly know where to begin, Father. Three days ago, we didn't have Annie with us, but I thought things were starting to look up and we'd weathered the storm. The house we've just moved into works very well for us all as far as I can see, and as we all have our own space it means we're not treading on each other's toes.

'And I had a little something too left over after I sold Joyce's house and put my chunk into the big house, and so I haven't been working, although I must think of something to do. It doesn't suit me to be at home too much, I'm finding, as I'm not used to it and I feel like a spare leg on a donkey. I liked that all the girls seemed content and full of purpose.'

Father O'Reilly grinned when Maria said 'donkey', and immediately nodded to keep her talking.

'And then it all went wrong in just a few minutes at our posh Christmas lunch,' she said.

'An argument?'

'Oh no, nothing like that. Not exactly. But Charity got upset over a baby crying and she fairly ran out, and when I found her breaking her heart on a bench in the cold outside, she told me that she and Little Danny have been trying for ages, but she can't get pregnant. She's terrified the marriage is going to fail, as aside from herself longing for a kiddie, Little Danny is really keen they have one. I tried to say they are young yet, and to give it time, but she wasn't finding that a comfort.

'And the more I think about it, the more I can see that maybe Charity has a point. She'd be a lovely mum, but life doesn't always work like that, does it? And the chances are Little Danny could have a child with somebody else, and if that were to happen if he and Charity remain childless, then who would blame him? I don't think I could, hard as that would be on Charity, and I don't think she would blame him either even though she would hate him a little for it.' Maria drank some tea, and the father snapped a biscuit in half.

She went on, 'Little Danny came to find Charity and I left them to it, but neither of them have looked happy since. You'll have come across this situation quite a lot, I'm sure, so you'll know how it goes. Anyway, then I went back to the table in the dining room to find that Hope had dropped a bombshell.'

The bell to the presbytery's front door clanged, and both Maria and Father O'Reilly heard the visitor say

Hope

something, and the housekeeper answer that she'd let the father know but it wouldn't be today.

'That visitor doesn't sound as important as this, so go on, Maria,' Father O'Reilly said.

'Father, I'm sure there is no way on earth that what I'm about to say you won't think a bad idea, and I feel the same too. I'm certain you are aware that Hope is a mistress at Chantal's, doing all sorts of things I can't bear to think about—' Father O'Reilly nodded '—and it certainly would never have been the choice that I would have made for her, but she's so determined once she's decided something.

'And now Hope has got this madcap idea that she is going to auction her virginity to the highest bidder, and she announced it to the whole table while I was outside with Charity. In fact, she was boasting about this being a great idea that she's had, so I hear. I was just flabbergasted when I heard. I think it's horrible and crude, and plain wrong.'

For the very first time ever Maria saw Father O'Reilly looking shocked. Maria hadn't wanted to burden the father with her problems, in part as she felt ashamed about Hope's brazenness, which she knew was rich considering her own background, and in part as this was the sort of thing that she'd always gone to Annie and Joyce with.

But of course Annie and Joyce were gone, and aside from Lisa, who was likely very tied up with what Little Danny was feeling about his and Charity's problems in conceiving, sadly Maria didn't have any friends. She'd thought about having a word with Faith or Charity, but had decided against that; Hope was a law unto herself, and Maria was cautious about escalating tensions should Hope ever feel her mother was talking behind her back to her sisters.

'I thought she abhorred the very idea of ever having physical relations with another person,' he said cautiously.

'Well, that's what I thought too,' said Maria, who didn't want to draw attention to Father O'Reilly inadvertently confirming what Hope must have said to him at some point during confession, in case he hadn't noticed the implication of his comment. She added quickly to give him something else to think about, 'But, I don't know – maybe she's got a bit power hungry as, please don't be offended, Father, she spends all day telling people what to do. Or maybe she's just changed her mind. I suppose people do sometimes about things like this.'

'Oh, I know all too well what goes on at Chantal's, Maria, never you mind about that. I might live a sheltered life personally, but I have long stopped being surprised by what people admit to me in the oratory that they get up to,' the father said. 'I must say though that I am surprised by Hope wanting to do what she's described, as it seems to go against everything I know about her.'

'I agree, Father. And what's worrying me—' Maria's voice dropped to little more than a mumble '—is that

Hope

Hope says that she might not go through with it at the end, the sex bit, I mean. And this scares me. Although it scares me too the thought of her maybe going through with actually having relations – for whatever she thinks *that* will be like, I doubt it's going to be what she expects.

'But if she is on her own with a man who has paid a lot of money for this virginity, then who knows what will happen if Hope suddenly says she's changed her mind and the intercourse bit is off the agenda? She'll have seemed to be treating her body as an object, so she won't be able to blame someone if they think of her as no more than this too and are furious if she doesn't go on to deliver on the service they've paid for. All my life I've seen that men don't like women promising one thing and doing another, and in some ways perhaps they can't be blamed for that. Father, I can't think that any of this will end well. But I know how headstrong Hope can be, once she sets her mind on something . . .'

Maria looked down, and then she raised her eyes to Father O'Reilly's and said, 'We all know that Hope only has to peek at my face to see what can happen if a man loses his temper. If the way I look isn't a warning to her that she is about to play with fire, then I don't know what would be, as I feel a walking advertisement in how life can change for the worse in a mere moment. I think she's overconfident, but when I tried to say this to her on

Christmas night when we got home, she nicely enough but very firmly told me to mind my own business, and then she added that I should concentrate on putting my feet up and having a rest, and leave her to get on with living her life as she sees fit.

'Aside from me wanting to shout back at her that I'm not yet forty-five and I'm not appreciating this insinuation about being put out on the scrap heap quite yet, I'd like to tell her how wrong and stupidly I think she is acting. But exactly like with Charity at the moment I feel like anything I do say to Hope is likely to make the situation worse, and so it is all combining to make me feel I can't say anything to anyone. I've quite often felt a bad mother before, but never quite so strongly as this.'

'You know, Maria, that a man should never push a woman to do anything she doesn't want to do?' said the father.

'Do you, or anyone of my generation, really believe that?' said Maria. 'Perhaps for my girls, in time that will be true, but as far as I can see right now, there's precious little of this going on.'

There was a silence as they both thought about this.

'And what about Faith?' asked the father.

'Ah, Faith. Well, that's not the best either. I'm very aware that she and I need to talk about her father. She saw Ted Walton at Annie's funeral, and after she asked about him just before the wake began, and I said he was her

Hope

grandfather,' said Maria. 'But then I got all panicky and I didn't know what to say, and so we pretty much just changed the subject because neither of us wanted to spoil Annie's send-off, and I haven't found the courage since, although she must be wondering. It's not so much I'm scared of what Faith will think of me, but more that I can't paint her father in any flattering light at all, as he's just a cruel and selfish pig who did this to my face in temper when I told his father about being pregnant with Fred's baby, and who wants to hear a man who thinks like that – and does *this* – is half of who they are?

'But I will have to talk to Faith – I should have done it years ago, and Annie always told me I should, but there never seemed the right time. She is being very patient as she waits for me to say something, but I see her looking at me sometimes, so I know that's not going to go on for ever.'

Father O'Reilly sighed and then said, 'Maria, you and I have known each other a long time, and one thing I know for certain is that you are neither a bad person nor a bad mother. All parents would find dealing with your three daughters at the moment to be very, no, *extremely* challenging, and to have these crises blow up at the same time is going to feel nigh on impossible for you to navigate until you get a bit more used to the *idea* of what they have told you. Would you like me to have a word? I'm not sure how helpful I can be, but I feel they see me as a father figure of sorts.'

Maria nodded. 'That would be very kind of you, Father, if you can bear to, as I know how busy you are and we're not in your area any more. But I can't talk to our new father as I can do to you.'

'Flattered.' Father O'Reilly smiled.

Maria didn't join him in this, but said seriously, 'I doubt it will do much good in any practical sense, but at the least you and I can feel we've tried. And a conversation needs to be had by someone they respect with both of them to make sure they are thinking things through properly.

'If Charity really can't get pregnant, there's going to be other options for her, or perhaps medical intervention, but I think that right now she's too panicked to think more widely about the situation, and if she doesn't calm down she might go on to wreck the marriage just through her panic. In any case she might need help with Little Danny whose machismo will be suffering and he might not be able to accept any of what's going on. All I've said to Lisa and Big Danny is that I think we need to allow Charity and Little Danny a bit of space, but if I know, then Little Danny's parents will know as well.'

'I hear you, Maria. But let's take it step by step. As they say, Rome wasn't built in a day,' Father O'Reilly told her.

Hope

'And, you never know – maybe each of your girls is thinking differently already.'

'I'd love to believe you, Father,' Maria answered in a way that told the father he hadn't alleviated her fears.

'Trust in God that you will find yourself the best way. God and I believe in you, remember,' the father told her.

Maria wished she shared the father's optimism, but she promised him she would do her best.

And then although she'd not been other than a conflicted believer for years in spite of going to church, she bent her head as Father O'Reilly closed his eyes before saying a prayer.

But neither found the comfort in this they sought, and the father was left sitting deep in thought for a long while after he had heard the front door close behind her, his hand making scratchy sounds as he stroked his slightly stubbly chin.

CHAPTER FIVE

It was nine o'clock in the morning, and Hope hadn't yet gone to bed after assisting Chantal run the New Year's Eve celebrations at Chantal's.

Indeed, quite a lot of the partygoers were still in the building after seeing the new year in, with some of them looking bleary and worse for wear.

Hope was starting to droop a little, although she was determined not to show it. She had been constantly on the go since mid-afternoon the previous day, and now that the adrenaline of the previous evening had passed, she was tired and her feet were aching from her high heels. She told herself that given the chance, she could sleep for a month.

The year 1993 had certainly been well and truly rung in though, with everyone at Chantal's in fine fettle.

Carefully planned by Chantal and Hope, it had turned out to be the sort of wild shindig that nobody was going to forget in a hurry, which was exactly what they had wanted. But Chantal and Hope couldn't stand down just yet, even though the finish line was tantalisingly in sight, and they had sneaked into the staff's private room for a twenty-minute flop at four o'clock, the pair so close on the sofa that their shoulders touched as they caught up with each other over how the event was going as they drank cans of cola for some much-needed energy and caffeine.

Five hours later the doorbell rang and without being asked a sub called Nick sprang to get it. Hope thought she had trained him well.

It was a couple of the clients from the previous evening who'd been instructed first thing to go out to find breakfast for everybody.

Now they were back bearing laden trays, and with a lad carrying a big cardboard box of goodies, after they'd discovered a café open nearby that could serve them bacon butties and large lidded paper cups of teas and coffees, which was exactly what everyone needed after the shenanigans of the previous twelve hours.

The box was put on the table with a pile of paper napkins beside it, and the two clients walked around with the trays so that people could choose what hot drinks they wanted. And it was when one of the men who had gone out slipped off his City overcoat that Hope smiled when she saw he was still wearing his bondage harness on his naked torso, his pelts of chest and back hair curling around

Hope

the leather, although he had slipped his trousers on top to go out. It was certainly a look.

The New Year's party had had the theme of leather, and Hope had chosen to wear a velvet sheath dress the same colour as her lips, with a snug corset over her ribcage in matching velvet that hoisted her breasts as high as they would go, the corset extravagantly laced with intricate leather straps all the way up her back. Tight black leather evening gloves pulled all the way to Hope's upper arms completed her outfit.

'Nick,' commanded Hope. 'Before you eat, run downstairs and free the puppies. I fed them earlier so ignore any woofs for more; if they growl, say for each growl, they will have to wait an extra fortnight before I'll even think about scheduling their next visit. And after that I may allow you to undo the buckles on my shoes. But only "may", mind. Off you go quickly, now.'

Nick's eyes were bright with pleasure at being the sub chosen to do Hope's bidding. He licked his lips in anticipation, his own bacon buttie forgotten. He headed to the basement where two men were kneeling in kennels, morning bowls of dog food empty beside them.

One of them, Harry Stewart, came upstairs and prostrated himself on the floor before Hope, while the other man stayed downstairs to take a shower.

'Did you have a good night, er, *Harry*?' asked Hope,

and he nodded as he made a 'ruff' sound, his body giving a quiver of delight. This was provoked through Hope saying his real name in front of everyone. Usually names were kept to special monikers only used at Chantal's to preserve the anonymity of the clients, but although Harry had never said so, Hope had suspected that he would get a thrill by being outed in front of the others, and one look at the shine in his eyes and his suddenly reddened lips told her she had been correct in her assumption. She thought he had liked what had happened a bit too much, and she wondered if he were on some sort of medication.

'Doggy play is now over. You are no longer a puppy. You will sit on a chair now and behave as Harry again,' she told him firmly. Harry looked disappointed but did what she said.

It was the first time he had tried this sort of experience, and Hope could tell he'd needed her to tell him it had all ended before he could come out of his role.

She thought he might have taken it a bit too seriously, and so she held his gaze with an expressionless face. If a client had gone to a place in their minds that was very deep, they could sometimes be a bit unpredictable as they reverted to normal.

But all was well this time as, after a pause, Harry nodded acquiescence, and then he pulled himself up onto a chair, and immediately in his normal voice wished Hope

Hope

a happy new year as he tilted his head to one side so that he could unbuckle the thick leather collar around his neck. He'd asked for a collar in brown leather; Hope had given him one in lavender leather.

But it was when Harry began chatting about maybe going skiing that Hope thought how strange her job was.

One minute it was making men howl (in Harry's case, quite literally, like the husky he'd wanted to be as he'd crawled down the corridor pulling her along in a small specially made hardboard sled as now and again she alternated flicking his arse with a dressage whip, and throwing ice cubes at his bare behind), and the next talking about their everyday lives as if they were the most conventional men imaginable who'd never heard the terms 'kink', 'play', 'slave' or 'safe words'.

There was always a point where it was as if what they had been doing previously and what they had come to Chantal's for hadn't really happened at all and while Hope never found her subs going *into* a role disconcerting, oddly she sometimes felt rattled as they came back to the real world.

When she wasn't actually at Chantal's, Hope found the snapshot her work gave her into human nature to be endlessly fascinating.

But now wasn't the time for anyone to ponder on this as there were heavy footsteps from the stairs, and a couple of other clients came in from rooms on the upper levels, and wordlessly Chantal pointed to where the paracetamol and plasters were.

Nick, who was CEO of a major bank, fairly trotted around to make sure everyone had some tea or coffee.

'Right!' Chantal clapped her hands and then announced, 'Fifteen minutes and everybody out. We're closed then until next Friday, January eighth, when that weekend all we will be offering are our infamous "Spring Cleaning" adventures. Anyone wanting to wear a pinny and Marigolds, and to get down on their knees to scrub the floors, you know how to sign up.'

Spring Cleaning happened every couple of months or so, and was so popular that it often had a waiting list of eager men. It was surprising the number of clients who got aroused to the smell of bleach, and who were delighted to be instructed to lick the rim of a toilet bowl whether it had just been cleaned or not.

All the mistresses loved Spring Cleaning, as they didn't have to do much other than point to imaginary areas that hadn't been cleaned quite thoroughly enough.

'But, before you are allowed to go,' Chantal continued, 'I am not finished yet. I want everyone to know that very soon we will be making an extremely exciting announcement concerning our one and only Scarlet. It's top secret for now, but Scarlet, why don't you give us a clue?'

Hope

Hope stood up, the balls of her feet stinging painfully although she didn't allow herself to flinch as she stared around with the most supercilious expression on her face that she could muster.

Very slowly she pushed the spaghetti straps to her dress off her shoulders, first one and then the other, each time tantalisingly slowly running the forefinger of her other hand back along her collarbone towards her throat, with her little finger inching across the swell of her corseted breasts. She didn't say a word, then unhurriedly she slid the straps back to their proper place with just as much care and sat down again.

The silence was so intense that quite literally anyone could have heard a pin drop, so rapt was the attention of every single man in the room as they tried to work out what Hope was teasing them about.

CHAPTER SIX

Still, Hope was pleased that when Father O'Reilly turned up two hours later, she was back in her beloved jeans and T-shirt once more after a long and scaldingly hot shower, all make-up gone and her damp hair wrapped in a turbaned towel as she packed her bits and pieces before heading home. She looked innocent and at least ten years younger than she was.

In fact Chantal had just told her as much when she'd come into the shower room to drop off two fluffy towels that were still warm out of the industrial-sized clothes dryer in the utility room. In an establishment such as Chantal's there tended to be a lot of washing of sheets and towels.

If the father had arrived even thirty minutes earlier he might have seen a very different version of Hope, and neither of them was quite ready for that yet.

Hope wondered why he hadn't visited her at home, but only very briefly, because the moment he sat down and said, 'I hear you caused quite the stir over your Christmas lunch. What with your auction plans and all . . .'

'Ah. So Mummy's been to see you then? I suppose I should have guessed she would.'

'Correct. But why don't you give your side of the story now? If you feel like confiding in me.'

'Are you sure you want me to?'

'Not really. For my sins . . . But I'll be in your mother's bad books if I don't.'

'Take it from me, Father,' Hope said with a laugh, 'that's not a good place to be.'

'Amen to that!'

It took Hope a little while to be able to articulate what she wanted to say, and Father O'Reilly waited patiently.

At last she was ready. 'If I were feeling uncharitable, I'd be telling you Mummy would say I have middle-sister syndrome. That I have a chip on my shoulder that I wasn't made enough of a fuss of when I was born, at least not in the way Faith was. That I struggled to be a twin, and couldn't allow myself to be the baby of the family in the way Charity always has. And perhaps there is an element of all that in me, as none of us can pretend that we were proud to tell our friends growing up what Mummy and Granny did for us to get by, and so I told myself I had to be a tough nut.'

Hope looked at her nails, clear now of the red polish of

Hope

the previous night, and then she unwrapped the towel from around her head and ran her fingers over her scalp to loosen the strands of her hair.

Father O'Reilly leaned towards her. 'Hope, nobody would pretend to you and your sisters that you had the easiest of childhoods. But from what I could see you all grew up in a household where you never needed to doubt that all three of you were loved and cherished. I don't mean in a way where money was tossed about, but in the way of clean clothes and meals on time, and Maria always going to the parent–teacher evenings at school, and Annie ironing your uniforms. Faith and Charity have both built on this and opted for something more conventional, and so it's hard not to wonder why you haven't too . . .'

'I've thought about that also, Father. And I don't know the answer really. Only that I would suffocate if I had the life that my sisters, and most people, want. It's as if I'm not quite a whole person, but having people value me in the way they look up to legal-eagle Faith, or to find everything I need in the arms of another as Charity does, isn't the answer somehow. I need . . . Well, I don't know quite what I need, only that it's *more*!'

Father O'Reilly said, 'I get that. But you've always been a very clever one, top of the class and schoolwork a doddle – yet you've always gone out of your way to make it difficult for anyone to challenge you should they worry about your choices. Even as a tiny tot.

'Perhaps we've all been guilty of being a bit scared of your reaction, and have taken the easy option of standing back from you to let you get on with it. I feel now I should have tried harder, and so I hope you forgive me that I didn't. But with your strong mind, your accountancy skills and your other talents, I know you must understand that Chantal's is but only one, dare I say, lesser option for you . . .'

Hope cut in. 'You're right, Father. I do see this, and I understand that me feeling as I do just doesn't make sense for anyone; I've spent years with it not making sense to me either. And it's clear that you and Mummy and everyone else worry about what I do here. But I cannot imagine anyone ever finding the thought of physical touch romantic, and a resulting emotional response from me at all enticing – I just don't seem to have the button for romance. Instead, when I hold up my whip – and I can't quite fathom the exhilaration of this – it's the closest I've yet found to what feels like that missing piece of me.'

The father studied Hope's face carefully.

'No, I don't understand, not really,' he said quietly. 'I see that you do feel strongly about it though, and that you have spent time thinking about it all.'

Hope gave a half-nod and then she shrugged with a

Hope

smile, her damp hair shimmering in a shaft of lamplight as she moved.

'But help me with this, Hope. What you are proposing, this so-called auction of your, ahem, um, your virginity, seems you walking into exactly what you are just telling me you find abhorrent, no?'

Hope bit back a smile at the father's stumble over getting the word 'virginity' out.

'Yes, it is that, Father. It is a puzzle for me too, if I'm honest. But the more I think about, the more I wonder if the auction is perhaps, for me, really about exploring and embracing my own power. My virginity, or sex, feels to me like it's no more than a conduit to this. And perhaps on some level I crave my own submission to my power. It's hard for me not to recognise the power of power, especially with what I do for a living – no one would want my services if I wasn't the one more powerful in the moment than my clients.'

Hope didn't think this was the moment to mention something else that she was increasingly wondering about, which was whether the real power in the sub-dom world lay with the one allowing the whip to be smacked on their arse, rather than the person bringing it down, and so she said instead, 'Of course the fact that I will probably make enough money to take a year off through it, should I want to, is a factor too. And I like to shock. All I know for certain is that when I first thought of the auction, it felt right. And very me. Or at least the me I want to be in 1993.'

The two stared at each other for a long while.

The father got slowly to his feet as he buttoned his coat. And then he turned towards Hope.

'Tread carefully, Hope. Please don't break Maria's heart for a third time. It's easy to underestimate the strength of one's heart as that is always going to be stronger than anything you can do with your clever words or the sound of some handcuffs closing,' he said.

'It's easy to forget that hearts are funny things – they have a way of getting involved with one's actions, no matter how much that's not intended. I know you think you can hold yourself above your feelings. But have you ever considered that perhaps, deep down, you don't want to go to your grave having always pushed away those who love you and who want to be close to you? Could this be your way of you giving yourself permission to try a new path for yourself, and this auction is something of a dummy run on the path to that? Indeed, I would argue that the most powerful thing of all is to let the right people close.'

Father O'Reilly smiled at her, and then added, 'I shall pray you make wise decisions, my dear.'

He left, and as Hope turned her hairdryer on, she was

Hope

left musing that although she felt confident the auction wasn't much to worry about, really, had Father O'Reilly hit upon a grain or two of truth?

And then she told herself not to be a ninny, and that she should man up and just get on with it, as to back out now would be a failure of spirit.

Wouldn't it?

CHAPTER SEVEN

Maria was back at the presbytery early on Saturday afternoon.

Shamus answered the door to her, his gaze still avoiding hers, and she said, 'Good afternoon, Mr... Um. Actually, I'm sorry but the father didn't tell me your last name.'

'Just Shamus is fine, missus,' he muttered in a thick Irish accent, flicking his eyes to her face for less than a second before looking down, his cheeks pinkening under her stare.

'In that case, I'm Maria,' she said, used to people – not her previous clients, of course, as their eyes were nearly always greedy – averting their eyes when they first met her. 'Is the father in?'

Shamus escorted her to Father O'Reilly's office as when they went by Maria could hear that the visitors' room was occupied, and he politely held the door open after he had tapped to alert the father's attention.

'Maria, come in, come in. I was just thinking about Hope,' he said, and nodded to Shamus that tea for both was required. 'I fear I wasn't able to help,' the father added. 'Indeed, I'm not certain that I haven't made things worse, which is the last thing I wanted to do.'

He sounded so down-hearted that Maria quickly said, 'Oh, my goodness, Father, Hope wasn't rude to you, was she?'

'Oh no, not at all. Very polite in fact, and honest too, I think. We had quite the chat as it turned out. She seems to have thought it all through though.'

Maria nodded with an expression of weary acceptance. 'It was always going to be a long shot, Father, and so you have nothing to blame yourself for. Hope is a dear girl but she's never allowed herself an easy option, and of course I think her religious faith, and dare I say your influence, has lessened as time has gone by, not that she ever had much to begin with, and so there's that. Over the years I've tried and tried to get her to soften in all sorts of ways, but she never has. But thank you so much for taking the time out of your busy day – you'll never know how much I appreciate it.'

Father O'Reilly reminded Maria that Hope's very name suggested there was always the possibility for change and positivity. And then he began to ask about Maria's plans for the early months of this new year, now that she had a bit more time on her hands, time (as he pointed out) that

Hope

she could spend on herself more than she had been able to in the past.

It was quite a short part of their conversation as Maria realised she didn't really know how she wanted to spend her time now her days on the streets were behind her, with all her daughters and herself settled in their new living accommodation, and not needing anything doing for them as much as they had in the past.

One thing Maria did know though was that it was time that she spoke to Faith about her father, and she told Father O'Reilly so.

'I'm pleased, Maria, as I'm sure you'll feel lighter after you do. I know you'll find the right words,' he said.

'I wish I shared your confidence, Father,' she replied. 'And when that's done, I'll need to turn towards Charity again.'

As she walked down the hall a few minutes later, she couldn't shake a growing sense of trepidation, as well as bafflement over how she should spend her new-found freedom now she had time on her hands. In fact she was so consumed by her thoughts that Maria barely heard Shamus telling her to mind how she went as he held the front door open for her.

CHAPTER EIGHT

Back home, Maria found Faith in the kitchen, having let herself in. She was putting some groceries away that she'd brought her mother.

'What a nice surprise,' said Maria.

'Turned out I'd won the raffle for the Christmas hamper at work, but as I had that case in Manchester and then the one in Surrey, I didn't know about that until I was back at my desk yesterday, and I can't possibly eat or drink all the goodies myself.'

'Tom not going to be helping you?'

Tom Jarrett was the detective inspector that was Faith's closest thing to a boyfriend, her very first in fact.

He seemed nice enough, but Maria knew Tom had been in the Special Branch before it had been disbanded, and she knew too that he and Big Danny seemed close, and so the likelihood was that Tom wasn't squeaky clean in his police life, especially as he and Big Danny went back years together. And Faith had said on several occasions she wouldn't associate with a bent copper, as that was asking for trouble.

This was understandable as Faith was a criminal barrister, mainly on defence cases, but occasionally on behalf of the Crown Prosecution Service.

All in all, it didn't bode well for Faith and Tom becoming serious about each other, as one or other of them would probably have to step into the other's world, and it didn't seem as if either would be prepared to do that, Maria had decided a while back.

However Tom never quite seemed to go away completely, although he and Faith certainly didn't spend a lot of time together.

And Maria thought Faith was happier when he was around. Faith had never really been one for having friends of any description, and so Maria supposed that having Tom on the scene might be a better option than not having him around.

Secretly, she harboured thoughts of becoming a grandmother. And with Charity's conception problems and Hope not liking men much, perhaps this was going to fall at Faith's door, not that Maria would ever suggest as much to Faith. Hence she wasn't above a little manoeuvring now and again.

'Mummy!' Faith made her voice sound a little shocked at her mother's insinuation about Tom and her, but Maria caught sight of a smile.

Hope

'Well,' said Maria as she inspected a jar of black cherries in kirsch and then lifted up by its ribbon a vanilla panettone in a cheery Christmas cardboard wrapping, 'this scran seems a bit more you and Tom, than me.'

'Rubbish, you deserve a treat. But if you must know, Tom is picking me up in a minute – he and Big Danny have just popped out to the dogs – and then we're going to the cinema.'

Maria knew this meant that Tom and Big Danny had gone down to the scrubland on the Isle of Dogs that Big Danny had purchased early in the 1980s at a knock-down price when he needed a fair bit of open ground in which to park up his huge fleet of Transit vans, as back then a lot of the land and buildings there were more or less derelict and empty, and land prices were dirt-cheap, as nobody could see much of a future in the area.

Now, the Transits were used in Big Danny's ring of part-time drivers who'd drive down to the ferry from Dover to Calais to fill up the vans with cheap alcohol and cigarettes that would then be fed out to a host of corner shops throughout the South East in order that everyone could make a healthy profit that was well beyond the bottom line of above-board trading.

The 'dogs' Faith mentioned wasn't the Isle of Dogs in spite of where they were going, but Wolfie and Simba, the two Alsatians that guarded the Transits, who were let out loose at night to prowl around the site and deter any opportunistic crims.

Presumably Big Danny and Tom needed some privacy to talk about something, or they needed to pick up or drop something off, as that land could hide a multitude of secrets. One thing Maria knew for certain was that Big Danny had made a very astute purchase of the Isle of Dogs land.

For, where once she and Annie had plied their trade in run-down streets and underneath crumbling lintels on doorways, now big-city firms were moving in, with property developers building huge skyscrapers for them, some with outside walls made totally of glass and atriums tall enough to house real trees. Developments of posh flats were going up apace too, and Lisa had let slip on the QT to Maria that most weeks Big Danny was approached by property developers eager to acquire his prime East End real estate, offering eye-wateringly huge sums of money. Lisa boasted that Big Danny was having the last laugh on rivals from other gangs who'd taken delight that he'd been ripped off when he originally bought the land.

Maria expected that Big Danny would sell at some point, not least as he was concentrating on making as many of his business interests as possible look legit, even if only on the surface.

And the fleet of Transits would at some point interest

Hope

the taxman and probably the occupants, too, of the highrise offices. Also the vans definitely wouldn't be quite the impression Big Danny would be wanting to give to his business interests when attempting to drive a hard bargain over the land price, and so they would most likely go too, unless Big Danny moved the base of the Transit operation to somewhere like Ashford or Dartford, which were on reasonably good road links to the Dover ferries.

Maria rather hoped that if Big Danny did decide to close down this part of his multi-faceted business interests, though, that Wolfie and Simba would be pensioned off rather than being sold on as guard dogs (or worse, euthanised), and come to live with them all at Cadogan Terrace. With time on her hands, walking two dogs in Victoria Park might be quite a nice thing to do, she wondered.

'Anyway, Mummy,' Faith interrupted Maria's train of thought, 'you just missed Charity and Little Danny. On the spur of the moment they've decided to go to Paris to have a little bit of quiet time together, and they jumped in a taxi just before you got back. They called City Airport, and were able to get on a flight leaving later. I think Little Danny wanted to spoil Charity a little, which is why they've gone to Paris rather than the timeshare.'

Charity and Little Danny spent a lot of their time at the timeshare on the Costa del Sol in Spain, and they often said they really hoped the newly opened and very close City Airport would soon start offering regular flights to Malaga, in the way that it currently did to Paris, Luxembourg and Frankfurt, as this would be really convenient.

'I hope they have a few days to relax,' said Maria. 'Charity has been very quiet and upset since Christmas. Has she talked to you about it? I've tried, but she closes it down, saying she was just tired on Christmas Day and her tears were only a blip.'

Faith shook her head. 'She's not said anything to me at all. On Boxing Day I said I was sorry to see her so miserable, and I gave her the opportunity to talk about whatever she wanted. But she didn't nibble, saying instead she'd just had bad PMT.'

'Let's hope it does the trick and she comes back preg—' Maria stopped talking as the chirp of the ringtone of Faith's 'Mars Bar' Sony portable phone interrupted their conversation.

Whenever Maria saw Faith's Sony she remembered Charity calling it the Mars Bar at a house tea several weeks earlier, and Big Danny's look of confusion when he heard this.

It was because in his East End world a 'mars bar' meant a scar, while he always called the telephone the 'dog and bone', and Lisa had had to break it to her husband gently that for the next generation, some words and phrases dear

Hope

to him were being adopted for other meanings, and this meant Mars Bar was how many under-thirties spoke about this model of the Sony mobile phone.

Maria hadn't known if Big Danny's slightly crestfallen expression was designed to make her girls and Little Danny laugh, or because Big Danny had stumbled at an unexpected example of the state of flux that life now and again threw at them all.

If it was the second reason, she knew the feeling and sympathised with Big Danny. For, until Hope joined Chantal's, Maria had thought her own sex work to be very near the knuckle, but the more Hope described what she saw, the more Maria came to feel that her own heterosexual sexual exchanges, frequent as they had been and often coming with a level of danger to her, were in many ways quite tame. There was something about the needs of the men who went to Chantal's that suggested a pushing of sexual boundaries was becoming increasingly commonplace across society, and Maria didn't like to think about where it might all end. She wasn't so silly as to think that bondage and all the rest hadn't been around since well before she and Annie had begun working the streets, but it was something she had no personal experience of, other than her clients with the obvious fetish for the scars Fred Walton had inflicted on her.

'Oh shoot, Tom. Yes, I understand. Speak soon.' Faith

ended the call and looked at her mother with a frown wrinkling the skin between her eyebrows, adding, 'Something's come up at work. Apparently.'

Maria didn't want to draw attention to the distinct tinge of disappointment in Faith's voice, and so she said, 'Thank goodness then that those cherries in kirsch will go well with the panettone. But to work up an appetite, why don't you and me go for a stroll in Victoria Park?'

Faith looked at her mother suspiciously, as Maria never normally suggested anything like this. 'Should I see if Hope wants to come too?' she asked.

'Best not, Faith. I think it's time that you and I had that chat about your dad that I've been putting off for far too long.'

Faith stared at her mother for a long moment, and then without taking her eyes off Maria's, she reached for her coat that had been slung onto the back of a kitchen chair.

Mother and daughter linked arms, and walked side by side with solemn faces in the deepening shadows. Victoria Park was large and splendid, but neither of them were thinking about that. There were few people in the park as it would close at the fast-approaching dusk.

'I was fifteen in my last year at school – my father Gary wouldn't allow me to stay on longer even though I was bright, and Annie couldn't persuade him otherwise – and

Hope

all Gary wanted was for me to work at the local factory. That was my nightmare, and I dreaded the day I'd be leaving – but back then once you were fifteen and a parent requested it, you were out. At the time Annie was working as a "hostess" at Ted Walton's illegal gambling club, because Gary owed a lot of money to Ted, who all the local criminals looked up to, and Annie had to work the debt off on Gary's behalf,' began Maria, her voice so low that Faith had to strain to hear.

'Obviously hostessing included some sleeping with the punters, and some of his rivals, as Ted wanted them kept happy in order that they would keep going back to the card table, which was where the real money was made at the club. Annie told me that that's where she met Joyce, who was a bit older and one of Ted's favourites, and Joyce took her under her wing and looked out for Annie, and so she had a better time at work very often than she had at home in spite of what she had to do at the club.'

'Yes, that sounds like Auntie Joyce,' said Faith.

Maria smiled, and then went on, 'But one day I was in Woolworths in Kirkdale, and I saw a young man looking at me, making eyes in my direction, as Annie would have said. Faith, you have no idea how naive and inexperienced I was. Annie had got married to Gary when she was a teenager, and she was determined for more in my case. All I did was go to school and work hard at my lessons; at home I avoided my father, and I never had friends as I couldn't risk anyone coming to my house and seeing how Gary treated Annie, and it felt too odd to be in anyone else's house as I didn't understand what happiness meant.

'So when this young man, who I admit was quite handsome, followed me around Woollies, and then asked me to a coffee bar, I was flattered, and curious too. Of course, I went. He was Fred, Ted Walton's son. And we began courting, and at first he was very gentlemanly. And he could be funny too. Later, Annie told me how horrified she was when she found out it was Fred Walton I had a crush on, as she knew a very different side to Fred than the one I was seeing – he was never a nice person and he felt entitled to whatever he wanted because of how respected Ted was. But I refused to listen to Annie's cautions, as I felt I knew best, and I thought my mother was just trying to spoil my fun.

'It was when one thing led to another and I became pregnant that Fred's true nature showed through. I honestly thought he would marry me as he had said he loved me, but he didn't, and he was horrible and took no responsibility. And I began to feel desperate, in part about what Gary would do to me when he found out, so much so that I went to Ted's drinking club to plead with Fred – and when Fred saw what I'd done, he attacked me. Joyce, who by then was living in London, said Fred had shown off to her about having a razor blade inserted into a gold ring, and it was this Fred used to wreck my face.'

Faith opened her mouth to say something, but Maria held up her hand to stop her daughter and went on speaking.

'Fred did this in front of Annie and Ted. To give him his due, Ted was livid, although this may have been only because I was bleeding all over the place and the club was about to open. He bundled me and Annie in the back of an old car that was kept purely for bleeders – they even named the car the "bleeder", Annie told me, as they used to take away the bleeding men who'd been injured in fights at the club – and we were driven to a doctor on Ted's payroll and he did his best to patch me up. My injuries were so severe and the doctor was so shocked at the sight of my face that he even gave us forty pounds of his own money so that we could do a flit.

'We never even went back home to get any clothes or anything else as we were terrified of Gary's response, and so we got a taxi to the station. And that night we were sneaked onto a post train down to London by a sweet guard – we sat with the sacks of mail. At dawn we got to King's Cross, and travelled by bus to Stepney to where Joyce was living. And from there, Joyce and Father O'Reilly helped all three of us make a new life, for that baby I was carrying was you, Faith.'

Faith pulled her mother into a comforting hug.

Maria murmured into Faith's shoulder as she clasped her daughter tightly, 'I want you to know though that while you weren't planned, and although your father was a despicable man, you were a very loved and wanted baby, and never have I regretted for a second giving birth to you. Your name, Faith, was chosen because I had faith in *you*, as well as in all of us having a better future.'

'Did you ever see Ted Walton or Fred over the years?' Faith asked as they let each other go.

'Never,' said Maria. 'It was as if we'd hadn't existed to the Waltons, although now and again Joyce would say the odd thing and so I knew that she and Ted kept in touch occasionally. But Ted read about Annie's murder in the newspaper, and I'd put a notice in the paper about her funeral. He came down, hoping to see Joyce, I think, although of course she'd died too within days of Annie. When he spoke to me at the funeral, he said it had long weighed heavily on him that he'd not looked after Annie, me and you after what Fred had done, but Fred was his only child and back then he felt that he couldn't give up on him.

'But over the years things have changed as Fred, Ted told me, has remained a bad, violent person who has caused all sorts of trouble at every opportunity. And the punishment of the Walton family has been that although

Hope

Fred has been married several times, Fred has not gone on to father any children other than you, and right now Ted has sent him to live abroad as he was bringing too much police attention Ted's way and he's had enough of Fred. Ted is in his seventies now, and his wife is poorly, so I think they both regret never meeting you as you are their only grandchild.

'At Annie's funeral, I said to Ted that you didn't know anything about Fred, and indeed precious little about our life back then in Wakefield. He told me he understood, but a few days later he sent me this, inside a letter.'

Maria reached into her pocket and drew out an envelope.

'Faith, you don't have to read this if you don't want to,' Maria said as she handed it to her daughter. 'You don't owe anything to the Waltons, remember. And you don't owe anything to me either.'

Faith stood still as she stared at the envelope. Her name was handwritten on the front in neat writing.

The bell for the park closing rang, and Faith pushed the letter into a pocket as she and Maria hurried towards the exit closest to the house on Cadogan Terrace.

It wasn't until she was back in her own flat later in the evening that Faith reached for the letter.

She put the slightly crumpled envelope on the coffee

table in front of her and regarded it carefully as she drank a large glass of red wine, and then a second glass.

As two police cars raced past her flat with their sirens blaring, at last Faith felt ready, and she slid her finger under the stuck-down flap. It felt a large moment playing out in a subdued and strangely mundane manner. She wasn't at all sure about what she hoped Ted Walton's words to her should be.

And even when she had read the letter several times, Faith still couldn't decide what her feelings about it were.

It wasn't long before she had finished the bottle of wine as she sat on her sofa lost in thought. She even ignored Tom's phone call when the trill of the mars bar rang, the first time she had ever not picked up to him.

Dear Faith,

You may remember that we caught each other's eye at your grandmother's funeral. It might be wishful thinking or just my imagination, but I felt we both recognised something in the other one. And if you are reading this, then your mother will have told you that my son Fred is your father.

I am afraid that over the years neither myself nor Fred have treated your mother or you as you deserve to

Hope

have been treated; my wife Martina remains, sadly, unaware of your existence.

The time that has passed since Annie and Maria left Wakefield has not been kind to my family, and as I get older increasingly I find myself thinking about the wrongs that have happened, and whether I can go any way to put things right.

Basically, my business has been successful and I've made a lot of money, but the biggest failure of my life has been Fred – he was totally despicable to your mother, and nothing much has changed since. I tried to give him every opportunity, but he has behaved appallingly at every turn. He is an abomination in human form.

When I saw you at the funeral, it really came home to me what an exceptionally foolish, selfish, stupid man I have been.

You were dealt a tough hand of cards, but it is clear that you have triumphed wonderfully. You were lucky to have Annie and Maria in your life; for me and Martina, I've seen now that it has been a crying shame I cut you from ours.

I think the realisation of this is something I will never recover from, especially as Martina could never forgive me for keeping you secret for all those years when she longed for a grandchild so.

I understand you very probably despise my weakness, and you will certainly hate the way Fred treated your mother in all respects.

But it is only fair that you know that Martina is these days not at all well.

And this means that if you did feel able to meet her, I would be prepared to tell her about your existence, and I know she would embrace you with open arms and that she would love to meet you, as would I. Martina is a sound woman with a good heart – she is a much better person than me, and I know that she would embrace everything about you.

But I will not say anything to her about you until I hear back from you, because as her health is declining, I do not want to risk her feeling excited about meeting you, her only grandchild, and then be left disappointed should you decide not to come up to Wakefield to meet her. I don't think she could bear that, and frankly I couldn't bear to see her suffer so.

Obviously this is a lot for you to think about and I would quite understand if you decide not to reply in any way to this letter. I know that I have not done right by you over the years, and that is a regret I will take to my own grave.

However, if you felt you might like to see us, I can promise that it would only be me and Martina, or just

Hope

Martina on her own if you preferred. Of course Maria would be welcomed by us too, should she want to accompany you.

If it helps, I can promise you both that Fred will not be in the country; I have made sure of that. I would advise you that whatever you decide to do from here, do not under any circumstances invite Fred into your life – if you do, you will rue the day.

Yours faithfully,
Ted Walton

CHAPTER NINE

Chantal ended up with a waiting list of eager punters who were desperate to participate in Spring Cleaning, and so she focused on those who were now deep into their kink journey.

She hadn't been going to include Harry Stewart as he had only recently upgraded from relatively vanilla bondage and being verbally abused by Hope to become a puppy, and the rule at Chantal's was that clients had to 'earn' the privilege to make it through to a chance of attendance at special days.

It was when the police arrested Harry at two o'clock in the morning for cleaning the downstairs windows to Chantal's, standing in the street outside stark-bollock naked (other than his red-framed specs), even though the establishment was closed and he'd not been asked to perform such a service, that Chantal relented and said he could come in for pre-Spring-Cleaning spring cleaning. This was a special deluxe session that was being offered to just six regulars, at a premium sum of double the price of the normal Spring Cleaning.

This premium pre-session had been Hope's idea, as some of the clientele loved the idea of being singled out for special attention, so much so that most of them didn't mind how much they paid for the honour.

Chantal and Hope hadn't believed when they first heard that Harry had been arrested. Especially the fact he was naked for anyone to see when he was shy about his round stomach and flabby bottom. Other clients maybe would have found it sexy to be stripped off in the street outside, but dull old Harry had never shown any signs of having that sort of gumption.

It took Tom Jarrett verifying that Harry had indeed been taken down to the station, where he had ended up with a caution, before Chantal and Hope were convinced.

Apparently, Tom explained to Hope, Harry had been almost blue with cold by the time he was placed in the police car as there was a thick hoar frost that night, but this was caused – according to his arrest sheet – more because there'd been a fifteen-minute stand-off, during which Harry flatly refused to put on his clothes or shoes until Hope told him to, as he'd snubbed the officers' assertions that Chantal's was standing empty, which in fact it was.

Eventually handcuffs had been slapped around his

Hope

wrists and a blanket slung around him, before Harry had been manhandled into the police car, his clothes and shoes in a dustbin bag slung into the car's boot.

'Tom says the officers who'd dealt with him had let the whole station know that Harry had found the incident, the blanket and handcuffs, and the arrest itself, *most* exciting . . .' Hope told Chantal with a snigger after she'd got off the phone with Tom.

'It was a sight those who saw won't be forgetting in a hurry by all accounts. A certain respect is due to Harry, I guess – it's a creative way he found to make you notice him. I'm still struggling to believe he had it in him. Tom said he kept asking for me in the station, but the desk sergeant knew I was Faith's sister, and Faith and Tom Jarrett are – well, who knows what they are, but whatever – and so as a favour to Tom, I wasn't tracked down. Thank Christ for that as I think Harry may be getting a bit of a thing for me.'

While Chantal and Hope liked clients to want a regular mistress, they tried not to let anything develop beyond a mere business arrangement.

'Mad as a hatter!' Chantal laughed.

Then her expression changed to one of seriousness. 'Gawd, Harry is so mild-mannered normally, that something as extreme as this is hard to believe, although it's definitely got my attention. I hope what he's done doesn't start a thing with the subs though, who then go out of their way to be arrested themselves. We've had such good relations with the local plods – and a couple of them have been here to sample our services – but that will change if Harry starts a trend, as it wouldn't take much until we're accused of engineering a waste of police time.'

'You're right,' said Hope. 'I know, let's reward Harry for effort by asking him to the pre-session, which I'll take with him, and make sure the message gets over he's had his one misdemeanour, and next time he's out.

'But let's also put out a very clear "This Is Not A Drill" bulletin on the noticeboard in the hall, saying that from now on any further deliberate attempts to get arrested by bona fide police officers will lead to a lifetime ban here.

'And if anyone ignores our instruction and goes on deliberately to provoke any sort of arrest, we'll immediately ring around every BDSM club we can find saying that punter is banned for life from Chantal's and they pose a high-level risk of unwelcome police attention at any further establishment.'

It went without saying that the doms and the subs would know any client deemed a known police risk was very likely to be banned by new establishments, other than from the most exclusive and extreme clubs, and these clubs would be nigh on impossible to get into if Chantal's didn't provide a reference.

Hope

'Wow, harsh. And firm. This is why I love you. But deserved as we must protect ourselves, and it'll be no surprise to anyone that your sister is a lawyer as some of that has clearly rubbed off on you,' Chantal told Hope with a grin. 'Just don't speak in that provocative tone of voice in front of any of the subs, otherwise they won't be able to control themselves. And definitely not in front of Harry, as I don't think I'd be ready for what that might lead to!'

They should have taken Harry more seriously.

A few days later the session for the six specially chosen men, for pre-Spring Cleaning, took place. The men were put on bathroom cleaning in the main bathroom used by the puppies, and once the door was closed behind them Harry announced to Hope he was ready to lick the rim of the not-yet-cleaned toilet bowl the very moment she told him to; in fact he was champing at the bit to do so, he added.

Harry was wearing a bridle with a rubber bit between his teeth, and Hope wondered if he'd been trying to joke with her, but his eyes were looking up at her so pleadingly from where he knelt on the floor in front of her feet that she thought he'd not noticed the irony to his comment.

The dirty toilet hadn't been attended to since before the New Year's party, and after a discreet glance down into the bowl, secretly Hope was horrified at Harry's desire to revel in the dirt, although she took care not to let him see this. She was concerned as well that he might get some sort of bacterial infection from doing as he wanted, and that wouldn't be good in any sense for business.

Her voice curt, she said immediately, 'I don't know what you expected today, Mister Stewart, but that is not it. You must never offer suggestions when we are at work. This displeases me very much, as it is my job to decide precisely what you shall and shall not do. The agreement is set out always before we begin, an agreement you signed the chit for when you arrived here today. Consequently you are banned for a fortnight from when we reopen with our normal hours, regarding any puppy play you might fancy. Right now, instead you will bleach this toilet clean over its every nook and cranny. And JoJo will supervise your work, and then watch you licking every single bit of where you have cleaned. After which you will bleach it all over again in front of him. You will not see me again today as I am going to call for JoJo.'

As they waited for JoJo to arrive, Hope felt she had now averted any potential crisis, especially as she had called Harry Mister Stewart, to signal her disapproval, as normally he was plain Harry to her. JoJo was the only male member of staff working that day, and Hope knew Harry found the thought of male staff doms terrifying rather than tantalising.

Hope

Harry looked crestfallen, his lower lip trembling as if he might cry. He tried to catch Hope's eye.

Calmly, Hope inspected her nails and totally ignored him. She knew that withdrawing her own personal attention from him was the real punishment.

Hope should not have been so confident though.

And while it was true that Harry didn't see her again that day, a couple of hours later he did catch sound of Hope's voice, and he couldn't help stopping to listen.

'I'm sorry,' Hope said, 'I like you but I can't . . . You know why.'

'You kill me every time you say that.'

'I kill you?' said Hope. 'You know how it is. It kills me, more like – it's too much and yet not enough. I can't bear it. In fact, I will have to kill you before you kill m—'

Hope and Chantal's voices faded as they moved out of earshot. And neither realised somebody had heard a snippet of their exchange, while even if they had, they wouldn't have been concerned.

It was only insignificant little Harry, after all, with his porky belly and floppy buttocks.

And they'd have been flabbergasted to think for a second that Harry was left under the impression that Hope was really threatening Chantal.

His ears buzzing through a sudden rush of blood to his head, Harry had a wild idea, and in his eagerness to think about it more, he jogged to the cloakroom to get his coat so that he could hurry home in order to consider it more deeply on his own. He had a few things to work out, and he needed quiet to concentrate.

It was a shame that he hadn't stuck around for longer though, as within a minute Hope and Chantal could clearly be heard laughing with each other.

And it was regretful Harry never understood this was a well-trodden verbal exchange between the two women that happened most months.

For Chantal – who was polyamorous, not that she would have used that particular term, preferring instead to deem herself just 'frisky and determined not to die wondering' – felt it her duty to declare every few weeks how horny Hope made her feel and how much she loved the fantasies she had about her.

Meanwhile, Hope, who'd made it very clear that in the event she started to experience any sexual impulse at all and subsequently leaned towards the lesbian or bi-curious, would be more than happy to indulge Chantal in exploring her fantasies further.

Her regular refusal to agree to Chantal's overtures wasn't because she didn't think Chantal attractive, as it was clear Chantal was very beautiful, as well as enviably funny and whip-smart and intelligent, and indeed pretty much everything someone like Hope could want.

Hope

But, Hope would add, she just never felt physical attraction to anybody, which by necessity would make any sort of experimentation a depressing experience for any partner as up close it inevitably would be apparent that Hope was acting a sham, at which point Chantal would always end the conversation by saying 'You can't blame a girl for trying', and Hope would stress 'You'd be top of the queue if I was that way, I promise'.

Quite what Harry would have made of these comments was anyone's guess.

But by then he was already a mile away on the 309 heading towards Canning Town, eagerly drumming his fingertips on the thighs of his polyester trousers as he stared out of the window, not noticing a single pub or bookie that the bus drove past, or that he still hadn't picked up the prescription waiting for him at the chemist.

CHAPTER TEN

At King's Cross train station, Faith hesitated and then took a deep breath to fortify herself before going through the turnstile.

On the other side she turned, and gave an encouraging smile to Maria, who sighed and then came through the turnstile herself.

There had been several conversations between mother and daughter about what was the best thing to do now that Ted had dropped a grenade into the Wills family with his letter to Faith.

Sitting in the kitchen two days earlier, Faith said she was worried that going to meet her own grandfather and grandmother properly might upset Hope and Charity, as the twins didn't stand a chance of ever discovering any blood relations they didn't already know about.

Faith was also very honest in confiding to Maria that she had conflicting feelings about Ted's surprisingly eloquent letter.

Maria read it very slowly, and then nodded thoughtfully as she passed it back to Faith.

'Well, you must take Hope and Charity out of your thinking,' said Maria, 'as this is a big thing for *you*, and they are big and ugly enough to come to terms with it in whatever way they will, no matter what you decide to do. As for Ted Walton penning a letter like this, I suppose you don't hold on to a business empire as Ted has done for so many years without having a lot of smarts about you and being good at getting what you want from people, although I don't think this is as deliberately manipulative as I suspected it might be. I've never heard anyone accusing Ted of being a stupid or silly man.'

Faith read the letter again, and then looked at her mother, who said, 'I'm not going to influence your decision either way, Faith, or tell you what I think you should do. But what I would say is that while I don't know Ted really, and I've never met Martina, I do remember that although Annie always said she hated Fred with a passion, she remained reasonably positive when speaking about Ted. Within reason, as of course she was working for him, I think he treated her quite well. And certainly Joyce and Ted were on good terms with each other, and we all know that Joyce wasn't the type to suffer fools gladly.

'Annie admitted Ted had a temper and was tough when he needed to be, but she said too that he had a kinder side.

Hope

He was a man of his times, of course, but it's probably in his favour that he didn't try in the slightest to stop Joyce leaving him when she wanted, even though she was his top earner. And even Fred said to me his father played by the rules, not that that impressed Fred in the slightest.'

'Mummy, if Ted and Martina aren't the devil's spawn, then how come they had a son who turned out like Fred?'

'Hmmn. That's a tough question to answer,' Maria replied. 'I have wondered before. But who can say? These things happen. Maybe he was just born twisted.

'There was always something dark about the Fred I knew, something that was deep down inside him. He seemed someone who revelled in violence and being malicious. But I didn't see it like that at the time, as compared to my father Gary, who was all I had to go on, at first I found him dazzling and exciting to be around more than anything else, and he made me laugh with his bad jokes, and when I first became aware of that sense of darkness, stupid me felt intrigued and like he was a puzzle I might be able to work out. Until that last day anyway, when he just seemed nothing more than a cruel, cruel brute.

'But from what I heard from Annie and Joyce, Ted could inflict pain on his business rivals with what seemed like very little compunction, although this was nearly always a last resort, as he never seemed by nature a vicious or vindictive man, and he would try to resolve things before they ever got that far. And I can't remember Annie or Joyce saying anything negative about Martina either; they were more inclined to say that she seemed nice enough on the occasions they saw her, although I don't think they met often.'

Faith thought about what her mother had said, and then added, 'You know what, Mummy – I am going to ring Ted, and say let's meet, otherwise I shall always be on the back foot about this, and I don't want to be left wondering what they are, or were, like for the rest of my life. I'd appreciate it very much if you came with me, but only if you want to, and not just because I'd like to have you there.'

Maria nodded. 'Just ask Ted once more if there is even the tiniest chance Fred will be there. If the answer to that is he isn't, then of course I will come along.'

Faith embraced Maria.

If her mother had asked her not to go, she would have done Maria's bidding, and done it happily. But now Faith realised she was excited at the prospect of going up to Wakefield to meet her relatives, even though she also felt a dip of apprehension somewhere deep within her chest that caught her breath.

Ted collected them from the station in a green Jaguar so sleek that its engine quietly purred, driving them in what

Hope

was actually quite a companionable silence to an upmarket and very leafy residential area of Wakefield. He pressed a device to open some electric gates and the car slid through.

Ted and Martina Walton lived in a large and comfortable-seeming house, just the correct side of seeming ostentatious. Inside, it was immaculate, with expensive furniture and tasteful decorations, and not a mote of dust to be seen anywhere. And as he led them down a corridor after he'd taken their coats, Faith glimpsed through an open door one of the biggest televisions she had ever seen in an expansive living room.

In the kitchen at the end of the passage they sat at a kitchen table in front of French windows to a pretty garden as Ted offered tea or coffee. A kitchen clock ticked on the wall nearest to the table.

He joined them with a tray, and said, 'Thank you both for coming – it means a lot. I'm sorry to say though that Martina has taken a turn for the worse, so the visit to her room will need to be short.'

And when Ted took them through to Martina's bedroom, which was an airy room overlooking the garden along the corridor from the kitchen, it was clear she was a dying woman, with sharp cheekbones and a yellowish tone to her papery skin.

Faith and Maria exchanged a glance to say this visit

wasn't happening a moment too soon; in another month it might well have been too late.

Martina was tiny and frail in a hospital bed, with her veins showing blue through white skin. There was a pungent synthetic scent to mask any unsavoury sickroom smells. A nurse who'd been sitting beside Martina pressed a button and the bed whirred and tilted at one end so that Martina was propped up, rather than lying down, and then the nurse left the room to give them some privacy. Martina was wearing a coral-coloured crocheted bedjacket and what there was still of her white hair looked as if it had been freshly washed and bouffed that morning.

But poorly and thin-skinned as Martina looked, her eyes were bright and lively, and she held out bony hands to Faith and Maria as she smiled and then said in a surprisingly strong voice, 'Come to me, my dears. Let me have a look at you.'

Maria sat on one side of the bed and Faith on the other, Maria saying, 'I'm sorry you aren't so good at the moment. I should have bought you a gift, but I wasn't sure whether you'd want me here.'

'Both of you sitting with me is a feast for my eyes, and a gift enough,' Martina said, her voice quavering with sentiment suddenly. 'It means the world to me.'

Unflinching, she stared at Maria's face and she raised a hand as if to run her fingers over Maria's scars. 'Our

Hope

Fred did *this* to you? Shameful. You poor, poor love. I had no idea. Please forgive me, and forgive Ted for not having the courage to tell me all those years ago. I am ashamed of our son.'

Maria believed her, and so she said, 'One good thing came out of it – Faith.'

'And she is a blessing,' said Martina, slowly turning her head towards Faith.

Maria stayed only for another minute or so, as she didn't want to tire Martina, who was naturally going to be more interested in speaking with Faith.

But at the doorway, Maria turned and saw Faith clasping both of the old woman's hands between her own – they seemed to be smiling at each other and in profile they looked remarkably similar to one another. Sat like that, there was absolutely no doubt that Faith was a carbon copy of Martina.

Back in the kitchen, Maria found Ted, who was setting some slices of ham and a bowl of salad out for them as he had promised them lunch before driving them back to the station.

'Let me do that,' she said. 'Why don't you sit down, as you look done in? It must be very difficult for both of you. It's hard to see a loved one nearing the end.'

She had nothing to thank Ted Walton for, as she remembered how he hadn't been able to stop Fred when

Fred had attacked her. But the man before her now was nothing like the man of thirty years earlier, or even the dapper older gent he'd been at Annie's funeral not a year since. Now, he looked as if he had shrunk in size, and the collar of his bespoke shirt gaped at the neck; Maria was unbearably touched somehow to see that although his world was clearly turning upside down, he had put on a tie that morning so as to be as respectable as possible for her and Faith.

Ted sank onto a chair, looking exhausted, his voice weary as he said, 'Thank you for helping them meet, Maria, as I know you didn't have to do that. It means the world for Martina to have these few minutes with your daughter.'

Maria heard Faith laugh, and then Martina laugh as well.

'Sounds as if they're getting on like a house on fire,' Maria said, and then paused before adding, 'I'm sorry you didn't make it to London in time to see Joyce, as I know you were fond of her. I should have let you know, but what with Annie going as she did, I wasn't thinking at my best.'

'Don't apologise, Maria, please, as that'll lead me to Fred, and I'm too used up to think about him today,' Ted said and gave a wan smile. 'Instead, why don't you tell me what you are up to?'

'Well, until recently I was always busy, what with

Hope

Annie and the three girls, and working too – I was a street girl for many years, and Annie worked alongside me so that we could look out for each other. But Annie is gone, and all the girls are living their own lives, and I'm not working now. If I'm honest, I'm finding time weighing quite heavily . . .'

Ted lifted his brows in recognition about time weighing heavily, and Maria realised there was something unguarded and soulful about him that made her feel she could speak to him honestly.

She surprised herself by adding, 'I was reading about Erin Pizzey and her women's refuge in Chiswick, and last week I went to a meeting at Joyce's church about battered women, not that I heard there were any easy solutions, which I guess we all know already, and not that it makes it easy to accept this. I haven't told anyone this, not even my daughters – I don't know why, and it's odd to say it to you as Fred's father and you looking at my face – but I am wondering about maybe volunteering in some respect in this area. On behalf of Annie, I mean, and not me.'

Ted leaned back in his chair and gazed at her without blinking. Time seemed to stretch and Maria felt her breathing slow, and then he said, 'You would have made a good daughter-in-law, I think – it's a cry—'

He was interrupted by Faith coming into the room, wiping a tear away.

'Was it all right?' asked Maria.

'Better than all right,' said Faith. 'I'm so glad to have met her. Mr Walton, your wife is a lovely woman and you must be very proud of her.'

'Yes, she makes people feel like that.' Ted clambered to his feet, and went to fetch the loaf of bread on the kitchen island.

Faith sat down and then placed a small box on the table. 'Mrs Walton gave me this. I said I couldn't take it, but she insisted, and so as I didn't want to exhaust her more than I already had, I said thank you and that I had to go but I was pleased to have met her, and you too, Mr Walton. Her eyes were shut by the time I left the room. But I absolutely can't accept this.'

'Ted, please,' he requested, 'and Martina.' His hand had the slightest tremor as he reached for the box, and when he opened it Maria couldn't prevent a small gasp at the sight of a ring with several huge diamonds in it. It looked incredibly valuable. Gently, Ted ran his finger over the diamonds.

'Oh,' he said, making the word sound like a soft cry, his voice a little stronger as he went on, 'it's her favourite ring – it was my mother's, and her mother's before that. And my mother gave it to Martina on her wedding day and Martina had the setting slightly altered to one that was more modern, although it probably looks very old hat to you, Faith.

Hope

'Back then Martina said she would give it to Fred's wife on their marriage, but he's been married three times, and she's always kept the ring as I don't think she's ever thought much of any of his wives. This ring has been very precious to Martina, and I don't mean in the sense of its value, even though it is a real family heirloom. She wore it when we christened Fred, and she wore it at our fiftieth wedding anniversary.

'I think if she wants you to have it, then you should accept.' Ted closed the box quietly, and placed it in Faith's hand. 'Please take it. For Martina's sake. And for you being the granddaughter anyone would wish for.'

Maria had never felt such a huge knot of bittersweet emotion in her throat as, in that moment, and judging by the gloss in both Ted and Faith's eyes, they felt just as moved too.

CHAPTER ELEVEN

At a knock-down price, Faith bought herself a smart second-hand Peugeot 106 with only five thousand miles on the clock from the trader who sourced and supplied Big Danny's fleet of Transits, her slapping down a wad of cash she'd just withdrawn from her building society account on his shabby desk.

She'd taken a month's leave from work so that she could drive up to see Martina and Ted as often as possible while Martina was still well enough to have visitors.

Although Faith passed her driving test back when she was twenty-one, she hadn't been behind the wheel of a car since, but Tom, who had passed the police advanced driver test top of his cohort, sat in the passenger seat beside her for what felt to him like a whole weekend until she got used to London driving.

And then with his encouragement vibrating in her ears still, she felt comfortable enough to tackle the M1 with her first solo drive northwards to Wakefield, her route mapped in a blue highlighter on the huge AA British Isles road map book Maria gave her on the day Faith bought the car, with, belt and braces, a neatly written description of the route tucked behind the pages of maps and the lengthy index, just in case.

She was the first person in the Wills family who learned to drive, and the first to own a car. Faith was also the first person in the Wills family to be ribbed for her 'audacity' in these things, her sisters enjoying their teasing, especially when they insisted on naming the car UMG, pronounced um-ger, for Upwardly Mobile Gladys.

Maria thought it was good the twins didn't seem to be holding it against Faith that she had connected with her blood grandparents, and Faith gave no sign of minding her sisters' kidding, but Maria couldn't shake the fear that on one of these visits Fred would come back to see his mother and run into Faith. Fred was too dangerous a man for this ever to be a good option.

Ted did his best to put Maria at ease, saying he had told Fred that it was best that he kept his distance, as Martina needed peace and quiet, and if Fred cared for his mother at all, he would understand the best thing was for him to stay well away. Ted had added Fred had never been much of a mummy's boy or paid his mother much heed, and so it was unlikely he would be keen to embark on any sort of mercy dash.

Hope

And Maria relaxed a little further when Tom found out there was an outstanding arrest warrant in Fred's name that meant should he fly into the country on a scheduled flight, or come in by ferry, then a police alert would be issued on him presenting his passport.

It did mean Fred could enter the UK should he charter a small plane to a private and non-commercial airfield, but Tom reassured Maria that the local police had let it be known among Fred's old cronies that the police had heard his mother's health wasn't great and consequently they would be keeping an eye out for him. The bush telegraph of the Yorkshire underworld would be sure to let Fred know that if he didn't want to end up in the Wood Street custody suite, he'd best stay away.

'What's Fred wanted for?' Maria asked.

'I doubt I'm supposed to know, and so I'm not going to tell you so you never have to lie on my behalf. But it's five offences, all with potential prison terms,' said Tom. 'And the rumour from the dinner queue is that Fred Walton is holed up in Spain, giving the Policía Nacional and the Guardia Civil quite the run-around and so he's got a lot to think about over there. He went out and Ted Walton called in a few favours from his old cronies that Fred be given some opportunities. But Fred seems to have upset quite a lot of people of the sort one shouldn't upset.'

*

On the afternoon when later Hope would be auctioning her own virginity, Faith dropped Tom off outside the boxing club where the auction, illegal obviously, would take place with brick-shithouse-sized bouncers on the door, and then she set off to spend the night at Ted and Martina's.

Inside the club, Tom looked around, sizing up potential risks and benefits.

The boxing club was closed for the day, and a hardboard cover had been laid over the boxing ring itself, where Hope would stand for the auction.

Tom was going to be there for the auction as the eyes and ears of the Wills family, with Big Danny and Little Danny strolling around too, so they could help things run smoothly but also blend in with the crowd, looking like people who might want to put in a bid so that those there who were one-time bidders and weren't regulars at Chantal's didn't get unnecessarily rattled.

Tom had been told to get to the venue early to give it this final once-over, leaving ample time to get put into place any further safety measures he felt were needed.

And Big Danny thought there'd be a lot of his fraternity there, which again would be a sign that nobody step out of line if they didn't want to face a slap or two from one or more of his henchmen.

People in the know understood that Big Danny had

Hope

long owned a financial stake in Chantal's (and it had proved a very good investment for him), and his interest in the business was why there was very rarely trouble there, either from the clients, or from other gangs who might want a piece of the action. Neither Tom nor Big Danny expected there would be trouble later on.

Hope had been very strict about reminding Tom, and Big Danny and Little Danny too, that they weren't to call her by the name Hope at all. They must all take care to remember that she was 'Scarlet' for the whole night of the auction.

Over at Cadogan Terrace, Charity and Lisa were helping Hope doll herself up, and they would go in the taxi with her to the boxing club, although they wouldn't go inside and the taxi would take them straight home again after they had seen Hope safely collected by one of the bouncers, as other than a few drag queens who wanted to see the spectacle, and Chantal too, this would be a men-only affair.

Rather against her better judgement, Faith had been persuaded a few weeks earlier to write the rules of the auction, and as Chantal had widely circulated them, this meant that everybody – bidders and spectators alike – knew that whoever won the auction, the top bidder, and Hope were not going to go any further later in the night to conclude the agreement in any physical sense. The most the auction's winner could expect was a simple handshake with Hope to seal their deal.

In part this was to allow the winning bid to be paid by bank transfer at some point in the following week, with twenty thousand pounds going to the boxing club's owner as he was taking perhaps the biggest risk of the night, and the entertainers and security staff were also being paid enough to take it all very seriously too. Chantal would be splitting the remaining profit fifty-fifty. Should the bidding not reach a sum that would see them clear at least fifty thousand pounds, the auction would be abandoned; the money already in from the seats sold to the spectators was enough to cover their other running costs.

Hope was brilliant at speedy mathematical calculations in her head, and so she would be able to let Chantal know immediately after the bidding concluded exactly how the auction had ended in terms of money, without any need to resort to a calculator.

While the various arrangements had been put in place over a space of ten days from when Chantal put up a notice on the board confirming that what Hope had teased on New Year's Day was the auction of her virginity, Maria refused to listen to or to comment on any of the family's discussions concerning the auction.

She could not make peace with the idea on any level.

Hope

And so she planned on spending the night of the auction itself holed up at home, watching videos of *The Bodyguard* and *Ghost*.

The man in Blockbusters had put up a spirited defence for Maria also renting *Pretty Woman*, but Maria knew she didn't want to watch a romance with a passing similarity to her own experience, especially with what Hope was undertaking.

As the hours ticked down and it got to when Hope had to leave Cadogan Terrace, Maria was able to go outside to hug her dramatically made-up daughter right before she got into the black cab that would ferry her to the boxing club, Maria unable to resist saying, 'You don't have to go through with it if you change your mind, Hope. Please remember that.'

Hope shrugged and told her mother not to worry as she'd be fine.

That Maria could tell Hope and Charity had downed at least one bottle of fizz between them, and maybe even two, wasn't reassuring.

But she just said, 'I love you,' through the window of the taxi as Hope scooted across the cab's back seat.

And then Lisa linked her arm through one of Maria's, and Charity did the same on the other side.

'We'll see her there safely, and be back here soon, and then me and Lisa will be up to join you on the sofa,' said

Charity, and she kissed her mother, adding, 'First one to cry in *Ghost* has to buy the takeaway.'

As Lisa and Charity climbed into the taxi, Maria called, 'Deal,' after them, as she realised she'd rather be watching the films with these two as a welcome distraction, than trying to concentrate on a film while sitting on her own when her thoughts would be dominated by what might be going on at the auction.

Chantal and Hope had decided that holding the auction on neutral territory was a safer situation for all, as if it got too raucous at Chantal's should they have held it there, it might have been hard for them to control things, as some people would be wanting their kinks satisfied while being a bit too fired up by watching other men get excited, while others might have wanted to watch, and the establishment just wasn't designed for that.

In the normal run of things, most of what went on at Chantal's happened in a relatively private manner, with punters being usually catered for on their own in small separate specialist rooms. And even in the larger rubber-leather room with its chain-link fencing attached to the walls, it was rare for more than about seven or eight people to get together when discreetly supervised orgies were occasionally allowed to take place, with everyone knowing the safe words and play immediately being stopped for everyone the moment anyone called out one of the agreed words.

Chantal was exceptionally safety-conscious as she had once heard of a BDSM establishment that had allowed a large group of men into an unsupervised meeting room, after which things had gone too far, with the result that a man nearly suffocated when his gimp mask twisted and nobody understood he was calling his safe word as he struggled to breathe. Charges had ended up being brought against the club's proprietors, and robust damages had had to be paid as the man had been left with life-changing injuries, and Chantal was determined that nothing like that would ever happen at her own venue.

The biggest issue of the auction had previously been them wondering how would they answer should anyone question whether Hope was in fact a virgin, but actually nobody had raised this. Hope had been prepared to get a sworn affidavit from a doctor to the effect, but it turned out she hadn't needed to.

The next biggest worry for Chantal and Hope was how Hope was going to be snuck away in case of anyone following her, and so the plan in place was a female double of Hope, dressed in the same outfit, setting off after everyone had left, with a security man lying on the floor in the taxi.

Hope herself would leave immediately she was out of the boxing ring, exiting through the fire escape at the back of the building with two bouncers, and heading to the back door of a pub in the adjoining street, where she would spend the night in a spare bed made up in a closet in the eaves of the pub's roof. The bouncers would stay outside the closet's door but inside the locked door to the bedroom the closet opened into. Hope would be in mufti the next morning, her distinctive hair tucked up inside a hat, as Tom drove her home.

It was undeniable that there had been a growing sense of excitement about the auction, especially when it was announced that only men who paid a joining fee of at least one thousand pounds would be allowed to bid, ideally all registered beforehand and with their bank details checked.

Several others had asked if they could pay cash, as they didn't want their wives and/or business associates to question a large sum leaving a bank account. If Chantal knew them and thought them reliable, she decided she would make the odd exception and they could join the auction, although she pointed out firmly to each man that if a cash bidder won on the night but then couldn't pay in full before leaving the venue, the auction would default to the underbidder. Specialist security staff had been booked to ensure the safety of the cash and to see unsuccessful cash bidders home.

So far, forty-two men had formally let it be known they planned to bid and had paid the joining fee, and in addition

Hope

Chantal had sold over one hundred seats to spectators at two hundred pounds a pop. Entertainment bookending the auction itself would be provided by the more risqué artists who'd performed in the annual Secret Policeman's Ball.

The auction itself would take place mid-way through the evening's entertainment, at nine o'clock precisely, and it would last only a few minutes, with Hope being her own MC.

The doors to the boxing club weren't going to be unlocked until seven-forty-five and all identities would be checked on arrival. The entertainment would be at eight-fifteen, with no entry permitted after that point. This timing had been chosen after a lot of discussion, as it would enable the bidders to loosen up through two or three drinks, but not have so much that they were rowdy.

Hope, or more exactly 'Scarlet', stood close to the sound system, ready to greet everyone individually as they came in.

She'd felt more than a bit giddy with excitement when she'd been saying goodbye to Maria, but now the time was nearly here, those feelings had given way to ones of icy calm.

She knew what she had to do, and she was determined to acquit herself well.

Chantal had her hand on the walkie-talkie to the staff at the front door, and she looked at Hope, who nodded.

The walkie-talkie crackled into life with Chantal's instruction to the doormen, and the door to the street was unlocked.

For the next half hour Hope mingled, trying to spend a little time with everyone so they could see up close her trim figure and clear skin. An overexcited and slightly wild-looking Harry Stewart kept getting under her feet, but Tom noticed this, and the next time Hope looked around neither Tom nor Harry were in sight.

Big Danny and Little Danny knew quite a lot of people there, and they, and Chantal, made sure the drinks flowed until ten past eight, when a bell was rung for people to take their seats on the gold chairs with red velvet seats that Chantal had hired that had been placed around the ring. Big Danny was in his element as he introduced the various acts; he kept things moving swiftly along, and then at a minute to nine o'clock, he did a countdown to Scarlet stepping onto the stage, the audience joining in. And Chantal and Hope were pleased that Big Danny's gang connections meant the crowd were remaining good-natured and well behaved.

Hope strutted slowly around the ring so that everyone could get a last good look at her, and then she stood in the centre of the ring calmly, smoke from the

Hope

audience's cigarettes and cigars swirling ethereally around her.

She kept her voice low as she said, 'Good evening to everyone. I am Scarlet, and I thank you for coming. Which of you gents am I going to be lucky enough to be paid a fortune by to spend some private time with?'

'Me!' somebody squeaked, and the whole room laughed. Hope didn't need to be told that it was Harry who had called out.

'Let's go then,' she said in an even softer voice, in her mind thanking Faith for this courtroom tip in making the whole room concentrate on her. 'Who's going to start it off?'

The bidding went high quickly, with most punters being knocked out almost immediately, and it ended up in a contest between two middle-aged men.

Hope could see wedding rings on both of them but this wasn't a surprise particularly.

One was a gaudily dressed and somewhat rumpled cowboy-boot-wearing American businessman called Bud Metzler who had thinning hair and a little beer gut, while the other, an industrialist named Hans Smit, was wearing a smart grey suit with a shirt so polar white that it almost made Hope's eyes hurt to look at it, and he had told Hope that he had flown in especially from Frankfurt for the event.

Hans was well over six foot and definitely better-looking, and his taut body suggested that he spent a significant amount of his life at the gym, as there didn't look to be an ounce of fat anywhere on him.

But Hope felt there was something engaging about Bud that she warmed to more, and she was pleased when he triumphed in the auction with a ridiculously high final bid.

Amid a cheering crowd, Bud scrambled into the boxing ring and stood beside her with his face beaming happily, as from the corner of her eye Hope noticed Chantal shepherding an obviously overcome Harry out of the room. His bid had been one of the first to be trumped.

'You are one of the most stunning women I have ever seen, and I am honoured to have won, ma'am,' Bud told her quietly so that the audience wouldn't hear, and as they shook hands and Chantal took several photographs, Bud deliberately made his eyes cross to make Hope laugh. He was shorter than she was in her high heels, and she'd noticed the crinkle of laughter lines around his eyes as he folded both his hands around her hand in its black silk evening glove.

Hope stepped back and blew him a chaste kiss, as she said, 'Until next time then, Mr Bud Metzler.'

Little Danny escorted Bud down from the ring, gifting him a chilled bottle of Krug champagne in a shiny ice

Hope

bucket once his feet were firmly on the ground. Meanwhile Hope made sure to commiserate with Hans Smit and thank him for being so game.

And then as the first entertainer of the second half of the evening was distracting everyone as they clapped him up and into the boxing ring, Big Danny spirited Hope through a heavy curtain that hid a passage and deposited her into the safety of the two bouncers Big Danny had picked from his crew, who would protect her during the night. They were huge and beefy, with thighs bigger than Hope's waist, and Big Danny had told Hope they were perfect for the job as they were in a relationship with each other, and wouldn't be distracted by any thoughts, other than making sure Hope didn't come to any harm.

Chantal nipped through the curtain and called down the passageway after Hope, 'Good going, girl!'

Hope suddenly felt a wave of exhaustion crash over her as the excitement of the previous few minutes left her, and so as she turned towards Chantal she mimed ringing her the next day, and then the huge heavy-guys quickly bustled Hope out through the fire door.

As the comedian began telling some very lewd jokes, the catcalls and sounds of loud belly laughs made clear that the audience was now very ready to let off steam and spend lots of money at the bar that had been set up.

All, that was, except Harry Stewart who was creating

merry hell in the street outside in temper at not winning the auction, kicking parked cars and swearing like a trooper. Tom was trying to be patient with him but was on the point of saying that Harry was about to be arrested if he didn't get himself under control, and if that happened then charges would be brought and Harry needn't think he would be given a caution for a second time.

Harry stopped his hullaballoo, and Tom signalled to one of the staff that Harry should be escorted home, calling out 'thirty' as Harry was put in a car, so the man knew he had to spend thirty minutes inside with Harry after they got to his house, in order to give Harry a decent amount of time to cool down and get control of himself.

CHAPTER TWELVE

At the same time, although up in Wakefield, Martina had just woken up.

Faith had been about to go to bed, but Ted tapped on the door to the guest room, saying that if Faith was awake still, then Martina would love to see her.

'Just coming,' said Faith. She slipped into her pocket the box with the ring that Martina had given her.

Martina looked brighter than when Faith had met her previously, and when she told her that, Martina answered that she damn well should do as she'd been asleep most of the day.

'Mrs Walton,' Faith said after she had asked after Martina's health – although Ted had previously said it was fine to call them both by their Christian names, Faith felt odd about doing so – but the older woman asked if Faith would please call her Martina.

'OK.' Faith paused, and then said, 'Martina, this is the most lovely ring, and I am very honoured you thought of giving it to me on the day we met. But it is obviously valuable, and although I think it is amazing, I need to see if you felt you acted a bit hastily, as I would one hundred per cent understand if you wanted it back.'

'Don't be such a daft ha'p'orth! Of course you must have it, Faith,' Martina insisted. 'Give it here.'

And Martina slid the ring onto the third finger of Faith's right hand. It fit perfectly, the diamonds sparkling in the low light of the bedroom.

Faith studied it for a long time. 'I rather hoped you'd want me to keep it, although I would have given it back instantly if you had asked. I feel really lucky. I want you to know that I am so pleased to have met you and Ted. And I don't think I am ever going to take the ring off as every time I see it I shall be reminded of you.'

Faith reached then into her pocket and drew out a second small box, which she placed in Martina's hand. 'Go on, open it,' Faith told her. 'I chose this for you.'

Inside was a delicate white-gold chain, onto which a tiny pendant hung that was engraved with two hands clasping.

Martina held it in the pool of light the lamp made beside the bed. 'It's perfect – thank you. What a fool our Fred was all those years ago . . .'

'Let's not think about him just now. Instead I want to hear all about you so I know much more about where I

Hope

come from. My mother, and her mother Annie, have always been very economical with the truth about their time here.'

Then Faith helped fasten the chain around Martina's neck, and as Martina lay stroking the pendant, she began to tell Faith about how she and Ted fell in love.

When Martina was too tired to speak any longer but couldn't bear the thought of settling down for the night quite yet, Faith began to read to her from the library book sat on the bedside table, not stopping until long after Faith's gentle voice had lulled Martina to sleep.

Faith stayed quietly where she was, staring at her right hand. The ring felt as if it had been made for her. And then Faith realised that the ring, and Martina and Ted, had made her feel as if she had come home. They wanted so little from her, and yet here she was, being gifted so, so much from them in every sense, in return for her merely spending time in their home.

CHAPTER THIRTEEN

The next morning Ted showed Faith around the local haunts, including the street where Gary, Annie and Maria had lived together, the secondary school Maria attended and the Woollies where Maria and Fred had first met.

His gambling club was still in business. And although it was too early in the day for it to be open and they had to wend their way around the cleaners, Ted was obviously proud of the club, which he'd taken legit.

He explained that about ten years previously he'd stopped any prostitution taking place on the premises with the hostesses, as he thought it was too distracting for the clients and he'd become more interested in hooking them into the higher-value card or craps games, as he'd built a reputation for having an establishment where big money was there for the taking.

The result was men with deep pockets came from a much wider area to gamble, many going on to become regulars, and percentage-wise the financial returns for the house were better in every way with this business model, when compared with how much the hostesses could earn for him, no matter how great the sex was they gave the clients, especially as without the distraction of a pretty face, it kept the men at the tables. And about a year later Ted had taken the plunge in taking everything above board, and now he paid tax on his earnings.

Faith got the impression that if the hostesses had been bringing in a fortune then Ted wouldn't have had an objection in keeping their sex work going. It was more that times and tastes had changed, and so Ted's business had changed accordingly.

Part of the club had been converted into a traditional licensed casino, complete with a roulette wheel at the head of a large green bias table, and Ted explained that the club's hostesses focused these days on keeping the drinks coming and in looking decorative as they stood beside the punters to encourage ever bigger bets, each hostess being assigned a punter to tend to and spoil the moment he came in through the door, unless they brought their wives or girlfriends.

'Your club is more upmarket than Annie made it sound,' said Faith, as she glanced up and noticed a plethora of security cameras set into the ceiling. 'My sister Hope would love it.'

'Perhaps you'll bring her up for a night sometime – it's

always good to have new faces, and I'd make sure she'd be a VIP.'

'I suspect she'd wipe the floor with your bottom line. Hope's just a bit too good with figures.' Faith laughed.

'I like the sound of her already! Still, back in the fifties in Annie and Joyce's day, I confess it was pretty basic. These days, it's mostly about sophistication and talking posh, and men in suits and women doused in a bottle of perfume. And those cameras you clocked are for keeping my staff honest as much as seeing what our guests are up to – constantly handling large wads of cash can be tempting in time even to the most loyal staff,' Ted told her.

'So it's all on the straight and narrow then?' Faith asked.

Ted shrugged. 'More or less – a bit more periodically, and a bit less at other times. And I have a pit boss nobody – staff or clientele – would want to get on the wrong side of. Any line I cross now, it's largely just to keep my hand in, or to let my competitors know Ted Walton is still very much in business in the way he was thirty-five years ago. But with this club here, having a proper accountant and local authority inspections of the club has taught me that it's less of a headache in the long run as at least it operates according to clear rules, while the crim side of the fence goes a bit wild west now and again.'

'Do you get much trouble with other rival gangs?' Faith

slipped in this question to let Ted know she was under no illusion about the man he was.

'Only if Fred's here, as he will go after a turf war given the chance. But no, not so as you'd notice otherwise. But then I – and Martina – don't hold with having anything to do with drugs or hardcore porn. And I think these days that most of the other gangs focus on that and other things I can't abide, like bringing in girls from Eastern Europe and taking their passports and then pimping them out, or stealing expensive cars to order and shipping them abroad, or the odd bit of extorting protection money from shopkeepers, or running rings of illegal taxi cabs, or people trafficking, or feeding rings of kiddie fiddlers, or whatever. So if I don't bother them or step on their toes, and I keep schtum with the police if there's trouble among them that I know about, then they pretty much leave me to get on with what I do, knowing that I've cut out most of the other stuff, as I don't want the heat. I have eight bookies, and clubs in Leeds and York as well as this one, and everything in those is clean, and generally, that's enough for a man of my age.'

Faith laughed. 'I won't be rude enough to ask your age, or what the small interests on the wrong side of the law you still hold might be, although having seen the things in your house, I'd hazard a guess at something to do with maybe antiques or jewellery . . .' Ted looked taken aback

Hope

at Faith's comment, a bit like a little boy who's been caught by his mother raiding the snacks drawer. And so Faith suspected she'd guessed correctly, but to smooth the moment, she added, 'But how does Fred fit into all of this?'

'Truth be told, not much, as he's a bit of a waster, and he's not that bright. I've done my best with him, but there it is. Years ago I tried to set him up with a bit of a property portfolio that I would get a percentage of the profits from, seeing I was the only investor, but although it had lots of potential, he's never done much more than collect a few rents, and I think it's almost bankrupt now. He's part of some sort of shady timeshare operation in Portugal, I know, and with all the building on the Costa he's got some skips he rents out that he swears is a gold mine but I'm yet to be convinced,' said Ted.

'Really, I think he dreams of owning a golf complex, and a corresponding village of accommodation for visitors, but he doesn't seem to have much of a business head. I didn't think his figures stacked up when he showed me the plans, and I told him so, which didn't go down well. He's got to pay the alimony for three ex-wives, and they're not the sort to avoid the designers, so it's time he concentrated on doing a bit of graft as he knows that I'm not going to be around and bankrolling him for ever, otherwise he's going to end up without a pot to piss in, excuse my French, and the thought of this makes his temper vile. The problem with Fred is he thinks every problem can be solved with muscle, when nearly always it should be the last resort. Most gangs understand this eventually, but Fred has never understood. Our lives are much easier now he's abroad.'

'Are you and Martina in touch with any of his former wives?'

'Probably a bit more often than Fred is, as they all send cards at Christmas. But me and Martina never really got on with any of them, not that we saw them unless Fred asked us to his for a barbecue. He never had children with any of them, and even if they wanted to be close to me and Martina, they're probably scared of what Fred would do to them if he thought they were going behind his back. He's got a girlfriend called Anna now, but from what we can tell, it's very off and on.'

Hmmn, Faith grunted quietly to herself, mentally making a note to remember Anna's name.

When she got back to London just before teatime, and went to Cadogan Terrace, Faith found Hope thrilled with how the auction had gone, and Maria looking relieved.

She joined them for some tea and got all the gen on the auction from Hope, but afterwards when Faith took some cake down to Charity's flat in the basement, it was to hear the muffled sound of Charity violently sobbing the other

Hope

side of the door, and Little Danny trying to comfort her, saying they could try again soon and it might be a very different story next month, at which point Charity's sobs became a wail of agony.

Faith padded backwards as quietly as she could, and she headed back upstairs to Maria's flat, her mother's suddenly tense expression when Faith came in seeming to understand at once why she might be back upstairs so quickly, especially as she was still holding the plate of uneaten cake.

'Mummy, I don't think Charity and Little Danny's trip to Paris did the trick,' said Faith.

Maria gave a deep sigh. 'Oh no, I'd so had my fingers crossed for them,' she added as she began to stare with unfocused eyes out of the window.

Looking back on it later, Faith, Hope and Maria agreed that it was from this point on that the bubbly and fun Charity they knew and loved seemed to disappear, giving way instead to a cold and snappy young woman nobody really recognised or indeed liked much.

The Day-Glo wardrobe and hair-sprayed big hair were replaced by a more sombre way of dressing that they all found hard to get used to, and it wasn't long before Charity had a hard glint in her eyes and a stroppy, dissatisfied edge to her voice that seemed to have completely subsumed her previous playful and generous nature.

Little Danny looked increasingly wary of his wife, with Charity very obviously pushing him away at every opportunity, while Big Danny and Lisa were obviously concerned, although they felt they couldn't do much to help as Little Danny insisted on standing up for his wife if they dared to voice even a hint of criticism.

Maria found it heartbreaking to see a once-close couple now barely able to look at each other. Charity and Little Danny had been obsessed with each other since they'd first met as toddlers, and they had never wavered in this. Maria wasn't certain how either of them would cope if they did separate, as their lives had always been so entwined with one another.

Still, this didn't stop Charity becoming increasingly silent and tight-lipped, and no matter what anyone suggested in an attempt to cheer her up, she didn't seem even to hear. Her enthusiasm for everything drained, other than the one thing in her current frame of mind she shouldn't be doing – hoisting.

And although Charity was out of practice in this, since serving a short prison sentence for numerous shoplifting offences that had all been rolled into one a couple of years back, she began to go 'up west' with a vengeance, taking silly risks as she shoplifted from the luxury department stores all manner of items that she had no interest in and couldn't sell on.

Lisa, a much more experienced hoister, did her best to accompany Charity in an effort to try and keep her out of trouble, but on more than one occasion, Charity gave Lisa the slip, and soon Lisa confided to Maria that she was at her wits' end over the risks her daughter-in-law was taking, and that this behaviour was terrifying Little Danny too. Maria said she felt the same, and she didn't really know how to help Charity.

For Maria, and Faith and Hope, had all tried on different occasions to speak with Charity, urging her to be cautious and that she should rest up and let Little Danny take care of her as she was exhausting herself.

But Charity brushed away their concerns as furiously she stared them down, saying in various ways that they should keep their advice and sympathy for someone who cared, and they could save their breath in trying to make her feel guilty, because she certainly didn't care what any of them thought.

It felt nothing short of a disaster waiting to happen.

CHAPTER FOURTEEN

An official-looking letter arrived for Maria by registered post. The business-sized envelope was made from thick and expensive cream paper that had a real weight to it, and there was an embossed solicitor's stamp on it that showed an address in Wakefield.

Maria frowned. She was at a loss as she wasn't expecting any sort of letter, and she couldn't think why a Wakefield legal practice would be contacting her.

Indeed the sight of the letter gave her the heebie-jeebies, and she went to Hope's flat immediately beside hers, and knocked at the door, placing the unopened envelope in her daughter's hands when Hope asked her in, saying, 'What do you think this is?'

'I think it's an envelope,' said Hope, but one look at Maria's anxious face told Hope that now wasn't the time for being facetious, and so she added more seriously, 'Do you want me to open it for you, Mummy?'

Maria nodded, and carefully Hope slid her finger under

the envelope's flap, pulling out a single folded page of the lush cream paper, and Maria glimpsed a deep maroon logo at the top of the paper.

Hope glanced at its contents, then beamed at her mother.

'It's good news. Following your discussion when you visited Wakefield, it seems that Ted Walton plans on gifting you what the solicitor describes as a substantial sum of money, in order that you can put it towards what you had been talking about. He had planned on leaving you a sum in his will, but he is bringing the gift forward as he thinks it will be more use now.'

Speechless and unable to think of anything that she and Ted had been talking about which might warrant a response like this, Maria could only stand stock-still and blink at her daughter.

Whatever she thought the letter might say, it certainly wasn't this.

'I'm not sure that is good news.' The note of doubt was clear in Maria's tone.

And then she remembered mentioning that she might volunteer to do something to help battered women.

Hope ignored her mother's comment, saying instead, 'I'm assuming what the solicitor isn't saying to you right now is that a gift at this time, and then provided Ted lives for another seven years, means that the sum won't be

Hope

included in his estate upon his death and therefore won't be liable for tax. That's sound thinking on his, or his financial adviser's part.'

After a long pause, Maria murmured, 'Er, um, is . . . is a sum mentioned?'

'That is the best bit, Mummy. Some investments are being liquified apparently and so there isn't a final figure yet, but the sum you should get is predicted by the solicitor to be in excess of half a million pounds,' said Hope.

'Holy Mary mother of God!' Maria's voice sounded close to a yelp, and she became so pale that Hope had to help her to a chair.

'I don't want it. I can't possibly accept,' Maria kept muttering. 'It's far too much responsibility for me.'

'Mummy, calm down,' said Hope, 'and take a day to think about this. Please. Then maybe speak to Father O'Reilly to see what he thinks, and to Ted too – actually the letter says that the solicitor is going to courier a personal letter to you tomorrow that Ted has written for you, so that may help.'

'I'd been to a meeting that Father O'Reilly allowed to take place at his presbytery that was about battered women, and I mentioned to Ted I'd found it very moving, and I'd wondered about volunteering. But I never said I wanted funds or actually to *do* anything concrete,' said Maria. 'Being a kindly ear to these poor girls is all I was considering. Something like what Ted seems to think I had in mind just isn't me at all.'

Hope didn't feel she had done enough to reassure her mother, and so she added, 'I understand it feels like a lot of responsibility and quite a burden, really I do. But you could set up a charitable trust, I would think, and that money could end up doing a huge amount of good. I'd put some money in too, and so would Big Danny, I'm sure, and so perhaps it could be something of a family enterprise. I can certainly mention to Bud Metzler too, as he strikes me as someone with an expansive chequebook. But don't think about details now. Take some time to get used to the idea.'

'I don't want it, Hope, really I don't.'

Hope made her mother a strong cup of tea, and put three heaped teaspoons of sugar in it, and then she sat beside her mother, holding her hand.

Although Maria had had what Hope honestly believed was good news, her perplexed expression suggested she was still in shock.

Hope thought it a pity that Maria's life had been so tough that she had been conditioned to find bad news easier to bear than something positive and amazing like this.

Of course everyone at Cadogan Terrace was up into the small hours talking about what had happened, with Charity looking momentarily interested and Faith joining them too, but when she went to bed, Maria still felt as confused as ever.

Knowing this, early next morning before breakfast, Hope rang Father O'Reilly, saying she was going to be deliberately cagey in how she spoke to him, but something unexpected had happened and she thought her mother would appreciate it very much if he came over for a chat, as Maria had had news she needed to talk to someone about.

So at noon Father O'Reilly arrived, and Maria immediately said, 'I suppose Hope rang you.'

'That she did,' he admitted. 'But I can go if now is not a good time or she was being presumptuous.'

Maria shook her head and stood aside so that he could come in. She made some tea and then showed him the letter as she told the father about the comments she had made to Ted Walton.

He read it slowly, and when he'd finished, he looked at Maria, his expression hard to read as he scrutinised Maria's face, trying to gauge what she felt about it.

Maria guessed this was what he was doing, and sniffed in recognition.

'Father, I don't know what I feel. And Ted's letter hasn't arrived yet. I don't for a moment believe that I am the right person for this, even though I know one should never look a gift horse in the mouth, and all the rest. I hate the idea of having such a burden of responsibility. But somehow I find I can't quite turn it down out of hand, and yet I can't bring myself to like the idea of having this money and being the person who has to decide what to do with it either. My head feels such a muddle, and I feel scared, and yet a little bit excited too. I'm just an ordinary person, so it feels too much for me.'

Father O'Reilly leaned towards Maria.

'You and I have known each other for many years, Maria, and personally I think you are much stronger than you know, and "ordinary" is something you could never be. But this is a big thing and it's not to be undertaken lightly. If you don't want to, you don't have to accept the money – no one could blame you for that.'

The father didn't break eye contact and then he added, 'But if you wanted, you'd have the help every step of the way of your three girls, and both the Dannys too and Lisa, and me of course. I could rustle you up some great backup to help you too. Shamus knows how to make himself useful, and I've a couple of others with no side to them who'd be willing to back you up too, I'm sure.'

He stirred some sugar into his tea, and Maria listened to the tinkle of the spoon on the rim of the mug as he tapped it to shake off a last drip or two.

The doorbell rang and they heard Hope running down the stairs, and then belting back up to Maria's flat. The solicitor's missive that contained Ted's letter had arrived.

Hope

Dear Maria,

Firstly, let me thank you on the behalf of Martina and myself for not trying to keep Faith away from us – that is the biggest gift anyone could ever make us.

And now I want to do something for you. You seemed full of life, and actually not so different to how you looked as a teenager, when you told me about maybe doing something for a cause that is close to your heart. And so in the memory of Annie, and in a small recompense for Fred's behaviour to you, please accept the money order my solicitor is preparing. Martina and I are in no doubt you will do something valuable with it.

Best wishes,
Ted Walton

Maria passed this second letter across to Father O'Reilly as she said, 'Faith wondered about some sort of pressure group that would campaign on behalf of these women, and she mentioned last night that she knows a judge who always gives heavy sentences to men who are violent to women, and she wondered if he might be prepared to help in some way, perhaps by drumming up some support among the judiciary.'

Father O'Reilly looked up. 'It sounds to me then as if

it's not a definite no on your part, then, to accepting this money?'

'Maybe,' whispered Maria, her voice so low that it almost wasn't there at all.

CHAPTER FIFTEEN

Bud Metzler asked Hope to lunch.

Through Chantal, he had asked for the message to be passed on to Hope that he would love to take her out and get to know her a little more before they had what he described as their 'special night'.

And Chantal passed the message on by phone to Hope, saying that if they ate at Harvey Nichols, Bud had stressed that he would be very happy to treat Hope to a complete new outfit, head to toe, that she could wear for what they had contracted to do, which would take place on another occasion, and of course he would gift her whatever she chose so that she could keep them afterwards.

Hope couldn't help feel dubious, but then she decided to go. Her virginity could only be disposed of the once, and so she might as well make it as relaxing an experience as possible for herself, she reasoned, and the best way for this to happen was probably to get to know Bud a little.

'As far as I can see you don't have anything to lose as it's in the sort of public place where everyone behaves well,' Chantal told her. (Hope thought of the number of times Charity had been shoplifting at the store, so she didn't think that Chantal's good behaviour comment was strictly justified.) Then Chantal added, 'And I gave Bud your sizes so that he can use the personal shopping service at Harvey Nicks and you won't have to spend hours trailing around the store.'

Hope didn't answer as she was thinking.

Her idea of auctioning herself, so bold-feeling and titillatingly out there when she'd first come up with it, was seeming much less so now. The closer she got to having to follow through the deal had been done, the more mixed her feelings were about it.

And, if Hope was honest with herself, there was a growing part of her that wished heartily that she had never announced anything about her idea, and that, later, she had allowed herself to be talked out of holding the auction by Maria and her sisters, and Father O'Reilly too. Chantal had been the only person who knew her who had supported the idea, but of course she had a vested interest to protect.

To fill the silence, Chantal chattered on, 'In other news, it's feeling very quiet and drab here without you, now all the excitement is over.'

'I'm not sure it's ever quiet or drab at Chantal's. But is Harry behaving himself? He didn't cover himself in glory at the auction.'

Hope

'I wouldn't know, as he's not been in – the last time I saw him was when he was creating mayhem in the street outside the boxing club after it was all over. But I've a couple of new puppies just come who seem hot to trot, and so I can't say that I'm missing him.'

'Me neither. There's something just a bit too much about him,' said Hope. 'Um . . . um, did Bud say anything else about what he wanted to happen on the night?'

'Not exactly. But I didn't get any sense of him wanting anything that you need to be worried about – I think it will all be straight-up vanilla. He's never been to Chantal's and I rang around the other clubs, and nobody has seen him there, so he doesn't seem a player in the fetish world. I expect he heard about the auction at the golf club or somewhere like that,' said Chantal.

'But do be prepared to be spoiled, Hope, as he did ask me what music you like, and what your favourite food and champagne is, and perfume too, and was there anything he might do that you'd find really off-putting. For two pins, I'd swap places with you, as I could learn to love a bit of spoiling on that level.'

'God, Bud Metzler sounds better than an actual boyfriend.'

'Yup, doesn't he?!' squealed Chantal, and then they laughed.

And at their lunch, Bud didn't do or say anything to dissuade Hope that he wasn't a perfect gentleman.

She'd toned down her normal look so that she wore no eye make-up and her lips were only lightly glossed and her nails bare, and she was wearing a simple black dress and boots as Hope thought her full-blown goth attitude would prove to be too much for him in daylight, and in case it would draw the sort of attention to her in a posh restaurant that right now she'd rather avoid.

Bud stood up to greet her when she arrived, and he didn't sit down until the waiter had seated her and placed a heavily starched napkin on her lap.

'I confess this is strange, Mr Metzler,' said Hope, after they'd said the usual pleasantries. 'I've never been on any sort of romantic date before, or actually even had lunch with a man on my own.'

'Never? And by the way, everyone calls me plain old Bud rather than Mr Metzler.'

'No. It's not been my thing, plain old Bud.' Hope smiled to show she was being playful rather than rude.

'So what has been your thing?'

'I'm not sure really.' Hope thought about it for a few seconds. 'Maybe working people out?'

'That's one of my favourite things too, Scarlet...' said Bud.

And before they knew it, the conversation was flowing

Hope

easily between them, with quite a lot of banter that made her laugh, and Hope was relieved once more that it had been Bud who'd won the auction and not Hans Smit, as she was one hundred per cent certain he would have been much harder to form a connection with.

Hope was surprised how much she liked Bud, as she had felt very nervous on her way over to Knightsbridge, which wasn't a feeling she was particularly familiar with. Bud proved an aimable and talkative lunch companion, despite him being at least twenty-five years older than her.

He was good with his questions, and he seemed genuinely interested in her answers. And she asked him his opinion on stories in the news and what Bud thought the new US president would focus on primarily. And about what it had been like for him growing up in Houston in Texas and then starting his business there, and why now was the time for him to be in the UK. Each time he gave a full and honest answer to her probing. He was sweet and respectful too in talking about his wife, which Hope hadn't really expected.

In fact they got on so well that just before coffee was served, Hope said, 'My name's not Scarlet, you know. You may call me Hope, if you'd like to, which is what I'm really called. Or you can keep on with the Scarlet. Whichever works best for you is fine with me.'

At the end of the meal, they were escorted to the personal shopping division. As Bud was no sharp dresser himself, Hope had expected some garish outfits to be waiting for her.

He told her he'd wait on the sofa outside the personal shopping area so that her outfit could be a surprise for him on the night.

Inside the room, a glass of champagne was placed in her hand, and then Hope was pleasantly surprised to find about a dozen sophisticated dresses hanging on a clothes rail for her to peruse, nearly all of which she really liked if she had to be non-goth.

Hope chose an oyster silk mid-length dress that dipped almost to the ground at the back, and matching heels, asking if they could alter the shoes slightly, with soft, wide silk ribbons in the same material as the dress being attached to their uppers near the back, the ribbons long enough so she could wrap them around her ankles and do them up with a large bow on her outside ankle bone. The dress was high and simple at the front and up into a plain collar neckline, but the whole of Hope's back was exposed, and she wanted to make a feature of the shoes. She felt good in the dress, liking the sensation of the cool silk skimming her body.

The personal shopper said they would match ribbons to the dress, and they would send the shoes out to a cobbler

Hope

for a professional job. Then she suggested a pricey clutch bag that matched the shoes, and a cashmere sloppy joe to keep Hope warm as the weather was still wintry, after which she showed Hope the underwear choices.

The last thing Hope chose was a cream coat that wrapped across the front and tied with a sash in the same woolly material, and reached down to her lower calves. She'd always wondered who wore such extravagantly impractical clothes as this coat, so pale it was likely to get grubby on its very first wear, and now she knew.

Hope was told that if she gave her address, everything would be sent to her home once the shoes were ready. And she learned that Bud had asked that Hope be reassured he wouldn't ask for, and the store wouldn't pass on to him, details of her home address. Again, Hope was touched by his level of attention to her psychological well-being.

As she signed the receipt for what would be sent over to Hackney, Hope felt her eyes prickle. She'd never thought about it previously, but she realised that she'd had no idea that a man could ever be as thoughtful as Bud appeared. It made her want to answer him with a really good girlfriend experience when they did consummate their agreement.

'Did you get what you wanted?' he asked when they were reunited.

'Yes, thank you, I did,' she told him.

'Good.' He grinned at her.

He led her to the waiting taxis outside, and put two twenty-pound notes in the cabbie's hand, with a 'wherever she wants to go', and then he offered her a hand to help her into the taxi, before he shut the door and slapped his hand on the cab's roof to say that Hope was safely seated.

As the taxi drove away, Hope turned to look at Bud through the cab's rear window. He was staring after her, looking just as gently rumpled and a little pudgy as he had on the night he'd won the auction.

With something of a jolt, Hope realised that although she would never have given Bud a second look on the street should she not know him and just happened to be walking by, she was – something she'd never believe could happen to her – actually looking forward to seeing him again.

In the small hours of the next day, Chantal was followed home from work.

Oblivious, her normal minicab driver picked her up as usual, and their journey was spent laughing about a man who'd wanted to be a pony, complete with a bridle on his head, and a tail inserted into his bottom. He didn't want to be whipped, but more for JoJo to shout 'hup' as he was made to repeatedly leap a red and white show-jump in the rubber-leather room, JoJo calling 'hung like a stallion' as the man cantered around the room neighing loudly, before he'd turn to come down to the fence again.

Hope

Neither Chantal nor the cabbie noticed the person on the moped who was weaving in and out of the traffic behind them, so wrapped up were they in the exploits of pony-man, not even when the moped also drew up outside Chantal's home in Limehouse, and right beside the minicab its rider pulled out a notebook to make a note of the number and the street name.

CHAPTER SIXTEEN

In the week between her lunch with Bud and the time when she would go to the apartment he was renting near Sloane Square, Hope spent her time mugging up on things she thought Bud might like to talk about. She'd decided that unless something terrible happened, she would stay the whole night with him if he wanted her to. After all, for the amount he had paid for her, she was determined that he have the sort of time that he would remember for evermore.

She was able to find out quite a lot about his business interests, which were mainly property, through going through copies of the *Financial Times* in the library. And in the society pages of the *Tatler* from the previous summer she came across a picture of Bud and his wife Dizzy at a charitable lawn party somewhere in the Home Counties. They both looked happy, and Hope was pleased to see that Dizzy was a little like Bud, being quite ordinary-looking and a little overweight, but having the sort of smile that suggested she was probably a really nice person. So many successful men traded their wives in for a younger model, but so far Bud had resisted the temptation, which Hope thought was yet another point in his favour.

Hope knew that while Bud might seem a perfect gentleman while lunching a woman he planned to have sex with, the fact he had paid for Hope's virginity showed there was a trickier side to him than was immediately obvious. But she suspected that almost all successful businessmen had a ruthless side, no matter how much they tried to disguise it. And Hope didn't hold the fact he was married against him, as her time at Chantal's had taught her that many of the men who frequented the establishment considered themselves to be very happily married, exactly as he'd told Hope he was, and who was she to say that this wasn't in fact true? Annie and Maria's time on the streets had proved time and again to her how complicated affairs of the human heart could be.

And in any case she and Bud were going to have a once-only night. Hope expected it would be the only time in her life she would ever have sex with anyone, and she certainly didn't have designs on Bud beyond what they had agreed.

As a teenager, Hope had sometimes looked at Charity who so enjoyed kissing Little Danny, and who would tell Hope she couldn't wait to be married, when they could have sex several times each and every night if they wanted to, discussions that would leave Hope feeling perplexed over why she never felt so much as a fanny flutter at the thought of getting up close and personal with anybody.

But one day Hope realised that maybe in their close-knit family, it was Charity who was the exception. For Maria and Annie actively seemed to dislike men, and Joyce didn't seem that keen either. And until Tom Jarrett came along, Faith had appeared to be on the fence about them too. Back then, Hope had told herself not to worry about it – if she met somebody she liked then she could think again, but until that happened there were lots of other things more deserving of her attention. And in the decade since then she never had met anyone to convince her otherwise.

Hope booked herself into a nice hotel just around the corner from Bud's apartment. The thought of getting ready for such a night had felt too weird for her to be thinking about primping herself up at Cadogan Terrace, and so a hotel felt a sensible choice.

Hope waited until everyone was out so that nobody would try a last-ditch attempt to prevent her going through with it, and then she called herself a taxi, leaving a note on Maria's kitchen table, and off she headed for west London, a knot of excitement just below her ribcage, or was it apprehension? Hope couldn't quite tell.

At the hotel Hope took a leisurely bath, and then

visited the hairdresser's just off the foyer to have her hair pinned into an up-do.

Back in her room, it was time to get dressed, and Hope liked the way her new shoes and dress complemented her milky skin and dark hair, and she kept her make-up minimal and innocent, the one concession to glamour an iridescent nail polish that was oyster in shade, albeit with a subtle pink or blue shimmer depending how the light caught it.

The cashmere jumper was loose-knit and light as a feather, and the coat luxurious and toasty warm, and when she caught sight of herself in a window during the one-hundred-yard walk to the flat, it took a moment for Hope to recognise the refined and stylish woman staring back at her as herself.

This was just as well. For although Hope knew that Bud was wealthy, she wasn't prepared for how just swanky the building where his apartment was, her heels clacking on the marble floor of the foyer, as a doorman escorted her across the foyer and then pressed the button marked 'Penthouse'. Nor did Hope feel ready when he opened the door to his flat and she could see his tasteful, luxurious interior design. Clearly Bud wasn't just wealthy, but enormously rich.

Bud smiled at her warmly. And after he'd taken her coat, he told her she looked fabulous. She went to take the cashmere jumper off, but he asked her to keep it on.

Hope

'These are for you, Bud,' she said, passing him a gold-wrapped box of Godiva chocolates.

His eyes twinkled as he looked into hers and answered, 'My favourite,' leaving Hope uncertain whether he was talking about the chocolates or her.

As music played softly in the background, they sat and shared a bottle of champagne, and then they moved into the kitchen where Bud served Hope a lavish meal. Beside her linen napkin were wrapped two presents and a single long-stem rose, and when Hope opened the first present, inside was a bracelet that Bud slipped onto her wrist. The second package contained a giant bottle of her favourite scent.

'Thank you. Much appreciated. You know the way to a girl's heart,' Hope told him. She didn't really believe that presents were the way to her own heart, but she wanted Bud to feel that his efforts had hit the spot.

After they'd eaten, Bud put a new CD into the Bang & Olufsen system, and after he'd gently removed the cashmere sloppy joe they began to slow dance together, Hope's fingers on his shoulders, and his hands chastely on her waist. It was the first time Hope had danced with or been that close to anyone, and as Bud didn't seem in any sort of hurry she allowed herself to explore how the experience made her feel, which was warm and mellow inside.

'Shall we?' Bud said at last, his mouth close to her ear,

and after Hope nodded, he led her through to the bedroom, where there was subdued lighting and a huge bed. A huge vase packed with an obscene number of white lilies gave off a heady perfume.

Bud sat Hope on the bed and then knelt on the floor before her as, one by one, he lifted her feet and slowly pulled the end of the ribbons to undo the large bows Hope had spent an age tying. He rubbed her feet and then gently kissed the insole of each one.

He stood up then, and suggested that Hope shimmy up the bed so that her head was on the pillow. Bud climbed up beside her, and lay on his side with one hand on her hip and the other supporting his head.

'Hope, I have something to tell you,' he said, his face serious.

She looked at him, a bit puzzled as the way he'd spoken seemed a little in contradiction to the romantic mood he'd gone to such an effort to create.

'I'm impotent,' he confessed. 'I have been for years, and if I'm honest, I never had much of a sex drive before that, and so I made my peace long ago with the situation, rarely thinking about sex as an act. Now and again I like to set the scene, like here, but it never goes further than this.'

'Bud, I'm confused. Why would you want to pay so much for me? I really am a virgin and horribly inexperienced, and I can't tell if this is your way of saying you

Hope

don't find me attractive and you want me to go? Or if I've done something wrong?'

'You are exquisite, Hope, in every way, I promise. Trust me, I have got more than my money's worth already; making someone like you happy is where the pleasure lies for me. If I could have sex, I would only want to with my wife, as I believe in marriage. But she doesn't mind me having a peccadillo like you've helped me with as she knows I'm not going to be unfaithful, and I'm not the sort of man who will want to enact this with the same person more than once, as for me it needs to feel as genuine as possible and it wouldn't with a repeat performance, so you and I will never do this again.'

'Aww!' Hope felt touched by the gentle innocence of Bud's fetish, as well as very slightly disappointed that they weren't going to have any sort of repeat performance, but his expression backed up his words that she had fulfilled what he had paid her to do. 'That's OK – I quite understand. I think your wife is very, very lucky to have found someone like you,' Hope told him.

'Please do stay a bit longer,' said Bud. 'You are such good company, and I can relax now.'

'In that case, shall I see if there's any more champagne in the fridge?' Hope got up to go and find her sloppy joe, as her dress felt that bit too exposed if she and Bud weren't going to be intimate, and as she slipped it on she heard Bud get off the bed and follow her into the living room.

And when Hope woke up the following morning, she found herself flat out on Bud's sofa and still wearing her jumper and dress, with her underwear fully in place, only now she had a tartan rug over the top of her clothes too.

Hope winced.

She and Bud had drunk the second bottle of champagne, and then a third, and possibly even broken into a fourth. She remembered them talking about book-keeping and what she thought was happening in the East End these days, and then them watching Martin Scorsese's *Goodfellas* and *Casino*, Hope realising she was falling asleep a few minutes into the third: *Mean Streets*.

As she struggled to focus her eyes, Hope realised that she had no idea of the time other than that through the half-open curtains she could see daylight, which made the colours of the tartan rug look a bit too vivid.

Her head felt alarmingly fuzzy, but Bud had placed a bottle of water on the coffee table nearby, as well as a bottle of paracetamol.

There was a note alongside, which Bud had handwritten. He'd thanked her for a lovely evening and explained that he'd had to go out for a business appointment, but Hope was to make herself at home.

If she left before he got back though, he'd be grateful if

Hope

she left her phone number as he'd had an idea he wanted to run past her.

She tried to recall what they'd talked about during the movies, but by then it was all a bit hazy.

She could picture a few fragments of teaching him some Cockney rhyming slang as they laughed uproariously, but beyond that it all felt very sketchy.

She sat up to reach for the glass, and as Hope made a vow to herself that she would never again drink champagne, her head banged painfully and for a moment she wondered if she was about to pass out.

It had been a really fun night though, and so the morning's payback was worth it. While it had gone spectacularly rogue as Hope had never expected to leave as virginal as when she arrived, and she couldn't remember ever having felt as rough as she did at that very minute, she hadn't enjoyed herself like that for years.

Not daring to have more than a few sips of water as she felt quite queasy, she lay back down and closed her eyes, but Hope then had to open them as the room had begun to tilt and rock, and she thought she must be still drunk. God, did she feel awful?!

As it turned out, Chantal wasn't feeling too special either.

While Hope and Bud were getting stuck into their final bottle of champagne in Sloane Square, over on the less salubrious side of London, Chantal poured herself a glass of wine after the minicab driver had dropped her home.

Then she slipped off her heels, and in the dim light of the living-room lamp on the side table she fiddled with the dial until she found the Home Service on the radio, the plummy accents of the world news presenters oddly soothing.

Closing her eyes and stretching her toes, she gave a contented sigh. Chantal's had done good business that night, and a new mistress had started, Chantal thinking that with a bit more experience, she showed all the signs of being able to step into Hope's shoes and become the new Scarlet. It looked like 1993 was shaping up to being a bumper year in the financial sense, even without Hope there.

WHAM!

Suddenly something was thrown over her head. Her assailant, who was standing behind her, as the sofa was positioned away from the wall, pulled what he was holding tight across the whole of Chantal's face.

It was a plastic bag, and it meant Chantal – or poor Alice Smith as she became again in her dying moments – couldn't breathe, her open mouth sucking a fold of the bag inwards with a crackle of plastic. It was a grotesque sight.

Her heels drummed and flailed on the floor and the lower front of the sofa, but the nylon on her nude tights wouldn't give her enough purchase to try and stand up.

Hope

And at the same time Chantal tried every trick she knew of, arching her back and trying to wriggle sideways, as she reached up and back with her hands in her efforts to escape his clutches, or to poke his eyes out or to scratch his face or neck.

But it was all to no effect. He was wearing a thick padded coat and his arms were longer than Chantal's and so she couldn't reach up as far as the soft skin of his cheeks.

And as Chantal's frantic efforts began to slow and then ceased, other than for the tiniest sporadic twitch as she slipped into unconsciousness, the man snarled and then jumped nimbly around to the front of the sofa, where he grabbed one of her stilettos up from the mat. He lifted it high and then bringing it sharply down, and fuelled by lethal levels of hate and frustration, he began pummelling the narrow heel repeatedly into her head and chest and neck in fury, as he chanted, 'Die, bitch, die!' again and again, now and again hearing the sound of a bone splintering as the heel cap connected.

Eventually – a long time after Chantal had stopped breathing – he ran out of breath too and, sweating and gulping, he folded to the ground with tears making his cheeks glisten, and his forehead pushed into her lap, the sharp smell of Chantal's urine in his nose as she had wet herself during the attack.

Something caught the vision of his left eye.

And Harry Stewart lifted his head and then pushed his torso away from Chantal, although he remained kneeling at her feet. He turned to the side to see himself in a large mirror on Chantal's wall, a mirror so tall it stretched almost to the ceiling, and right down to the floor, and the full horror of her death was splayed before him.

Transfixed, Harry stared at the blood splatters all over his dove-grey puffer, and the chips of bone and brain matter flecking his hair and face. His tears caught the light of the lamp and with a rasping sound coming from his mouth, and the undulations of the rise and fall of his chest and his stonewash jeans Jackson-Pollocked with splashes of Chantal's life-blood, he watched himself fighting to gain some sort of control.

And in one of his last seconds of lucidity, Harry Stewart realised he'd just gone too far.

He put his head in his hands as he began to rock himself forwards and backwards as he thought he probably should have kept on taking his meds.

And as Chantal's body started to very slowly slither sideways, Harry Stewart began to howl a mantra.

'*Scarlet, what have you made me do?*'

CHAPTER SEVENTEEN

As Ted was warming through some soup for their lunch, Faith was sitting close to Martina as they looked through some photograph albums.

Martina felt well enough that morning to get out of bed and sit on the sofa for an hour or two in the living room, a rug tucked snugly around her knees. She wore two pairs of bed socks to keep her toes toasty even though the room was as warm as a tropical hothouse.

Faith had driven up the evening before, and now she was heartened to see that Martina was having a good day. And meanwhile, the day nurse took the opportunity to change the bed and give the sickroom a good clean.

All the same, Martina's arms were noticeably more shrunken, being almost only skin, tendon and bone, and Faith tried not to stare at her tiny wrists peeping out from the arm of her dressing gown, nor her fingers that had so little flesh on them that they looked skeletal.

When Faith had hugged Martina hello the previous day, she'd thought it was like holding in her arms something as light and fragile as a bird, much more than a person, a feeling heightened when for a second Faith's own fingers brushed against the knobbly protuberances of Martina's backbone in spite of how bundled up in bed-jackets the elderly woman had been as she sat in bed.

Luckily the photographs were fascinating, and Martina became increasingly energetic as she described to Faith their backstories, often smiling at the nice memories.

There were pictures of Ted and Martina at various events in the 1950s and 1960s, when they looked to be quite the society couple in Wakefield terms back then, and Faith could in all honesty admire Martina's fashion sense.

And Ted had been photographed sitting on the bonnets of various motors that he'd owned. Mostly these photographs had been shot right outside the gambling club, which Martina said he'd opened on the QT right after he was demobbed.

The series of cars began with a very modest one that Faith thought might be an ancient pre-war Austin, perhaps even the motor that went on to be the vehicle used years later to take her mother to the doctor with her slashed face as Faith remembered Maria had told her that car was an ancient jalopy, although Faith felt it

Hope

tactless to ask Martina, or Ted, if that was indeed the case.

As the years passed, the cars grew more expensive as Ted became more successful and his suits and hairstyles signalled the time passing.

During the 1970s there was even a brief period he'd embraced burgundy suits with flared legs and wide lapels, worn with shoes that had a platform sole.

'He thought he was the *business* in that suit.' Martina grinned, and Faith realised that Martina had been proud of her husband. Faith told her it had indeed been a look.

Martina indicated Faith should open a different album, and so Faith suspected there were photos on the latter pages of Fred that Martina thought inappropriate to show her.

Faith knew what Fred looked like though already, as she'd begged Tom Jarrett to slip her a copy of Fred's police mugshot from his latest arrest, saying she really wanted to see a picture of her father's face to discover if there was any resemblance between Fred and her.

When Faith first saw the mugshot, she felt confused. For Fred wasn't an unattractive man as such looks-wise, and he didn't exactly come across like the obvious goon she was expecting to see before her, and so she understood how he'd managed to persuade three women to marry him. But Faith had decided then that he looked a nasty piece of work all the same because he had an arrogant sneer about his face and a slightly lazy eye.

This second photograph album contained at its start pictures of Martina and Ted courting, when they'd clearly enjoyed going out to countryside on picnics, and then them getting married. Ted and Martina looked very happy in their wedding picture from 1941, Ted smart in his naval uniform and Martina coy but glamorous beside him, dressed in a trim-fitting utility suit that had a skirt that just managed to skim her knees, and with her hair neatly pin-curled.

'We were served Woolton pie, which was popular in the war although not that nice to eat. And our wedding cake looks wonderful, doesn't it, with three tiers and elaborate icing, but it was all a sham. You couldn't get the sugar or the eggs back then, and so the icing bit and the tiers was only a cardboard mock-up of a real cake, with plaster of Paris "icing". The photographer used the same one for everybody's reception photographs, and really our wedding cake was a Victoria sponge made on the ration and we—' Martina stopped abruptly as the angry timbre of Ted's rising voice cut across their conversation, even though he was standing in the kitchen.

He sounded aggressive and rougher somehow, and Faith realised this was a side of the dapper Ted she'd not experienced.

Hope

'Fred, what the hell do you mean you're at the British Oak, with Anna? I told you expressly that you needed to stay put in Marbella, and you've downright disobey—'

Ted went quiet as presumably Fred interrupted him, and Faith glanced towards Martina, who clutched Faith's arm with a surprisingly strong grip considering how frail she was. Faith immediately put her hand on top of Martina's in comfort, and the two women stayed that way as Faith realised that although she had no idea where or what the British Oak was, Fred wasn't where he was supposed to be and Ted was furious about this.

Ted began to shout, 'Fred, I *fucking* told you that your mother needs all the rest she can get. Do *not* come here, and you just stay put in that fucking rathole of a pub. She doesn't want any of your games right now and I don't either. And we really don't need your latest girl swanning it about all over the place – Martina is too poorly for any of it, so just back the fuck off to the hole you crawled out of. Are you listening, Fred? FRED!! Oh, for fuck's sake . . .'

There was a clattering sound as Ted slammed the handset to the phone down in such temper that it sounded as if it had immediately bounced off its cradle and skittered across the quartz worktop above the incongruous homely cottage-style kitchen cabinets beneath.

Ted hurried into the living room, looking worried.

He crouched before Martina and said, 'I don't know what's going on. But that sod Fred and his bint are on their way here from the British Oak, and so I think you need to go back to bed as it might not be pretty.'

'I'd better leave,' said Faith, her promises to Maria to do everything she could to avoid ever meeting Fred face to face uppermost in her mind.

She headed to the spare room where she'd left her overnight bag, and quickly packed her possessions, taking care to leave the bedroom exactly the same as when she'd arrived so that Fred wouldn't become suspicious about anyone unknown to him having stayed in the house, and she smoothed out the bedclothes so it looked as much as she could make it as if it had recently been made up with fresh linen.

She used the en-suite bathroom, and went to the kitchen for a drink of water before she slipped on her coat, and then ran back to get her used towel, using it to give the handbasin and taps a rapid wipe to get rid of any splashes, and then she tossed the towel into the dirty laundry basket in the utility room.

She had to wait for a few moments while the nurse settled an ashen-faced Martina back in bed, but Faith couldn't bear the thought of leaving her grandmother without a final hug. She was sorry to see that gone was the smiling and animated person of just a few minutes earlier

Hope

who'd been so enjoying describing her wedding day; that contented person had been replaced now with a tremulous husk of a woman with blue-tinged lips and trembling hands.

'Drive safely, Faith.' Martina's voice was both weak and croaky.

'I will,' Faith promised, and she held up her right hand to remind Martina she was wearing the ring. 'I'll try and see you soon.'

Faith found Ted standing by her little Peugeot.

'I'm sorry, but . . .' Ted could only shake his head.

'I understand, and I know it's not your fault. You take care, Ted, and look after Martina.'

The electric gates opened and Faith left.

It wasn't a moment too soon, for as she indicated she'd turn right once she'd got to the T-junction at the bottom of the road, a car driving far too fast almost caught her front wing as it made a too-wide turn to swing left and into the side road where the Waltons' home was.

Faith's heart jumped at such cavalier driving, and then she felt adrenaline course around her body at the near miss.

Gingerly she inched across the road in the next break of traffic and headed towards the southbound junction of the M1.

If the traffic had been a little heavier and had kept Faith waiting for an opening at the T-junction for just a few seconds more, in her wing mirror she might have seen the car that nearly scraped her wing turn with a screech of tyres into Ted and Martina's drive.

Fred and his girlfriend had come to visit.

Ted stayed on the doorstep, his arms folded and his feet planted wide apart.

'What the hell do you think you're up to, Fred?'

'Not fucking interested, Dad. And why wouldn't a good son want to be seeing his ill mother?'

Fred pushed past his father without a second glance, leaving his girlfriend Anna struggling to pull their heavy suitcase out of the car's boot.

'You've never wanted to see her at any other time,' Ted called to his son's retreating back as Fred flicked him the Vs without bothering to look around, and then under his breath, Ted muttered, 'And you're not a good son.'

Ted sighed, and went to help Anna.

They'd met briefly only once before, and it hadn't gone well as Fred had been in a dreadful mood. Considering the disparaging way Fred had talked that time to Anna, although she'd seemed quite a sweet and devoted thing, Ted was amazed the relationship was still going.

She gave a weak smile. 'I'm sorry, Mr Walton – I didn't know until we were in the pub down the way that

Hope

we weren't supposed to be here. I should have realised something was up as I saw on the plane that Fred has got a false passport now. And then we had to meet somebody in the pub and so Fred went out to the car park to see him and was gone ages. But he's been in a good mood since, so I think it will be all right.' Anna sounded as if she was trying to convince herself more than Ted.

Christ on a bike, thought Ted, if this was Fred in a good mood, then things must be going worse in Marbella than he'd supposed.

Ted lugged the case to the spare room that Faith had just vacated, and said to Anna wearily, 'I'll get you some towels.'

He disappeared and when he didn't come back, and there was no sign of Fred as he had closeted himself in with Martina, the nurse having been yelled at that she should get the fuck out of there, Anna sat on the end of the bed, staring at the carpet and feeling too dispirited to make a start on the unpacking.

She might have given a fleeting wry smile had she known that at that very moment Ted was sitting on his bed also, feeling similarly discombobulated.

The next morning Fred disappeared for a couple of hours, and no one knew when he had gone; neither his mother nor father had seen him before he left, and Anna seemed clueless too.

At her suggestion, she, Martina and Ted endured mid-morning a rather painful cup of tea together, with Anna and Ted sitting beside Martina's bed but none of them knowing quite what to say beyond a little polite chitchat. Fred felt very much like the elephant in the room nobody dared mention, even though he wasn't there. And neither his mother nor father had the energy to probe with Anna who he'd upset in Spain, or who he had gone to see right now.

Martina had whispered to Ted when he'd gone in to say goodnight to her the previous evening that when the pair had arrived and Fred had come into his mother's room, he had closed the door after the nurse had gone. He'd then proceeded to march about as he made a series of telephone calls, bragging about this and that in a manner that made Martina wonder if there was anybody at the other end. And then he'd said just an offhand 'hi, Mum' before he left, giving her a perfunctory wave on his way out of the room, before immediately collecting Anna and the two of them then driving off.

Ted thought this had been a charade on Fred's part purely designed to show his mother that these days he was something of a player and that all manner of gangsters were ready to take his call, with the assumption that

Hope

Martina would then tell Ted. Fred wouldn't have dared try such a stunt in front of his father as Ted would have seen through it right away.

Whatever, Fred and Anna must have been on a pub crawl that evening, judging by the way they'd crashed about the house when they got in a long time after midnight, and Ted was thankful Martina now had to take a sleeping pill each night as at least it would have knocked her out sound asleep. Ted had hardly slept though, and he was feeling upset and fidgety.

Just before lunchtime Fred came home, and he pulled Anna into the bedroom.

It wasn't long before there were the sounds of loud sex, followed by several hours of laughing and loud voices.

'What are they doing?' Martina wondered.

'I dread to think,' said Ted.

Thinking they would be wearing themselves out quite soon, Ted gave it another thirty minutes, but when Fred and Anna were still making enough noise that Martina couldn't nap, he went and rapped loudly on their door.

'Tone it down,' called Ted, 'your mother needs to rest.'

It was as if he hadn't spoken.

Ted went back to the sickroom, where he plopped himself into an easy chair but couldn't stop shuffling his feet angrily about. He tried to follow Martina's urging that he should calm down, but he got more and more het up, to the point that he marched down the corridor and wrenched open the door to their room.

'What the fuck?!' Ted paused in the doorway and stared into the room.

Aside from his heavy gold jewellery, Fred was naked as he leaned over the chest of drawers with a rolled fiver in his fingers, and Ted could see several lines of cocaine had been got ready and Fred was about to snort. And Anna was almost bare too, wearing just a tiny thong and with her eyes showing she'd probably gone for it with the coke as much as Fred. Neither seemed perturbed by Ted standing there or even to care about their bodies being on such unashamed display.

'Wanna line, Dad? You know, live a little for once. Oh, I forgot. You don't approve . . .' Fred sounded excited as he goaded his father, and his immediate sniff when he stopped speaking was loud and as if he was acting. Anna thought it hilarious, to judge by the way she was egging Fred on.

Martina wasn't a naive person, and she could hear the exchange. Past experience meant that she didn't need to be told that Fred and Anna were on a cocaine binge. She recognised the edge coke gave to her son's voice – it was an unwelcome edge she had heard far too many times over the years he'd lived with them. Coke seemed to flip a switch in Fred's head that more often than not led to trouble, and once Martina said to Ted that she wished heroin was Fred's drug of choice, as at least that way he'd sit somewhere with his eyes shut and a nodding head. Ted knew what she meant.

Ted replied, 'No, I fucking do not want a line, you fucking *child*. The one thing I asked you to do was stay away. And the second thing I've asked of you is no fucking drugs if you want me still supporting you. Just look at the state of you both.'

Fred squared up to his father. 'Old man, fuck off, you fucking ancient dinosaur.'

Forgetting that he had told himself not to rise to Fred's taunting, Ted flipped at the word 'dinosaur' as Fred had found his weak spot. Losing his authority through his advancing years was something he'd wondered on and then worried about more than once, and in retaliation he screamed, 'Dinosaur my arse! Reggie Kray's old empire is up the shitter since his lock-up in the big house and the new guard can't keep it going, and so there's advantage to be had, and something in east London I've just been pulled in on, I'll have you know.'

Ted immediately regretted his outburst, and he didn't know why he'd allowed himself to be brought down to his son's level. But Fred's presence was making him feel at sixes and sevens, and he was worried about Martina, and so Ted suspected he was tired and not therefore as sharp as he was usually. And what he'd said was true, although Ted had learned a long time ago that it was sensible not to let his son know what he was up to, personally or professionally.

'Yeah, yeah,' mocked Fred. 'In your dreams.'

The mullered look in Fred's eyes, the pupils dilated so much across the irises that they were almost black because of the physical effects of the coke, suggested there was a fighting chance that Fred wouldn't be able to recall Ted's boast, which was something, Ted supposed.

Still, this didn't stop Ted and Fred Walton standing face-on as they tried to stare each other out, each determined not to be the one who'd back down. Fred looked proud he was squaring up to his father, and boastful of the sex and drugs binge.

Anna went to Fred, and put her hands around his waist with her head on his chest as she gyrated against him, saying, 'Look, babe, let's not make this a fight. Come back to bed.'

With a frown Fred looked down at her with narrowed eyes as if he'd just seen a bug on his pectorals, and then he peeled her off his body and swung his fist at her, catching her cheek so hard with his punch that it propelled her right across the room.

Anna hit the wall with a scream and a sickening thump, and she slowly crumpled to the carpet. Fred loomed over

Hope

her, and then staggered, and for a moment it seemed as if he might pass out. Anna couldn't stop shrieking.

'Fred!' shouted Ted, and stepped towards his son, although it was unclear whether he was going to pull Fred away from Anna or to pulverise him.

But Fred rallied and he turned and gave Ted a swift and hard push with both his hands on his father's chest.

And with an 'oof' Ted landed on his back on the bed, the rumpled sheets close to his face stinking of sweat and semen.

'Fred!' There was a cry from the doorway.

It was Martina, who somehow had found the strength to struggle out of bed and totter along the corridor, supporting herself by clutching the wall as she did so.

The nurse hurried to the doorway to announce that she'd phoned the police, and as Ted struggled to disentangle himself from the bedclothes, the nurse caught hold of Martina who looked on the verge of collapse. But as if he'd been cattle-prodded, Fred came to his senses at the sound of the word 'police'.

'Right, bitch,' he said to Anna. 'Cut the snivelling. We're off. And fuck the rest of you.'

Ted helped the nurse take Martina back to her bed. And when he came back, Fred was dressed and sitting in the car.

Anna was struggling once more with the suitcase, a

shiner of a black eye already forming, her eyelid so swollen that she couldn't see out of it.

'Anna, he's a monster. You don't need to go with him, you know,' Ted said. 'Stay here and we can sort something out that will mean you can let him go to hell on his own.'

She looked at Ted with her good eye, saying sadly, 'That's sweet of you. But I do need to go with him, Mr Walton. He'll kill me if I don't.'

Ted stood back to let Anna pass. He thought Fred would probably end up killing her either way.

Anna bumped the suitcase along to the car, and got into the passenger seat, as Ted yelled from the doorstep, 'Help the woman, Fred. And this is how you treat your mother, you filthy scum!'

Fred ignored his father other than mouth through the car's window a weak 'piss off', before he looked daggers at Anna for a long moment.

Then he got out of the car, dealt with the suitcase as Anna scampered around to the passenger side, Fred then nearly knocking Ted over as he reversed back at speed before accelerating out of the drive, the electric gates, automatic from the house side, only just managing to open in time.

Estimating he had about five minutes until the police arrived, Ted closed the front door and ran to the kitchen

Hope

and got some cleaner and some clean tea towels. He stripped the bed and put the linen into the washing machine on a hot wash, racing back to bleach the surfaces clean to remove traces of the coke.

He was just about to leave the room when he saw something peeping out from under a cushion on the bedroom chair.

It was a clear plastic bag of coke, probably worth more than forty thousand pounds by the time it had been cut, Ted calculated, judging by how pure it was when he put a grain on his upper gum. He had a pretty good idea which of his rivals Fred had been dealing with to get tasked with selling on such a big delivery across county lines. Ted was sure from the way Fred had behaved that he hadn't worked with this gang before.

Ted knew instantly that this meant Fred would be considered disposable by the dealer and that only an idiot would be taking such a risk on a first job with a new gang as Fred had. Ted knew too that Fred would have felt the big man and proud of himself, not for a moment seeing or comprehending the nuances of the gamble he was taking on an unknown entity's behalf, nor that he was a total idiot for getting involved. Crossing county lines usually threw out a challenge and the repercussions could be extreme. And the fact Fred had had the audacity to sample the product – well, many inept gangsters had had their bodies placed on railway tracks in front of an oncoming train for much smaller misdemeanours.

'Give me strength,' said Ted out loud, and as the police rang the doorbell exactly five minutes from the point Ted had guessed they'd arrive, he just had time to dash to Martina and say 'hide this' as he thrust the bag of coke in her direction.

And with a defeated look on her face, she took the baggie and slipped it under the bedcover as the nurse pretended not to notice.

By this point neither Ted nor Martina cared about creating a good impression in front of the nurse, and Ted knew already that he was going to have to give her a good bundle of cash to buy her silence.

Ten minutes after the police had gone – Ted had had years of practice in getting them to go away and leave him alone, helped this time by Martina looking ill enough that they didn't dare to stay long as they didn't want to be around and risk her actually dying in front of them – Ted went back to his wife, who wordlessly placed the cocaine in his hand. Seconds later Ted drove out of the drive, returning after half an hour.

It was nearly midnight by the time a mostly sober and extremely scared and worried-sounding Fred dared to telephone his father.

Hope

'Don't. You. Ever. Fucking. Do. That. Again. Or. It. Will. Be. The. Last. Time. You. Do. Anything. You. Bastard,' Ted told him, his words chilling Fred deep down inside, although nowhere near as much as the thought of what the dealer might do to him should he ever get wind that Fred had sampled the product when he'd been expressly told not to, or that Fred had got himself so out of it that he'd been twattish enough to leave the house without the damn delivery.

The horror of the situation he was in washed through Fred again, and momentarily he zoned out of Ted's tirade, only surfacing to Ted's final salvo: 'You should have the balls and the good grace to show a bit of respect for your mother.'

Fred couldn't think of anything to say that would immediately soothe his father's temper, and so there was a silence.

'Er, after we'd gone, did you find anything, Dad? Or did the police?' Fred said eventually in what he hoped would pass for a casual voice. He sounded almost reasonable for the first time in over twenty-four hours.

'Yes, I did. And I had to bring your mother into hiding it while the police were here, which I'll never forgive you for. It was such a large amount I knew I couldn't flush it, much as I wanted to, not while your mother is still alive, as whoever gave it you will come looking for you or want the profit you've agreed. And that gang won't be messing about when they know their delivery is AWOL, and I couldn't have your body on my conscience while she is still with us. I'll have you know it didn't take much for me to find out who you got it from, and he's the sort to sling you under the train soon as look at you. I'll get it back to him and pay him off, but I want to make sure the police aren't coming back. You need to get back to Spain pronto and stay there. And until I can sort it all out, the delivery—' Ted couldn't bring himself to say the word *cocaine* '—is in the safe in the lock-up where I hid the old bleeder. Along with the guns.'

He was secure in the knowledge that Fred had no idea where the lock-up actually was as Ted had paid cash for it before the war and he had always taken care that nobody else knew about it, not even Martina.

It had long been the perfect place to stash the bleeder, which was indeed the car in the photograph that Faith had wondered about. He'd never been able to get rid of the car as by the time they stopped using it to take away the cut men from the club, the age of the car had made it valuable again, and someone would have blabbed should he have decided to scrap it. And there was way too much blood dried black inside for someone not to have wanted to sell it to Ted's rivals should he have tried to pass it on to anyone, and Ted was determined that nobody would ever

Hope

use it as leverage against him. And over the years Fred had squirrelled away in the lock-up all manner of other things he thought might come in useful one day.

'Guns?' said Fred.

'For fuck's sake wise up.' Ted's voice became even more threatening as he added, 'And Fred, know that if you don't stay away from here, I swear to God I'm going to come looking for you myself, and one of us won't come out of it alive, and it's not going to be me who dies. Do you fucking hear me?'

'I do,' said Fred, his voice a whimper.

Fred might have done more than whimper if he had known that as his father was speaking, Ted was wearing some yellow Marigold household gloves as he clasped one of the large selection of weapons he'd previously stashed away in the lock-up, back when he'd fully expected that that side of his life was long past.

Now, the gun was still in the sealed plastic bag that Ted had slipped it into all those years earlier, thinking it might be good leverage one day but would remain hidden in the safe until then.

Even through the rubber of the Marigolds and the polythene of the wrapping, the weapon felt sleek and potent, for once anyone had ever held a gun, it was impossible not to remember the feel or the balance, or the sense of power it gave.

And, given the value of the cocaine, as Ted hung up on Fred's call, he thought he'd have been a fool not to take the gun home with him from the safe as there were some things that needed a bit of muscle, and nothing shouted muscle like a gun barrel. And this was a special gun after all, with a special history.

As the central heating clicked off for the night, Ted spent a good ten minutes familiarising himself once more with what it felt like to have a shooter in his hand, even though he'd promised Martina at least twenty years ago that he wouldn't fire a gun ever again.

Fred had got him so upset that the past thirty-six hours had felt a nightmare.

The heft of the gun calmed him in these few short minutes, and brought Ted back into himself.

And this gun felt good. Incredibly good, in fact.

CHAPTER EIGHTEEN

Hope was just getting out of a taxi after enjoying a second lunch with Bud Metzler.

This time it had been all about business. Traditional business, with Bud questioning her closely about her non-mistress work, being very interested in her accountancy qualifications and book-keeping experience, and about what she had learned from Big Danny in negotiation skills and preparing the books for the taxman.

And then he asked where Hope thought there might be property opportunities in London, Hope noticing the glint of excitement in his eyes. And with that, she understood that Bud was a wheeler-dealer through and through, and brokering deals of various kinds was where his passion lay. His soft-core fetish of chaste girlfriend experience with a virginal young woman might be an itch he'd want to scratch occasionally, but he'd be able to take it or leave it. In the business world, it was clearly a different story, one in which Bud wanted to be The Man.

She'd told him he was probably too late to the party to make much of a killing on the Isle of Dogs, but she thought around Elephant and Castle was interesting, as there were decrepit and crumbling blocks of flats there that would be pulled down in the next twenty years. And along the banks of the Thames on the south side of the river, with Bermondsey likely to become a property hotspot, as would Deptford and Greenwich.

'What makes you say that?' asked Bud as he leaned back as if to study her more intently.

'Well, it stands to reason, doesn't it? Elephant is walking distance for the young thrusters going up to the City, while Borough is already on the up and so that confidence in south-east London will spread from London Bridge going eastwards, as to the west is already developed. Bermondsey and Deptford are on the river and so yuppies who work in the City will be tempted to a waterside property and they'll pay top dollar more or less just because they can with their high wages. And Greenwich has the park and the observatory and nice areas with good schools already and so the price for new-builds between the traditional housing will hold a high premium. And so from Greenwich back to Borough, there's a lot of land across that whole sweep that's ripe for development, with excellent rail links into London Bridge or Charing Cross, and the Docklands Light Railway to go south of the Thames. It's not rocket science,' she said, hoping she wasn't sounding too know-it-all.

'So the consultant I paid to look at this expressly, who charged me extortionately, didn't have much more to add than you've said with a very welcome brevity, compared to how he put it.' Bud laughed.

'Well, if you are thinking of putting serious amounts into the South East generally, I'd be looking in the triangle too between the M20 to Dover, the M23 to Gatwick and Brighton, and the M25. There are good links to where most of the transport lorries come in at Dover, and where businesspeople leave from Gatwick – personally I'd be interested in outside the M25 in that triangle as it would be stockbroker belt. A lot of development has happened there, but I'm sure there are still opportunities, particularly if it was for posh executive properties near a commuter train station directly into central London.'

She and Bud had decided that they should go on a recce the next day, and Hope was pretty certain that if she played her cards right, she might be able to talk herself into some sort of job with Bud.

Since the auction, any desire that she'd once had to be a mistress had dwindled to nothing, and although she had a tidy sum to live on for a while, it wouldn't last for ever, and at some point she would need to rejoin the working world. There would be worse things than working in some capacity for Bud, that was for certain.

So Hope was deep in thought as to how she should play her cards in this, as she walked up to the front door in Cadogan Terrace.

'Thank Christ! Hold up, Hope,' she heard behind her, and she turned to find Tom jogging towards her, the keys to his car jangling in his hand.

'Oh, Tom, hello. Faith's not going to be here though.'

'No, it's you I need to see.'

'Me?' Hope was surprised as although she and Tom Jarrett got on quite well, she wouldn't have classed him as a friend.

'We need to go inside,' he said. 'I've tried to speak to Faith, but she's in court. And I've been ringing you for the last hour, but you've not answered.'

'I think I turned it off. I'm sorry.' Hope quite often switched off the ringtone to her mobile phone as she didn't like to think of herself as constantly available at the whim of others, something neither Faith nor Charity could understand.

Inside Hope's flat, which was decorated in a sparse Japanese style Maria found very austere, Hope looked at Tom. 'You're starting to worry me, Tom. It's not Maria, or Charity, is it?'

'No, but you do need to sit down.'

Hope

Hope did as he said.

'You won't have long. But you need to lawyer up, and fast.'

'I haven't done anything wrong!' Hope sounded affronted. 'This makes no sense, Tom. I think someone's having you on.'

'Hope, you need to concentrate on what I'm saying as there might not be much time and there are things you need to do. And there's no easy way for me to break it to you. But Chantal has been murdered – early pathology suggests it happened three nights ago, and it was an exceptionally brutal killing, with her, it looks like, being suffocated at her home and also stabbed with the heel of her own shoe.'

Hope gasped in shock as she understood at once that Chantal's stilettos could make the perfect lethal weapon.

And she realised that if the pathologists were correct in their time-framing, exactly as she had been having a good time with Bud Metzler in his flat, it was probable Chantal's life was ending in a most horrific way.

What a sobering thought.

Life was certainly shitty sometimes.

But for the life of her, Hope couldn't quite see why Tom was so worried about her being arrested as she'd had nothing to do with the killing of Chantal, and so she nodded that Tom should keep talking.

'I'm not allocated to the case, and of course I'm taking a professional risk in warning you,' Tom went on without pausing at Hope's second nod a moment later that she understood she mustn't drop him in it, 'but I know that right at this moment my colleagues are speaking to the CPS over whether they have enough evidence to charge Harry Stewart for Chantal's murder.

'My guess is that the CPS will deem that there is enough evidence realistically to be able to win a guilty verdict should he plead not guilty and it go to trial with a jury. He was brought in around midnight last night after a concerned member of the public reported him sitting weeping on the steps to Chantal's, which was closed. And then when he refused to move along, the WPC became suspicious that he had dried blood on his clothes. She thought he was a dosser at first, but he began raving that he'd "seen to" Chantal, "wiping the smile off her face for ever" – and this is the bit where you come in – that he had done this on Scarlet's orders, Scarlet putting the idea of murder into his head when Chantal was bullying Scarlet.

'So Chantal's was searched and it was clear from the burglar alarm log that it hadn't been opened for three nights, and that this was an unplanned closure – the police know this as clients who had been booked in left notes in the letter box saying how surprised they were Chantal's wasn't open for business. First thing this morning, officers went to her home where she was found deceased in her living room, forensic evidence suggesting that's where she died.

'It's a strong team working on this,' added Tom, 'and SOCO is all over her flat right now, but preliminary photos are doing the rounds back at base. And they've called in a forensic accountant to look at the books and so it's only going to be a matter of time before you get taken in for questioning, because there's going to be no way that they won't find out your mistress name is Scarlet, especially as I've heard Harry is singing like a canary. So basically anything you need to do, needs doing now.'

'Holy fuck!' groaned Hope. 'Harry jerk-off Stewart! That bastard weasel apology of a deluded gobshite – I'd give him what-for and beat him within an inch of his life, if I could get my hands on him, if I didn't think he'd enjoy it too much. Oh, poor Alice. Why does it always seem to happen to the nicest people?'

'Hope, you must keep it together,' said Tom. 'I need to go as it's not going to help you or me if I'm found here. I'll make sure to talk to Faith, as she'll be able to sort decent representation. Remember you mustn't say a word at any point when the officers take you in or question without your brief present – they'll try every trick to get you to speak, but anything you say will be used against you. Even with your brief, don't rush into answers – if they step in and answer for you or say you won't be answering that question, listen to them. Not doing what you are told, as usual, might lead to years extra in prison should you be convicted.'

'Thanks for the heads-up, Tom. I do appreciate what you've done for me. I'm not going to do anything daft, and I definitely do not want to do a runner so I'll be here waiting for them.'

'That's the spirit,' said Tom, and for a moment Hope understood why he and Faith had been in each other's lives for such a long time.

After they'd had a quick hug and as Tom's footsteps thumped away down the stairs, Hope called Bud, beginning, 'I'm so sorry but something has come up and so I can't come on the recce. Such a shame . . .'

And, sure enough, at five-thirty the next morning the front door was rammed open with an Enforcer and far too much shouting, and Hope was hoicked out of bed to be taken in for questioning, while the neighbours had a field day watching what was going on with the four police cars in Cadogan Terrace parked across the road with their lights flashing, and two officers with Alsatian dogs waiting outside the front gate who looked very ready to chase down a recalcitrant arrestee given the chance.

CHAPTER NINETEEN

Before eight-thirty, Shamus was opening the presbytery front door to a sobbing Maria.

'It's the day for early mass,' he said, 'so the father's not back yet.'

Maria visibly wilted. All she wanted to do at that moment was to hear the wise and calming tones of Father O'Reilly.

Shamus shuffled his feet and Maria saw him glance at her face and then look away with a flush of colour to his cheeks. But then he said, 'Why not come in and wait, missus?'

Maria sat in the visitors' room, and to her surprise Shamus sat down at the other end of the table after she'd refused his offer of some tea.

He didn't say anything, and neither did she, but as the clock ticked in the background Maria found it a very mollifying quarter of an hour as her sobs gave way to a tingle across her cheeks and the salt of her tears dried, tightening her flesh where they had been. Once she had calmed a little, she felt almost sleepy.

When Father O'Reilly's key was heard in the lock, Shamus got up and Maria could hear an indistinct burr of words muttered between them.

Then the father came in and said, 'Our Shamus tells me you are upset, Maria. What is it?'

'I daresay it will be on the news later again as the police will probably charge him and so they'll be seen to be doing their job and getting results, but that Limehouse woman who was found murdered yesterday is Chantal.'

Maria thought Father O'Reilly would make a comment, but he didn't, so she added, 'She was bludgeoned to death at home, and the police have one of the clients as a "male helping their enquiries". And while it was still dark, the police came to ours early and they took Hope in – the client has alleged that she told him to do it. We had a bit of warning she would be collared for it, and so I couldn't sleep with the worry of it, and now my worst fears have happened. It's ridiculous of course, but even so . . .'

Although she tried not to, Maria began to weep once more as yet again the tension spiked in her chest, and she felt dizzy and nauseous.

'I don't really know why I'm here as I know you can't do anything, but I feel at my wits' end,' she said so despairingly

Hope

that Father O'Reilly had to listen very hard to be able to work out what she said.

'Yes, so difficult,' said the father. 'I know, let's you and I go and sit in church. Sometimes that helps.'

Back at home Maria felt strengthened by her time with Father O'Reilly.

It was just as well, as the police kept Hope for the full amount of time they could, and then applied and were granted leave to question her further.

Eventually she was charged with conspiracy to murder, and at her preliminary hearing, bail was refused.

Hope was remanded to Holloway prison to await trial. And the name of the Crown Prosecution Service was mud in the Cadogan Terrace household.

Faith said Tom had told her that a behind-the-scenes deal had been brokered with Harry Stewart. While the team felt there was enough forensic evidence against him for a murder charge to succeed, as there wasn't any particular evidence against Hope other than Harry's allegation, her own brief, whom Faith had arranged, had told her that he would let it be known that she would be entering a not guilty plea. He thought that on the paucity of evidence the CPS would decide to drop the case, especially as it was in the discovery pack that Harry had at times in his life suffered from poor mental health and so could be deemed an unreliable witness.

Her barrister thought wrong, as it turned out.

For it seemed that the powers that be wanted a case that would grab the headlines and therefore prove to be a warning to others, and so the police and CPS felt confident they would succeed against Hope in spite of any not-guilty plea she may make. This was because Harry had had a plea bargain offered to him that he had accepted.

For his agreement to give evidence in court against Hope, Harry had been told if he pleaded guilty to manslaughter on the grounds of diminished responsibility for his part in killing Chantal, that plea would be accepted by the courts, with a directive to the judge that he was a danger to society and so should serve what would be in effect a life sentence, although in a secure unit such as Broadmoor, where life was much more cushy than it ever could be for him banged up in a prison, or 'the big house' as Big Danny always called it. If he pleaded guilty to murder, his life sentence would almost definitely end up as a prison term.

Either way, it meant at least a couple of decades incarcerated for Harry, and of course he'd have a nicer time in a secure psychological unit, so it was easy to see why he had agreed to the deal.

But nicer for Harry meant bad news for Hope.

While everyone batting for Hope felt the evidence against her was scant, and that in a perfect world this

Hope

should lead to a jury finding her not guilty, the reality was that trial by jury was notoriously unpredictable, with juries being lenient or tough according to prior unfathomable variables, such as the vagaries of jury selection, and once the jurors had been selected, the time in their jury service when the trial began, and this came down to how the cases would be scheduled at the court. Scheduling could be bumped, as should several trials collapse, with defendants changing their pleas to guilty part-way through the case, or the judge stopping a trial for legal reasons, it meant that cases could be shifted around.

And if Hope's conspiracy case was the jurors' first not-guilty plea in court they had had to sit in on, then a not-guilty verdict was much more likely. But should exactly the same case kick off in the jurors' second week of their two-week jury service, the following week the odds frequently swung towards a guilty verdict as the jurors grew more experienced in what they were witnessing, at the same time as they became less susceptible to a sob story.

What the most frustrating thing about it was that everyone believed that if Hope had been a man, then the CPS and the police wouldn't have persisted with the prosecution.

But old-fashioned values to do with fallen women and the idea of women being either saints or sinners – and damn those sinners – still permeated the legal system, probably because nearly all the judges for the most serious criminal cases were middle-aged or elderly men from privileged families and Oxbridge backgrounds who, quite frankly, looked down on the women who appeared in the dock in front of them much more than they did male defendants up before them for similar crimes, and the police and Crown Prosecution Service and press were all equally judgemental. Women were more likely to be convicted by juries; and for lesser offences, such as shoplifting, more likely to be sent to prison on their very first offence.

Faith had grown up feeling incensed over how badly some of the other prostitutes Annie and Maria knew were treated by the law when they appeared in court, with the men who used and abused them getting away scot-free, and the unfairness of this was what first made her want to work in the law, Faith's reasoning being that if passionate and intelligent women like her continued to shy away from the judicial system, it would never change, and she was fully determined to become a judge one day.

Maria knew all this, but it wasn't helpful to dwell on it or to listen to Faith explaining the ins and outs of the British legal system to Charity. For Maria felt as if she were going out of her mind with concern. If Hope were found guilty by the jury, a judge could sentence her to life imprisonment.

Hope

To distract Maria, Father O'Reilly began taking her around some empty properties locally that might make a good refuge for battered women, should Maria decide to use the money Ted had given her, either to buy, or to rent and refurbish, maybe employing some support workers and outreach counsellors should Maria want to take the second option. The father took care not to try to persuade Maria to commit to the idea, instead couching it as 'showing her mere options'.

Shamus had a lot of building experience and so he accompanied Maria and the father in order to give structural advice and talk through problems about taking water to upper levels or adding in more bathrooms or moving kitchens to different rooms. He had the knack of talking about what the work could lead to in a way that meant Maria could imagine how the rooms could be, rather than how they were before her.

Although she was still hesitant over whether she felt the right person to take on this extra responsibility, especially with Hope's predicament looming, and with Charity seeming still to be on a downward spiral, and now Lisa fretting that Little Danny seemed to be taking more risks than were sensible in his work for Big Danny, the more properties she looked around, the more Maria felt she could hear the murmur of Annie's voice in her ear.

And Annie seemed to be insisting more and more that

Maria must let both of her troubled daughters deal with their own issues as they were strong, healthy and intelligent young women who were perfectly capable of doing this, and there wasn't much that Maria could do in concrete terms to help either one.

Other women were not so fortunate, Annie seemed to urge, and it was these that Maria really could make a difference for, and Annie believed in her abilities to excel at this.

After a while, Maria started to believe too that she could do it.

Meanwhile, the next bombshell to hit the family was when Ted Walton telephoned Faith to let her know that Martina had died.

After Fred's disastrous visit, she had gone downhill very rapidly, and had been taken into a hospice, but that had proved too little, too late, and she slipped away on her second day there, with Ted at her side holding her hand.

Faith felt blindsided, even though she had only ever met Martina a handful of times.

To have found a grandmother she never knew about, and then to realise that she could grow to truly love Martina, and finally to lose her so abruptly felt just plain cruel.

Faith drove up to Wakefield, booked herself into a hotel, and went privately to the funeral director's offices

Hope

where Martina's body had been taken in order to pay her last respects in the chapel of rest. She had told Ted she would be in town for this final goodbye, but not at the funeral, and she wouldn't expect to see him, although of course she would be thinking of him in this difficult time, after which she would continue to keep in touch.

But the next day in the morning Ted telephoned Faith to say that if she wanted to come to the funeral, she could.

For Fred was under arrest, out on the Costa del Sol. It was something to do with a fight in a bar the day before his mother's funeral. And although Ted had arranged for a lawyer to help Fred, he'd stipulated that the representation wasn't going to start until after Martina had been buried to make damn sure there was no way that Fred could attend and spread his usual havoc.

'Thank you, Ted,' said Faith. 'I'd like to go. I won't come to the wake though, as I think it might cause awkward questions, and it might get back to Fred.'

She said she wouldn't speak to Ted at the funeral. And then she and Ted arranged that she would take him down to London with her when she drove the Peugeot back home. Ted told her he had business to attend to in the smoke, and this arrangement would give them some private time together, and when he had done everything he needed to do, he could get the train back to Wakefield.

And this is what happened.

Faith waited until the priest had begun the service before she crept silently into the back of the church and took a pew in a shadowy corner, leaving before the service was quite concluded.

It was a lovely funeral, with some heartfelt readings from Ted and also Martina's sisters – so she had great-aunts, Faith realised. She had never thought to ask Martina about her birth family, as Ted and she seemed such a unit together, and Fred such a large and wayward presence, that together they had expelled from Faith's mind any thoughts there could be other relatives she had yet to meet.

As the priest read a lesson, Faith couldn't help wondering about what Martina had been going to tell her as she described with a gentle expression on her face their wedding celebration, when Martina had been interrupted by the harsh sounds of Ted and Fred arguing when Fred was down the road in the British Oak pub. Faith hoped it had been one of her very best memories that Martina had been thinking of.

The next morning Ted arrived at Faith's hotel, and they set off for London.

As she drove, Faith couldn't resist asking, 'Ted, the more I got to know Martina, the more amazing I thought her. I couldn't have discovered a better secret grandmother; I absolutely mean that. And I'm pleased to get to

Hope

know you too. But what I don't understand is why Fred is like he is? It's hard for me to think of you both as his parents, and then Fred as your son, as there seems such a disconnect somehow.'

'Ah, Faith, if only we knew. Martina had influenza in the outbreak of 1946 when she was expecting and always blamed that. But I think Fred's nothing more than a bad apple. It's broken our hearts as he was a sunny lad until he went to school. But after that I could never make him feel confident, and when he was small he had nightmares and sleepwalked, and in recent years I have considered if Fred might have seen some things that he shouldn't when he was a child.

'Back then we didn't think it anything out of the ordinary when we cut Annie's husband Gary Wills when he defaulted on a debt for the umpteenth time. Not enough to kill him, mind, but we were used to doing it when we needed respect, and we knew just how far to go to cause maximum fear. So Gary ended with enough nicks with a Stanley knife that it looked bad. I'm not saying I'm proud of that, but Gary was a fist-happy moron, and he deserved it as he delighted in making Annie's life wretched, and Maria's too, I'll be bound – he owed us money too, and he was the sort of git that we had to do it, to stop him taking advantage of our goodwill.

'And to be fair to Gary, he knew he was only getting

what had been promised, and he took it well enough,' said Ted. 'Well, he was foul to Annie in temper afterwards, I heard from Joyce, and so I had to tell him then that we'd kill him, or good as, if he laid a hand on Annie again, as she was my top earner and she was working his debt off. Put like that, Gary finally got the message, and after that he never tried to get back at us, or Annie as far as I know, and then she and your mother had to do that flit, which is another thing I can't square in my head. And I suppose Fred might have seen some of that as Gary wasn't the only one, back when Fred was at an impressionable age.'

Ted spoke in a very matter-of-fact way.

Faith wasn't shocked or surprised by how casual he sounded about it.

Growing up with Big Danny in her life, even though he wasn't at Ted's level of notoriety, and even though he was a top-level player in the East End criminal fraternity at the moment, with a sizeable number of underlings, Faith had come to understand through her first-hand experience how gangland life operated. And so she knew by 'goodwill', Ted was really saying his empire had been bloody and rife with punishment meted out on those who disobeyed him, and the goodwill mentioned came down to Ted holding off on the violence or creation of fear, but only provided whoever he was dealing with had bent to

Hope

his will. Big Danny operated similarly, and so Faith had long been familiar with this sort of reasoning.

'Well, maybe Fred has found life a bit like a scary carousel that's hard to jump off,' said Faith. 'Perhaps he grew up feeling he could never be the son you expected him to be, and so he put on the act of a hard man as a way of hiding this, and now he's done it so long he can't think of another way, and he's skewed off into someone with no toe-hold on reality. I'm sure the drugs and drinking and fighting can't help. But maybe you shouldn't give up on him, as people can change. There's got to be a bit of Martina in there, and although I think you can be a tough man, to me you seem to have rules you follow that are designed to keep order, but that aren't cruel for the sake of cruelty, and so perhaps he'll calm down.'

Faith didn't believe what she'd said about Fred, but she wanted to see if Ted would try to defend his son.

Ted snorted. 'I think you're being too nice about him. He's getting on for fifty and he's never stopped acting like a stroppy fourteen-year-old. Personally, I think he's just a vicious thug who doesn't know when to stop. I told him that while his mother was alive I didn't want him to die. But now she's not here, it's a different story. I daresay the thought of that will keep him in line for a bit, but he's a touch of the Gary Wills about him that he's shit to a shovel, and the sort always to be in trouble.'

'He must be a worry to you,' Faith said. Now Martina had died, she too felt a freedom over how she might think about making Fred pay for hurting Maria so.

Ted sounded dismissive as he said, 'Oh, I haven't worried about Fred himself for years. I save any worry to thinking about what nightmare he's pulled or is about to pull me into. Time and again I've given him sound advice he's ignored, so I've long ago made my peace that one day he will get what's coming to him – quite possibly at my hands, and I'm reconciled to that – and he'll end up as food on some geezer's pig farm, and I really don't think I'll be sad for a moment should that happen.'

She knew that feeding a body to pigs was believed to be a good way of disposing of it as it would destroy all evidence of an unlawful killing. And as she thought about this, an unexpected quiver of excitement caught Faith between her shoulder blades. She had for a while felt determined to avenge Maria, a determination only strengthened each time she looked at her mother's face, especially now that Faith knew exactly how Fred had ruined her looks with his ring that had the razor embedded in it.

When she hadn't been able to put a face in her mind to Maria's attacker, her feelings had felt more under control. But now Fred was firmly in her sights, and Faith wasn't quite sure where that would end, and actually she didn't

Hope

much care, just as long as Fred Walton paid the price he should.

Ted looked at her. 'You seem remarkably composed about what we've been talking about, all things considered.'

'Well, I had a childhood growing up living right beside Big Danny, a right London hard man with a web of lackeys. Big Danny probably wasn't quite in your league, but he always had a lot of respect, and he played by the rules. In fact, he made sure us Willses were protected. I'm sure much of what was going on really passed me by, although I always knew we were never going to be burgled,' said Faith.

Ted laughed, saying, 'And who says crime's all bad?'

'To a degree, I suspect the police feel like that. Strong gangs means strong gang law, and it keeps the chancers respectful. My friend Tom, who used to be at Special Branch, told me that in Soho they loved the Triads operation as their power was such that it kept a lot of the other sorts of crime down, and that many of his colleagues felt gangs were a good thing because although they were violent, generally it was only members of rival gangs who were targeted. Maybe it's changing with the new types of drugs and people trafficking, but maybe not.'

Ted stared out of the passenger window as he thought about what Faith had said. 'Do you think I ought to meet your Big Danny? Now that Martina has passed?'

Faith only half-heard Ted's question, because as she flipped the car's indicator to turn along Piccadilly so that she could drop Ted off at the bank he wanted to visit, she wondered what Ted would say if he knew that she, Faith, fully intended to be the instigator of his son Fred Walton's downfall.

For a wild moment she thought she would confess this to Ted, and she even opened her mouth to begin speaking.

'Pull over here please, Faith,' Ted said, killing her moment. 'The bank's just here.'

Faith watched him enter through the heavy glass doors with their vertical brass handles, feeling unexpectedly and inexplicably touched by the sight of his smart suit and leather briefcase, and then she realised it was because of a slight droop in his shoulders that made him seem a tad vulnerable, a droop that hadn't been there, or he had been keen to hide, while Martina was still alive.

Droop or not, Ted looked the image of an older successful businessman still, and there was something fatherly and straight up about Ted that made Faith feel very secure with him, certain that he would never do anything to harm her in any way. She realised she was growing fond of him.

But Faith knew also that much of the image that Ted was presenting to the world today was a veneer, and that

Hope

not too far beneath the surface lurked a man who casually talked about giving out nicks with a Stanley knife, and who accepted that one day he might have to kill his own son.

And then she realised that with her own desire for vengeance, perhaps she – a sought-after barrister and A-grade student – had got a share of the same strands of DNA that fired the darker impulses of both Ted and Fred.

This was a thought that was equally terrifying and intoxicating, and in the corresponding fizz of emotion she stalled the Peugeot as she tried to pull away, Faith laughing at herself then as she restarted the engine.

CHAPTER TWENTY

The high level of anxiety Maria was living with couldn't stay at that intensity for long, and although she continued to wake each morning with a feeling of dread nestled in her stomach, the reality was that she found she could shake this feeling off quite quickly once she'd got up and dressed after the first month had passed, at which point Maria realised that she had got used to the idea of Hope being stuck in Holloway awaiting trial.

It helped that because she hadn't been convicted, Hope had the right to have more visits than the convicted women in Holloway.

Maria tried to go once or twice a week and always found Hope surprisingly upbeat, which made Maria pleased that she had made the trek over to the prison, as it was an annoyingly tiresome journey from Cadogan Terrace. Hope joked that the rock-hard mattress on the bed that she'd insisted on sleeping on as she grew up, and her life-long insistence of owning very few possessions, had proved perfect training for cell life.

Her spirits were kept up by Charity and Faith, and Bud too, all visiting regularly.

The one thing that Hope didn't like about her time inside was what she had to wear. Being on remand, she was allowed to wear her own clothes. But the prison hadn't deemed what ordinarily she wore at home to be acceptable for where she was now. Punky goth wear with chains and studs was no-no, apparently, while the vintage and now valuable Vivienne Westwood tees were deemed pornographic.

Charity brought Hope two pairs of stonewash jeans and pale primrose and light grey sweatshirts that all came from Topshop, and some floral underwear from Selfridges. Hope accepted everything with a glum: 'I knew it would be a mistake letting you choose something for me to wear. I hope you paid for it all, as I don't want to encourage you.'

'Get over yourself,' Charity snapped sharply, and Hope couldn't stop herself screwing her brow into such an affronted expression at being spoken to in this tone that for the first time in weeks Charity properly laughed.

'How's Cadogan Terrace life?' Hope asked, once she realised Charity wasn't going to admit if she'd stolen the items or not.

'Same as usual, pretty much. I'm being told off for

Hope

going up west. Himself is getting moaned at by his olds, and everyone wishes you were at home,' said Charity, knowing that Hope would understand 'himself' was Little Danny. 'And Mummy looks a bit death-warmed-up over you being in here, but mostly she's out a lot looking at properties – with the father and his skanky builder guy – that might work for the women's refuge idea.

'I think it will be an official full steam ahead on this soon on her part, as she was telling me this morning that they might've found somewhere that seems suitable with some work on it, and Father O'Reilly is going to have a quiet word with the planning department at the council to see how easily they might be able to get permission to convert it. And Mummy's got a solicitor theoretically trying to sort a long-term rental agreement for the property, as that will spread the money out for more years, and provide for the alterations and staff. So while having a sad face when your name comes up, when Father O'Reilly comes by Mummy gets a bit of a spark to her. She's even having driving lessons as going on the bus to the refuge is taking too much time, and Big Danny says he'll help her get a runabout once she's got her test.'

'Wow. Good for her. I can't imagine her driving though.' Hope really couldn't.

'Same,' agreed Charity. 'But when she's home, she's making me test her on the Highway Code *all* the time – in fact I know it so well now that Big Danny says I ought to take a crash course of lessons and put in for my test too. I'm not sure, but maybe I will. I told Mummy though that I knew she was making me help her as a way of keeping me out of the shops, and she did look caught out when I said that. But then I felt mean, as she does need to learn a lot as that Highway Code is b-i-g, and she wants to get the test soonest, so I am making sure to spend a lot of time with her when she's home, which isn't that much.'

Hope looked at her twin, and asked, 'How are you, really, Charity?'

Charity merely gave a moody shrug.

Hope tried again. 'You've hardly mentioned Little Danny, and that's not like you.'

'I'm fucking pissed off with him, if you must know.'

Charity indeed looked pissed off, and Hope was quite shocked as she could probably count on the fingers of one hand the number of times she had ever heard her twin swear, and Charity had been blessed with the sort of temperament that meant she was hardly ever bad-tempered.

There was a loud sigh, and then Charity added, 'He seems to think more sex is magically going to make me pregnant.'

'Well, he's got a point, hasn't he? Seeing as that is how babies are made.'

'Eugh. Well, not in my case. I've given up on it. I'm

Hope

even thinking I might need to get some sort of job now that I'm not going to be a mother, although doing what I have no idea.'

Charity gave a huff of dislike at the idea of work.

She had never had a job of any description. While both Faith and Hope had held down Saturday jobs from being young teenagers, Charity had always been so besotted with Little Danny that she had never been able to bear the thought of having a pull on her time that would keep her away from him, even giving up her coveted place at grammar school when she passed the eleven-plus and Little Danny didn't. She and Little Danny had pretty much been welded together at the hip since they'd first set eyes on each other well over twenty years previously.

'Steady on, Charity.'

Hope sounded so shocked by Charity even mentioning the word 'job', that it made Charity let out a rough bark of laughter once more, and then she said, 'I do miss having you around, you know, Hope.'

'Me too. I can't tell you how much I'd like to be at home listening to you banging on about your latest nail varnish or whatever else you're keen on at the moment.'

After Charity had gone, Hope thought about her twin. There was definitely something different about her, and after a while Hope realised it was because aside from some colour on her lips, Charity had gone out in public without any make-up, something which probably hadn't happened since Charity was about fourteen.

Maria had said on her visit two days earlier that Charity didn't seem to be pulling out of the slump she was in, and Hope was inclined to feel that things seemed to have worsened.

It wasn't so much what Charity had said that was concerning, but more what she hadn't.

Hope didn't like the glint in her sister's eye and the way that she had lost weight from her face so the tiny blue veins were visible on her eyelids, nor the jittery way she kept playing with her nails and hair, or the way she was talking, which was as if she was slightly distracted and was about to jump up and head off to somewhere more interesting. If Charity hadn't always been so anti-drugs, Hope would have thought she was coked up as she'd seemed so wired. And the make-up thing was just plain weird.

Charity had grown up a happy person, but she didn't seem like that now. And Hope could see precious few signs of the chirpy, glass-half-full Charity who'd shared the same bedroom with her for all those years.

While she herself was in a prison quite literally, thought Hope, somehow it seemed as if Charity was also locked in some sort of prison, even if it was only one of her own making. Hope knew which prison was the easiest to bear, and it certainly wasn't Charity's.

CHAPTER TWENTY-ONE

Christmas and New Year came and went, and at last, on a Monday morning early in 1994, everyone went to the Old Bailey when Hope's trial was scheduled to take place, and took their seats in the public gallery.

When she came up the stairs and stood in the dock, Hope looked smart in her tight-fitting suit, and she had been allowed to trim her glossy black hair into her trademark sharp bob. She glanced at her family, but then after she had been told to sit down, Hope kept her eyes steely and focused on the judge.

Whatever fireworks those watching expected, it wasn't this, as there was something dank about the atmosphere in the courtroom that made it feel like a very low-key start to a major trial.

Bud Metzler had agreed to be a character witness for Hope, and so he couldn't go into the courtroom, and he was on a seat outside waiting to be called. And after her plea of 'not guilty' to the charge of conspiracy to murder had been recorded by the clerk of the court, the laborious process of selecting the twelve supposedly random members of the public who would make up the jury 'of peers' had been completed, which took a whole morning, as objections to particular would-be jurors were made by both the prosecution and the defence.

Things took a strange turn at the start of the afternoon session, when right after they had all been asked to stand and the judge came back in, Hope's barrister asked to approach the bench and then he went forward and had a whispered conversation with the judge, after which the prosecution barrister was beckoned over. Both barristers then returned to their legal teams as Faith noticed a couple of police glancing at each other to see if the other one knew what was going on. It seemed neither did.

'This is irregular and tiresome,' the judge announced, 'but the court will be cleared of the jury and the public for legal arguments.'

Outside the Old Bailey Faith phoned a few people she knew, and then came back inside to tell the family that there was now a rumour around that the defence must have got wind of. Late that morning Harry Stewart was believed to have retracted his statement and was now refusing to give evidence against Hope.

In the autumn previously, he had pleaded guilty in

Hope

exactly the same courtroom where Hope was standing trial to the charge of manslaughter due to diminished responsibility, and as agreed under the plea bargain, the prosecution barrister said in open court that other charges of conspiracy to murder, and murder, had been dropped in return for the guilty plea with the proviso that Harry Stewart gave evidence for the crown in court against another defendant who had been arrested on a serious charge.

So Harry had been sent indefinitely to Broadmoor, although right now he was at Wormwood Scrubs so as to be readily available and within easy distance to pick up for appearing for the prosecution at Hope's trial.

The issue arising, Hope's barrister would likely be claiming, Faith supposed, was that Hope was facing a charge of 'conspiracy' and yet she was the only person charged with that offence, which was unusual in itself. And virtually all of the evidence of her complicity in the conspiracy charge lay in what Harry had alleged that Scarlet had asked him to do, which was from a conversation he had overheard, and therefore was 'hearsay' and therefore not admissible in court, especially if Harry wasn't going to appear himself. And all of this would mean that Hope's barrister would be suggesting to the judge that in order to save expense to the taxpayer when a conviction was not likely, the judge could, or should, declare that the case Hope had to answer had collapsed, at which point she could be released from court.

Relief blossomed in Maria's heart, but only momentarily, as Faith added the judge wouldn't be hasty in doing any such thing, especially as he was a judge known for his misogynistic attitudes.

Instead he would listen to legal arguments from both sides, and study case law for legal precedents that would be provided to him from both the defence and prosecution teams.

And the prosecution would also remind Harry Stewart about the agreement he'd signed that meant he should give evidence in open court, although the CPS probably wouldn't want the expense of bringing him back to court should he definitely refuse to budge, especially as it was a fundamental tenet of British law that a defendant couldn't be tried twice for the same crime, and so they would need a very strong reason to bring him back to court should he not go on to speak against Hope.

The prosecution would have written statements that had been prepared during Harry's questioning at the police station when he'd been originally brought in that they could use against Hope still, but these statements could be ruled out as hearsay, and in any case if the defence couldn't test the evidence in front of a jury, again it posed a knotty legal issue.

Hope

Basically, explained Faith, it was all a boggy, legal quagmire.

The trial was adjourned for two days as far as the public were concerned, but when the open court resumed, the assumption seemed to be that Harry Stewart was now prepared to take the stand, and the judge wanted the case to go ahead in spite of Hope being the sole person facing a conspiracy charge, and so on the Thursday morning everyone took their places in court once more and at long last the case finally kicked off, the judge looking pleased as punch that he hadn't allowed himself to be argued out of continuing with the trial.

Judges are supposed to be fair and impartial, but it was clear from the get-go of the trial proper that this particular judge had taken a fearsome dislike to Hope.

Maria thought the jury had noticed this, and she hoped this would be in Hope's favour, but she wasn't sure.

She'd watched the jury carefully as the prosecution barrister outlined the case he wanted to put before them, and at the mention of what sort of establishment Chantal's had been and the sort of things Hope had done there as Scarlet, it was clear that several of the jury were gobsmacked at the realities of mistressing in a fetish parlour, although Maria noted there were two male jurors who looked at Hope with new, distinctly admiring eyes as if they had been titillated by what they had just heard.

After the prosecution's opening speech, Hope's barrister got to his feet and outlined their defence.

Then the prosecution began bringing their witnesses to the stand to detail what had happened to Chantal. The police and forensic evidence came first, and the jury were shown photographs of the various rooms at Chantal's, those of the dungeons and the puppies' kennels, causing wide eyes of disbelief.

The jurors were also shown scene-of-crime evidence from Chantal's flat, that included the bloody and incredibly gruesome pictures of how her body had been found.

When Harry took the witness stand it was almost a relief, as his cheerful expression and demeanour was in stark contrast to the solemn faces of the police and expert witnesses, as he described how much he had loved being one of Scarlet's puppies, and what he'd done by cleaning the windows naked in the street outside on a freezing winter's night in order to be asked to join the pre-Spring-Cleaning session. This part of his evidence definitely gave some comic moments that lightened the atmosphere.

He seemed to have no difficulty in explaining all the rules of puppy play and he got over well how very much he enjoyed being a husky pulling Scarlet along the corridor in the sled as she whipped his bare behind and thew ice

Hope

cubes at him. Harry freely admitted having had mental health issues in the past, said that he had stopped taking his medication or going to his appointments at his local health centre, and that he had become unhealthily obsessed with Scarlet.

Then he described the fragments of the conversation he'd overheard between Scarlet and Chantal, and how he had bid on Scarlet's virginity in the illegal auction.

He was disturbingly matter-of-fact as he described following Chantal home, and how he returned another night with the express intention of killing her, and then answered the prosecution's questions to describe exactly how he had gone on to do so.

A chill rang through the courtroom when Harry Stewart added close to the end of his description of what had happened: 'I think picking up her shoe and beating her head with it was probably going a bit far, if I'm honest. I never planned to do that and it was all very spur-of-the-moment and now I can't remember much about it, but when I looked in the mirror afterwards I saw I was kneeling beside her with the shoe in my hand and bits of her skull and brains on my face, and I could taste her blood on my lips.'

There was a thump as a juror fainted, and there had to be a short recess while this was dealt with.

And then Harry said, 'I found a plastic bag to put my

coat into as it was now bloody, and sticky too. I didn't want it to make my moped seat dirty, you see. And I thought about taking the shoe away with me as a keepsake, but when I looked for it again I saw it stuck in her head as those heels were very sharp. If I remember rightly, I think I must have put it back there, and it may have gone through her eyeball . . .'

It was a surprise to precisely nobody when a second juror keeled over.

The judge looked to be verging on the apoplectic the further Harry got into his evidence, especially as Hope was sitting in the dock in a calm and relaxed way, her eyes never leaving the judge, not even to give Harry Stewart so much as a single glance. Maria would have wanted to laugh at the judge's expression, if Hope's situation wasn't so serious.

For although Harry was clearly daft as a box of frogs and he had long ago lost much of any toe-hold he may once have had on reality, nevertheless there was somehow a strange innocence about the way he talked about his fetishes and his obsession with Scarlet, and how he had gone on to kill Chantal.

And against the odds, and probably very unintentionally on Harry's part, somehow his childish enthusiasm for telling the truth exactly as it had been for him was slowly turning the case against Hope.

Hope

He truly seemed to believe that Scarlet had instructed him to kill Chantal, and he said several times that he'd been pleased to do this as a sign of his devotion to her, once even saying that he was really pleased to be able to tell her right now how much he had devoted himself to bending to her will, and he hoped she was very proud of him. Being incarcerated was a price he was happy to pay as he didn't believe he could think of anything that would prove to Scarlet that he could ever be a better slave to her.

When it came to the cross-examination, no matter how Hope's barrister couched his questions, it was clear to all that Harry really couldn't see anything wrong with what he'd done, and he had no idea why Scarlet wanted Chantal dead, but it wouldn't matter anyway as he always did his very best to do whatever Scarlet had asked of him.

Harry Stewart was told to step down from the witness box, and he stood grinning at the jury as his handcuffs were put back on before he was escorted from court.

And because Hope's barrister wasn't able to dent Harry's account in any way the judge began to look at Hope in a different way, as if he believed she really would lose the case.

Maria glanced at the two jurors who had been interested in Hope, and both of them were writing in their notebooks and not paying her any attention.

The next morning it was the turn of the defence to put their side of things, and Hope's barrister immediately asked for the case to be dismissed on lack of evidence and the prosecution being unable to provide a feasible motive for why Hope might want Chantal dead, pointing out that although the prosecution had tried hard, they hadn't been able to find a single witness to any cross words ever passing between the two women.

But Harry's turn the day before had damaged Hope's case badly, and so the judge refused. And in the cold light of a new morning it was clear the jury thought his refusal was the right course of action.

Hope took the stand, even though the game plan before the trial started was that she wouldn't give spoken evidence, as her legal team had been convinced there simply wasn't enough evidence for the trial to get to this stage. Defendants speaking in their own defence was always risky, as while the defence team could get her used to their questions during the preparation of the case prior to the trial beginning, it could all go very wrong with a smart prosecution barrister coming up with a question nobody on the defence side had prepared for.

She answered her own barrister's questions, and those of the prosecution, fully and clearly, but the judge did a bit of play-acting with raised eyebrows and dramatic flourishes

Hope

on the legal pad in front of him at inopportune moments that the jury definitely noticed.

The fact that Hope admitted in open court that she prided herself in coming up with unique ways of servicing her clients' fetishes, and that her mother and grandmother had been known prostitutes, with her grandmother being murdered, and it had been she who'd had the idea of the auction of her own virginity, all added to the growing sense swirling around that Hope was a bit too out there to be a good or valuable member of society.

She said she could barely remember her exact words to Chantal, as it was such a general conversation of the sort they'd had many times before that it hadn't stayed in her mind. But they hadn't been arguing and there was no way that Hope wanted Chantal dead as she was a close friend whom she loved. Under cross-examining by the prosecution barrister Hope did however admit though that she might have used the word kill, and he moved to another question before she could clarify further that it would only ever have been said in a colloquial, non-violent and non-instructive way. Her own barrister did try to rectify matters by getting Hope to clarify this, but it was clear that what the jury was remembering was what the prosecution had got her to say.

Bud Metzler didn't help her case either, as his clothes looked out of place for a courtroom and not nearly up to the gravitas of the situation, even if he was only there as a character witness. Then immediately it became clear he was married and more than twice Hope's age, and that he had been the highest bidder at the auction.

Most people smirked when he said he and Hope hadn't subsequently gone on to have sex as frankly nobody believed him, rather in the way undercover vice officers were known for saying in court 'and I made my excuses and left', when it was blatantly clear to all that they hadn't gone on to leave and instead had gone on to have sex with whatever prostitute they'd been in the process of building a case against.

The fact Bud was American and a very rich and respected player in the business world operating on both sides of the pond, and he didn't seem to mind who knew about him taking part in the auction, didn't go down well either.

And this was true even when Bud asserted that if the prosecution were claiming that Hope's motive for murder must have been greed and wanting to take over Chantal's, this was ridiculous as Hope had a brilliant brain and could easily work a single year in the commercial property world and make a take-home pay of three or four times the annual turnover of Chantal's, and that when she was back in civvy life he would be employing her in a legitimate role on which UK tax would be paid

Hope

as he wanted her brilliant brain as part of his business empire.

The case for the defence rested, and then both barristers made their closing statements.

The judge followed with his summing up for the jury, making very clear through his tone of voice how he thought they should find Hope guilty, although his words themselves never quite went as far as stipulating this out loud.

The jury came back with their verdict quite soon after they'd been sent out, and as the foreman rose to give their verdict the blood thumped painfully in Maria's ears as if she had tinnitus as the word 'guilty' was said.

And so Hope found herself convicted of a crime that she'd had nothing to do with.

After the jury had been released from their jury duty on this case and escorted out of court through their own side door, Hope's barrister did what he could in outlining various points of mitigation, but the judge's expression made it clear to all that he wasn't going to be deterred from his initial thoughts, with the expectation clear to all that sentencing was going to be hefty.

But before he got to this, the reports from social services and a psychological evaluation that had been prepared prior to trial were handed to the judge. He read them meticulously, and painfully slowly.

'Stand up,' the judge demanded at last, pulling his tortoise-shell reading spectacles from his large nose as Hope and her barrister got once more to their feet. Hope's unblinking gaze had never wavered from the judge since she had sat down.

'You have been found guilty by a jury taken from your peers of one of the most heinous crimes, that of . . .' he paused dramatically '. . . conspiracy. To. MURDER,' the judge told Hope, emphasising in a pantomime manner the word 'murder'. 'Those who play with fire, as you have, must expect to get burned.'

Hope made very sure she responded to the judge with as bored an expression as she could muster, and she jutted out a hip as she adjusted her weight on her needle-sharp heels.

The judge paused and reordered the papers before him, and then he declared, 'And as a result of your actions that have now been proven in this court, a person lost their life. That is a tragedy, a matter of the utmost seriousness.

'Therefore, as a lesson to others that they should under no circumstances behave as you have, I have no choice but to sentence you to a prison term of eight years, with the recommendation that you serve the full sentence.'

The judge had more things to say to her, but Hope zoned out of listening to him as she was already thinking about her next move. It was only when the judge snapped

Hope

at her, 'Take her down!' that she tuned in once more to what he was saying, and with a last disparaging look at him she turned to leave the dock, a court officer in front of her and one behind.

An hour later Maria was in a cell below the courts. She had been allowed to see Hope.

'Don't worry, Mummy,' an unbowed-looking Hope told her with a smile, after they'd talked about how the press would be handling the story of her conviction, with the red-tops set for a field day. 'I have a plan.'

Maria hoped this was true.

But there was quite a large part of Maria that just wanted to scream at her daughter that this was all Hope's fault, and that if only she'd listened to Maria's advice, and had never gone to work as a mistress first place, nor had the stupid idea about the auction, then none of this would have happened and Hope wouldn't have put her, Maria, through the wringer as she had.

Taking a breath to control herself, instead Maria made herself smile at her daughter, and then she said, 'I'm sure you do. You wouldn't be my dear Hope if you didn't.'

Although it had been a struggle to pull back her temper, as Maria hugged Hope and promised she'd come to see her soon in Holloway, and Hope hugged her mother back more tightly than she ever had done before, Maria wondered if the firmness of her daughter's clasp meant that the whole experience had upset Hope in a way that she wasn't letting on.

Whatever, Maria was pleased that her daughter didn't have to start her lengthy prison sentence with the sound of her mother shouting at her still ringing in her ears.

CHAPTER TWENTY-TWO

As Hope entered Holloway Prison through its big wooden sliding door for the first time following her trial at the Old Bailey, she realised that now she was a proper lag, it was a different feeling going through this door than it had been when she was on remand or during her trial.

Still, although she was disappointed the trial hadn't gone her way earlier in the day, and although she was no legal expert, she thought it clear there were grounds for an appeal, both against her conviction and her sentencing.

But this could take a while and so Hope knew that for now she just had to make the best of it.

And as she stood in reception with a prison officer beside her, she was struck as she hadn't been the first time by just how filthy it was, with tissues and cigarette packets and other rubbish strewn across the floor. It smelt funky too, as if too many sweaty armpits and unchanged sanitary wear was the norm.

Hope had expected to be called forward to the desk

before long, but after they'd been standing there for fifteen minutes, she and the screw in charge of her exchanged a glance and then they backed up to the seats to wait.

In front of them still were what looked like a group of organised hoisters who were feigning having little English just for the hell of it, and Hope supposed they were all there on remand and were feeling pretty cross about it. Eventually they all got their prison numbers, and one by one were chivvied through a side door for the next stage of the processing.

The woman on the other side of the desk indicated that Hope should step forward, and then she said, 'Back again, Ms Wills, and so soon. We must have treated you so well you couldn't stay away.'

Hope made sure to give the sarky woman a smile, just to be annoying in her own way.

'Prison number, phone and jewellery.' The woman sounded tired and gruff as she pushed a plastic box in Hope's direction for the possessions to be placed into, her sigh as she looked at Hope suggesting that her side of the counter kicking off the processing administration always led to her having a long day and seeing just too much of people.

After slowly saying her number so the woman could write it down, Hope took off her jewellery, looking regretfully at the matching designer jet-stone necklace, bracelet,

Hope

ring and earring set with a skull design that Bud had given her to wear in court for good luck, thinking how she would miss wearing them every day, as although she and Bud had met probably only a handful of times, somehow he instinctively knew that although she'd never been much of a one for jewellery, something like this very much answered the darker side of her goth sensibility. But jewellery with stones was not allowed on the wings and so Bud's present had to go into the box and as it dropped there was a weighty clunk about it that Hope liked, and she placed her phone on top.

'Next door,' said the screw beside her, and they went through to the next section where Hope was given a pillowcase and some scuzzy bedclothes. Her smart suit and heels went into a bag to be returned to her on release.

She had to hand over her own clothes she would be wearing in the cell, and also the underwear she still had on. Each item was carefully checked for razor blades and drugs before being handed back. Hope felt the screw doing the inspection spent an obscene amount of time checking her silk bra and knickers she'd worn in court, looking closely too at the inner gusset to the knickers; if this woman didn't have a thing for this sort of silk and lace frillies, Hope thought she would eat her hat, as Chantal's had taught her to recognise a fetish a mile off.

Then this screw ran her hands through Hope's hair, in case Hope had hidden anything there.

Hope sensed, or more precisely heard, the screw sniffing her as the larger woman stood too close. Even at the best of times, Hope didn't like other people she didn't know to be near her, but she forced herself to stand rigid and not give the slightest flinch when the screw's hand accidentally-on-purpose grazed her breast as she lowered her hands from Hope's head. It wasn't because the prison officer was a woman, but because she was taking advantage of her position to behave like this to Hope when she knew that Hope couldn't do anything about it that rankled.

Next there was a holding room where Hope was asked if she needed to see a doctor, and she said no, and it was explained to her that for her first night of the sentence she was going to be in wing C1, where the psychiatric staff would keep an eye on her. After that, if she wasn't thought to be a suicide risk, she would be allocated a single room because of the length of her sentence.

Hope was pleased about the single cell as while on remand she'd had a string of cellmates she hadn't liked much, mainly because most of them wanted to talk to her and make her sympathetic about what hard lives they'd had. Hope had remained tight-lipped about her own life, and what she was on remand for.

Hope

But while she wasn't exactly unfeeling for these women with their drug dependencies and rotten men in their lives, in the hard-life stakes, Hope thought her life hadn't been a walk in the park either.

Back when she was a teenager, her prostitute mother had been ridiculed to Hope's face almost every day at school for both her profession and her looks. And Hope believed she'd never be able to square in her mind that her granny Annie had been forced into prostitution by a weak and vindictive husband, before ending up brutally slain when just trying to protect Maria from a crazed punter. It was no wonder she was more than happy to remain a virgin, felt Hope.

Hope knew she would never dream though of trying to make anyone feel sorry for her, and so she didn't utter a word about any of this. And the advantage to this strategy was that she didn't allow anyone information that they might later use to hurt her.

Instead, Hope would listen patiently to what these women had to say, and then tell them, 'You know you never have to remain a victim, don't you? I'm not saying bad things haven't happened, and I am sorry you feel so sad right now. But while you can't change the past, you can alter how you feel about it, and decide too how you are going to live your life differently going forward and learn how to make better choices.'

More than one of the women in the shared cell had clapped back along the lines that the very fact Hope was in Holloway on a long remand, which in itself suggested her offence was serious and not a mere silly mistake, meant that Hope might not be best placed to tell others how to live their lives as clearly she had made some bad choices along the way, so what the hell gave her the audacity to offer any unwanted advice?

'I agree with you,' Hope would reply. 'But that doesn't get around the fact that none of us *have* to let the past keep repeating in our future. If that happens, then that is a choice, simple as – it might not feel like it at the time, but it really is, exactly as much as if you opt to change yourself or your situation.'

Hope wasn't a popular cellmate on her previous wing with the other women on remand, not that she cared much either way about this, although more than one asked to be moved away from her to another cell.

It had been surprisingly exhausting, Hope had found, to have a string of people she didn't know repeatedly brought in to room with her. And now her trial had finally ended, she was pleased that because of the eight-year sentence – which even with time off for good behaviour, would lead to her being inside for over three years, and with account taken of the time she had spent in the remand wing at Holloway – meant she would be able to find a modicum of psychological peace while in a cell to herself, something that had escaped her since her arrest.

Three-plus years was a long time, but if she had to, Hope knew she could get through it relatively easily if left to her own devices. Not that she thought she was going to have to, but she liked to fathom the ins and outs of the worst-case scenarios.

But Hope wasn't bulletproof, and there was a moment her nerve faltered once she got inside the cell on C1, clutching along with her clothes and bedding, her blue plastic plate, cup and bowl and white plastic cutlery, when she almost felt defeated.

She knew it was only for a night, but the sight of the bare mattress and a lumpy mass that passed for a pillow – both looking stained with shit, piss, blood and vomit – made her gag. She had to close her eyes and breathe slowly to get a grip on herself again.

And later, although the remand wing had often been noisy at night, with the sound of people crying, or yelling in frustration, Hope discovered she hadn't been prepared for how different and disturbing the sounds would be in a psychiatric wing.

For there was a lot of commotion that came from staff unlocking doors and banging them closed, and then weird silences from cells where the inmate had previously been making a racket, and so Hope supposed that this meant some women were being sedated. Well, she hoped it was sedation, as she didn't like to think of her fellow inmates going through anything else when they were clearly so vulnerable. And those who kept on crying or shouting sounded utterly desperate in a way those on the remand wing hadn't really been.

Worst of all though, was the jarring slam of the peephole door as screws flipped it closed as they repeatedly came by to check on Hope to make sure she wasn't trying to kill herself.

The next morning the prison's governor came by and told Hope that she would be moved to her permanent wing. Hope could have danced for joy.

On her new wing, yet again the atmosphere felt unlike what Hope had experienced previously. It helped a lot that this cell was much cleaner than the C1 one. And – this was unheard of – the pillow was in a good state, and nobody had come in to swap it with their shoddy one as was routine.

Indeed, Hope felt she had lucked out as it was at the quieter end of the wing, and the women seemed to congregate in the part of the recreation area furthest away.

As her first few days on the wing passed, Hope came to appreciate more and more the lack of footfall of people walking past her cell. It made it easier for her to keep herself to herself, and she liked too that there was a good view from her window over the exercise yard, and so Hope

Hope

spent quite a lot of time studying the women outside, making sure she knew who was friendly with who, and understood who would be best avoided.

There were further pluses and minuses of the wing.

On one hand, it seemed on the surface much calmer generally. The days felt quite organised and as if there was a real routine, with many inmates going to work each day and the screws not appearing to be quite as on edge. All the inmates were encouraged to socialise, and various sorts of education were on offer.

And Hope could see that by the time many of the women had reached this point of serving a long sentence, they just wanted to keep their head down and get through it with as little hassle as possible, which again helped promote a sense of routine and, whilst not of calm exactly, one of resigned acceptance.

There was quite a lot of laughing, and Hope could see obviously close friendships and some long-term sexual partnerships having been forged between many of the inmates and, sometimes, between a prisoner and a screw.

Generally, there was much less sound too of the screws moving about, as the prisoners weren't allowed to have so many prison visits, and nor were there the number of prisoners coming in and out for short stays as there had been on the remand wing, and so there was less to-ing and fro-ing by the prison officers who would be needed as escorts.

On the less-good side of things though, there was a clearly defined and sternly defended pecking order among the women, and each time a new prisoner joined the wing, they would be sorely tested as to where they would slot into the accepted order.

To be somebody near the bottom of this chain was to be avoided if possible, as those at the top of the food chain expected privileges and rewards from those down the order, and Hope saw some terrible bullying.

And if a scrap happened, which it did occasionally, it showed the allegiances that had already been established, so that what could begin over something laughably trivial could escalate more quickly into something larger and more sprawling as it sucked other people in.

When Hope had seen trouble escalating on the remand wing, she'd noticed there was much more of a sense of people being very jumpy and wary of everybody else, as when push came to shove, most people were only really out for themselves.

The allegiances Hope saw on this long-term wing probably had taken time and effort to build, and she supposed that on the remand wing, the population had always been in such a state of flux that loyalty couldn't be achieved in the same way.

*

Hope

Hope knew it was coming, but she couldn't predict when or what would be done to test her. She told herself she must be prepared at all times, and that waiting for it was probably more unsettling than whatever it would actually be when it came.

But when it happened, Hope thought it pathetic in its childishness.

She had rinsed out her underwear and carefully placed it to dry on the radiator in her cell, and then she had gone to the shelf on wheels that held a selection of the prison's library books to choose something to read.

As she got back to her cell, two of the low-ranking and routinely hen-pecked women – Kathy and Lil – slunk out holding her damp silk underwear.

Lil obviously came from some sort of desperate background, as although they could wear their own clothes, Hope had only ever seen her in a mismatch of garments that had clearly come from Holloway's poor-box of discarded clothes, with holey plimsolls that had to be at least two sizes too big, judging by the way they slapped the ground as she walked. Kathy's arms bore the silken lattice of scars of someone who has spent years cutting her arms with a razor blade, interspersed with marks and dents that suggested a long history of intravenous drug use.

Together, they were a sorry sight, and Hope knew they would never have dared to enter her cell unless instructed to. She didn't blame them. These were women already defeated, and just doing what they could to make each day a little less depressing than it promised to be otherwise.

Clearly not expecting to see Hope, they paused in horror at finding her so near to them.

Hope thought they were probably more used to readers who were mouth-breathers having to point at the words of a sentence they were reading, and so they had miscalculated how long she would be when choosing a book.

She seized the advantage and blocked their way, saying, 'You don't want to do that, I'm telling you.'

'Fuck off,' said Kathy, trying and failing for an aggressive tone, although she flung her bundle as far away as she could to the jeers of those watching.

'Who put you up to it?' asked Hope.

'As if,' Kathy tried to butch it out.

Lil looked too terrified to speak, but her lightning glance behind Hope was the tell she needed.

Quick as a flash Hope turned and ran back where she had just come from, barrelling full-on into the breastbone of the tallest and widest woman Hope had ever seen.

This was Suze, currently top girl on the wing.

Thanking her lucky stars for the self-defence training Hope had been given by one of her clients, she allowed herself to be slapped in the face and then wrapped in Suze's arms, as Hope gathered all her strength to kick her

Hope

assailant's thick shins as hard as she could, and then she brought her knee up hard into Suze's crotch.

There was a nano-second when Suze, who was frighteningly strong, twitched one arm in pain and dropped her face an inch, and Hope found this gave her enough leeway to shoot her hand up to jab Suze in the eye socket.

'Oi!' shouted a screw as she hurried to where they were, and Suze let Hope go, and Hope backed away too, the two women never taking their eyes off each other.

Suze was told to go to her cell and Hope was escorted into an office, where the screw said she'd seen it all, including Suze recruiting Kath and Lil for the shake-down, and so this time Hope wouldn't be punished, but it must never happen again. Hope resisted the urge to say there might be better ways of handling this new-girl-proving-it palaver without letting it actually play out.

A couple of days earlier Hope had applied for a visiting order for Maria to come, and her mother's gasp in visiting hour the next afternoon when she saw the slap mark on Hope's face told her she didn't look good.

'Don't worry, Mummy – it was something and nothing,' said Hope, in an effort to be reassuring, 'and the other one is wearing an eye patch right now.' Maria did not look reassured in the slightest by either statement.

A few days passed with Suze standing threateningly at the other end of the recreation area, pounding a closed fist into the open palm of her other hand every time Hope had to pass her.

Hope ignored her, walking past with her head held high, even though her heart would be beating furiously inside her chest. Suze didn't do anything to hurt her, but Hope thought this was merely to build up the tension in Hope's mind regarding what might be coming her way.

And then one day it was all over.

Every single piece of Hope's underwear was back on the radiator, and there was Suze asking if Hope wanted to join her in a game of chess.

Tentatively, Hope agreed, and then proceeded to beat Suze in just two moves, by employing the Fool's Mate. Suze frowned and suggested pontoon, and Hope nodded. It took a bit longer, but Hope made sure she won again.

And to Hope's surprise, Suze stuck out her meaty paw of a hand for a handshake, saying as Hope stood up to return to her cell, 'You should've said from the off you were one of Big Danny's.'

Hope looked at Suze as she thought about the extent of Big Danny's reach across the criminal underworld these days – was there no place he didn't hold sway?

But what she said to Suze was: 'You think I need Big Danny to put in a word?'

'Maybe not,' Suze answered, and as Hope turned to go, Suze let out a wheezy laugh.

Hope

Hope was never bothered by anyone again, not even when she refused to join Suze's crew, which she heard was something that nobody ever dared refuse once Suze had thrown the invite their way.

Big Danny's reputation must be at the level that even a hardened offender as Suze was understood that he would have a long memory for any signs of disrespect to somebody he was looking out for, Hope had to conclude.

CHAPTER TWENTY-THREE

It had taken a lot of dusty physical work but in a small and quiet cul-de-sac in Stepney, Maria's refuge for battered women was nearing completion.

The good thing about the street where the refuge sat were its other properties. There were clothing sweatshops on one side that looked to be employing mostly illegal immigrants judging by how furtive everyone seemed who went in and out through the door with its metal grille, and a couple of distinctly dodgy small warehouses on the other, while the refuge itself had yet more clothing sweatshops to its rear.

Maria didn't hold with sweatshop factories, where the machinists would be fined for leaving their sewing to go to the toilet, but then she didn't hold with women not being able to provide for their children either.

And at least the mostly brown-skinned women she saw hurrying to and from the sweatshops weren't having to ply their trade on the streets as she and Annie had had to.

Maria had been keen to find a place that wouldn't have too many nosy neighbours, as jobsworths living in nearby houses were always a concern, as at any time they might find a reason to blab to others that something was going on at the end of the street.

This was to be a safe refuge for terrified women, and it was of prime importance that its location was kept as low-key as possible so that husbands, fathers, brothers or boyfriends couldn't come to kick up a rumpus.

A huge advantage of this particular street seemed to be that nobody there already wanted unwelcome attention drawing to themselves, and so they pointedly ignored what was going on.

Best of all, there was a dog-leg towards the end of the cul-de-sac, and this meant that for anyone standing on the pavement of the busier road it edged away from, there was no sign of the refuge.

It really was a case of if anybody didn't know it was there, then they would never guess from the road at the top of the street.

The property itself Maria ended up buying was a job lot at auction as it was a stand-alone small terrace comprising a trio of three-storey houses that were structurally sound although cosmetically very run-down. A kindly planning officer helped with the plans to knock the three houses together and have the three front entrances brought down

Hope

to one to make security easier to be heard in-camera, as this meant the application was done on a need-to-know basis and members of the general public wouldn't easily find out about it.

The downside to the property was that the houses only had small backyards, and so there wouldn't be much outside space for children to play, as Maria knew that some women would come with their children. But this compromise was a small price to pay, when the property had so much else working in its favour.

Faith had been brilliant overseeing the legalities and the paperwork they'd needed to get signed off, and she had got her influential judge who hated wife-beaters onside, and he in turn had influence with some Members of Parliament and a few higher-ups in the police force. The judge wasn't going to be actively involved at this point, but it was more that should Maria need help from officials further down the line in some way, then a start had been made in lining potential people up already who said they were prepared to offer support of various sorts at a moment's notice.

Father O'Reilly and Shamus proved to be a godsend, and they organised various volunteers, Shamus ending up in charge of a crew of Irish navvies with all the building skills that were needed.

Little Danny proved a dab hand at decorating. He and

Charity remained under pressure in their marriage, and as he didn't have the concentration at the moment to do work for Big Danny, he found sloshing paint on walls and stripping woodwork to be very soothing. Shamus taught him how to tile, and Little Danny became very proud that he had done the tiling in every bathroom and toilet.

Everybody was pleased about this as Little Danny had got very drunk and leery one evening in a Hackney pub recently, and had ended up having to spend the night at the local nick, and being fined at the magistrates' court the next day for being drunk and disorderly. It was very out of character as normally he wasn't much of a drinker, but it was clear to those at Cadogan Terrace that although he never raised his voice or was mean in any way to Charity, he was feeling the pressure of their infertility just as much as she was.

Little Danny's arrest proved a bit of a wake-up call though as far as Charity was concerned, and she made an effort not to be witchy with him, and he promised to her that he would never do anything like this again. It was baby steps, with them still being very cautious of each other, but at least it was a start.

In the spirit of these small and fragile shoots of marital reconciliation, Charity suggested to her mother-in-law Lisa that together they should embroider a piece of linen

Hope

that they could have framed and fronted with unbreakable glass to give to Maria. Lisa, who normally hated any form of crafting, immediately agreed as Charity hadn't suggested anything like this for ages.

When finished, the embroidery read:

In memory of two strong women, ANNIE WILLS and her friend JOYCE. They were not treated well by men, but their minds were always stronger than those that did them wrong, and they never gave up hope. They truly believed life could change – for the better.

Maria went to the refuge almost every day, and quite soon she realised how much she enjoyed getting everything ready.

At Father O'Reilly's recommendation, Maria and Shamus interviewed a recent widow called Linda who was a member of the father's church. She was a former social worker, and had lost her husband to cancer at the start of the year. Her landlord had promptly then given her notice of her eviction as he didn't want a single woman in his property.

Linda seemed perfect to become the refuge's live-in manager, and although they hadn't interviewed anyone else yet, at a nod from Shamus, who seemed to have read Maria's mind, Maria offered Linda the job in the interview, knowing that Father O'Reilly would not have sent her a candidate if he didn't think her up to the job.

Linda burst into tears, her voice gulpy as she told them how delighted she was to get both a job and a new home in one fell swoop, as she'd had to stop work to nurse her husband through the final year of his life, and she hadn't quite been able since his death to face the demands of full-time work as a social worker as there was so much paperwork and people to see, and so she had been feeling almost as if she was going out of her mind. But she wasn't scared of hard work, and she would throw herself into helping the women who would seek their help.

After Linda had gone, Shamus suggested that in celebration of Maria having her first member of staff, he and Maria should hang the embroidered tribute to Annie and Joyce.

Maria thought that a good idea and she chose a spot over the mantelpiece of the largest sitting room. It looked very fine once it was up, and then bashfully Shamus gave Maria a wooden plaque he'd made that had ANNIE'S carefully burned into it, the whole plaque burnished with a soft varnish.

Maria asked him to put it above the cork noticeboard in the main hall, so that everyone would know the name of the refuge was 'Annie's'.

'She'd have been so proud,' Maria told Shamus as they

Hope

stood looking at it up on the wall. He coloured a deep puce, but by now Maria was so used to Shamus that she didn't take any notice.

Although things to do with getting the refuge ready to open were going much better than she could ever have hoped for, Maria couldn't stop a nagging sense of anxiety.

Faith seemed on edge, although she refused to be drawn on why. It took Maria a while to notice, but she realised Tom Jarrett hadn't been around for a while, although she had no idea why that might be. And Charity was definitely off-centre still even though she did look to be trying to find a way back to Little Danny. Maria was pleased to hear that, according to Lisa, Charity had enjoyed doing the embroidery on Annie and Joyce's tribute.

Oddly, the one daughter Maria was becoming less concerned about was Hope, as she seemed to have adjusted to prison life relatively easily. On each visit, aside from that time with the mark of Suze's hand on her face, however closely Maria studied her across the table as they sat in the visitors' room, she couldn't detect anything in Hope's demeanour that looked worrisome.

Then, one evening, there was a ring on Maria's doorbell in Cadogan Terrace, and when she got downstairs to answer, it was to find Ted Walton on the doorstep.

Maria was so astonished to see him there that she was struck speechless.

'I'm sorry, Maria, but we need your help,' said Ted. 'Fred's girlfriend Anna is in the car, and in a bad way. She called me from Malaga airport, saying Fred was trying to kill her, and she'd had to run with her passport and just enough money for a flight, and could I help as I had offered to her once before. I've just driven down from Wakefield and picked her up from Gatwick, and she's in the car right now, shaking like a leaf. I know it's a terrible imposition, but I couldn't help but think of you, as I don't know what to do otherwise.'

'Let me make a quick call,' said Maria. And she went to ring Linda and ask that a bed be made up.

And so Annie's got its first resident.

Maria went in the Jag with Ted and Anna over to the refuge, as Anna sobbed quietly to herself, and Maria (and probably Ted too) pondered the irony of him driving both of the women passengers in his car right now to safety after Fred had gone on the rampage, albeit with thirty years passing between the rescues.

'Ted, park here,' said Maria as they drew close to the side street where the refuge was. 'You can't come any closer as there's to be no men here at all.'

Once the navvies had left just the snagging to do, Linda had taken up residence, with exceptions made for Little Danny, Father O'Reilly and Shamus as the only males

Hope

who would be allowed through the elaborate security system and onto the premises as they would be finishing off putting the final touches in. Maria felt very firmly about this, to the point that she was wondering whether any male children should be allowed in the establishment once they had gone past the age of twelve.

But that was a question for another day as Linda opened the door and ushered Anna inside, saying to Maria, 'Leave her with me, I think that will be best – I'll ring if we hit any problems, but I'm sure we'll be fine.'

Anna went to follow Linda down the hall, but then she ran back and flung herself into Maria's arms, her face close against Maria's scarred cheek, as she cried, 'Thank you! You'll never know how much I have to thank you for, or how it feels to escape such a pig.'

'I think I do,' said Maria, and she clasped Anna firmly to her.

Maria went to find Ted.

'It looks like Anna will be OK with Linda, and we'll hear if she's not. Meanwhile you'd better come back to mine – as Hope isn't there you can sleep in her flat,' she said.

Ted looked very grateful for the offer, as he had been contemplating the unwelcome thought of the long drive back up to Wakefield.

*

As Maria unlocked the front door to the Cadogan Terrace house, Big Danny was coming down the stairs, and he did a double take at the sight of Maria bringing in a man to the hall. In all the years he'd known Maria, Big Danny had never seen her choosing to have any man near her, other than Father O'Reilly.

Maria said, 'Let me introduce you both. This is Ted Walton, the benefactor of the refuge, and Ted, this is Big Danny, who has been very, very kind to my family over many years. He lives upstairs, and I live above him. You are going to stay in Hope's flat, which is the studio beside mine.'

Big Danny shook Ted's hand warmly, as he said, 'So you're the gent who has given Maria a spring in her step. If you're going to be around for a day or two, me and my son Little Danny would love to take you for a drink in a traditional East End boozer.'

Ted looked a bit doubtful as he had been planning to leave in the morning. But he nodded when Maria said, 'Yes, Ted, do stay on a bit, as I know Faith would want to see you too.'

'Thank you both,' said Ted, thinking fate was a strange thing as now it seemed as if he would be going for a drink with Big Danny tomorrow or the next day, exactly as he had wanted Faith to broker, yet somehow it had happened without Faith having to get involved. 'Sounds good,' he added.

CHAPTER TWENTY-FOUR

The drink in the boozer ended up being quite an outing in the end.

Lisa and Charity came too, as did Faith and Tom Jarrett. Even Maria was persuaded to join them, although she only stayed for one, and Faith made sure not to sit close enough to her mother that Maria could ask about Tom.

Faith didn't know what she could say to her mother about him, as Tom had disappeared and then arrived back in Hackney weeks later without explanation and with the sort of look on his face that said to Faith he wouldn't tell her where he'd been, even if she asked him.

She liked him as he made her laugh, and she was pleased that he was now sitting beside her, but there was something about the time she had been spending up in Wakefield that told her Tom was never going to be reliable enough for her long-term, Faith was beginning to realise, even though the unexpected sight of him had made her belly flip. Be that as it may, the irony that Tom was a policeman who seemed unafraid of being outside the law if he had to, while Ted had a long history of organised crime but appeared much more law-abiding, wasn't lost on Faith.

In fact, in many ways, what she wanted after seeing first-hand Ted's devotion to Martina, was a younger version of Ted for herself, the crime connections aside. He'd told her during the drive down to London that he'd never so much as looked at another woman once he'd met Martina, even though he'd had some great-looking girls like Annie and Joyce working for him back in the day.

Faith believed him and as a tray of drinks arrived while they all sat in the corner of the pub, she could see that since Martina had died, Ted had lost weight and he'd abruptly aged by about ten years. Martina's death had clearly hit Ted hard.

She turned and smiled at Tom, who grinned back. It was clear Tom must have filled in Big Danny on just what a player up north that Ted Walton was, as Big Danny was going out of his way to make Ted Walton feel welcome and show him 'where history was made'. And both Big Danny and Ted were sizing each other up with appraising looks, although each was trying, and mostly failing, to hide that they were.

They began in the Carpenters Arms in Bethnal Green,

Hope

which the notorious Kray brothers had bought for their mother in the sixties, and then they moved on to the Blind Beggar in Whitechapel, where Ronnie Kray shot and killed a rival.

'It strikes me,' Big Danny said to Ted when they were in their fourth pub, 'that perhaps you and I ought to see if your interests might align with my interests. Now's not the night to talk, but soon?'

Ted laughed. 'Great minds . . .'

They were each taking great care to show respect to the other and not to try any one-upmanship. So far, this was a strategy making for a convivial evening.

The night ended up being a very boozy affair, although Little Danny made sure to stick to his word of behaving himself where drink was concerned, and he took Charity home at ten o'clock.

Everyone watched them leave, the family going 'aww' when they saw Charity put her arm around Little Danny's waist and pull him towards her as they went out through the pub's door.

Faith saw Ted looking slightly bemused, so she explained, 'They've had a few problems,' at exactly the same time Tom slugged the last of his whisky and said, 'Little Dan's luck's in tonight for hunt the salami!' making Faith roll her eyes and tut, and everybody else laughed.

At one point they were in Lord Napier in Hackney Wick, and a group of lads on a nearby table began drunkenly messing about and being that bit too raucous in their drinking game.

'Shut it,' called Big Danny over his shoulder.

They began to jeer at his back.

With a sigh Big Danny got up and went to stand close to the group, looking each of them in the eye turn by turn.

'Who the fuck do you think you are, old man?' said the ringleader. 'I'll have you soon as look at you.'

After a little while one of the minions dared to add, 'Yeah, piss off, fucker.'

A hefty barman came around the bar to hover nearby, while Big Danny stayed stock-still but continued to eyeball them.

When they had quietened under his stare and were sitting there meekly, which didn't take long, Big Danny turned and rejoined his table as the barman had a word in the ear of the first lad who had told Big Danny to fuck off. Big Danny hadn't had to say a word to get control of the situation.

But as the barman spoke, Ted saw the lad's face go white, and then he nodded and quickly got up to follow the barman to the bar.

An unordered fresh round of drinks arrived at Big

Hope

Danny's table, and the mouthy lad came over looking now very sober and contrite. 'Apologies. I didn't mean any disrespect,' he said.

Big Danny looked up at him. 'Name?' he asked.

'Carl.' Carl's voice was a squeak.

'I never forget a face, Carl,' Big Danny told him, and Carl looked as if he were about to pass out.

The drinks at Carl's expense kept coming to their table after that, and Ted Walton could see why Big Danny had grown an empire.

Quiet authority on top of a fearsome reputation was what every gang kingpin wanted but very few could achieve, especially when although still in the East End, this particular pub wasn't even in Big Danny's original stamping ground, as Ted knew that was over in Stepney. The fact his reputation had grown along with his experience made Big Danny impressive.

It was something Ted thought that, Fred aside, he'd managed to do too.

In fact, the more Ted looked at Big Danny, the more he thought they were brothers in arms.

It almost made up for how epic the hangover the next morning felt.

It was several weeks later when Hope had gone to bed early and had just fallen asleep, when there was a noise and she opened her eye to see a screw standing in the doorway to her cell.

'Pack up, mate, you're moving,' the screw told her.

'Where to?' asked Hope. 'It's the middle of the night.'

'Just do it, and pronto. Back to remand wing. Don't ask me any more as I don't know.'

With a sinking feeling, Hope knew something must have happened. She'd never heard anyone speak about being on a long-term wing and out of the blue suddenly being sent back to remand. But she couldn't think of anything that meant it would be to do with her as she had made sure to be a model prisoner. Well, other than when she and Suze had had words of course, but that was a while back now.

She scrabbled to get dressed, and the screw handed her a black plastic rubbish bag to put her things in.

'Bye, babe,' called Suze, and the prison officer unlocked the first of the doors out of the wing. It was the last thing Hope ever had said to her on that wing.

The energy of the remand wing hadn't changed from the familiar mix of nervy and frenetic, and Hope didn't like it any more than she had when she was first there.

A cell door was unlocked, and before Hope could properly get inside as she was having to look at the guard who was demanding the bin bag back as it was too much of a

Hope

suicide risk, a woman flung herself at Hope, and Hope dropped the damn bin bag. The screw upended it half in the cell and half in the walkway, and yanked up the bag so that everything fell onto the floor.

But Hope wasn't thinking about that.

For she had Charity in her arms.

But it was a Charity with unfocused eyes, trails of dried tears and snot on her face, and a strange sour yet sweet smell about her.

'Charity! What on earth?' said Hope as she guided Charity to the bottom bunk and went to sit down beside her.

But before she could do so, Hope saw a hand snake towards her pillowcase, clearly intent on nabbing it.

With a 'hold on, Charity', she sprang up and kicked the hand away as, while she was in Holloway, Hope was determined that she wasn't going to be the victim of theft twice, reasoning that once was par for the course, but for it to happen a second time was simply unacceptable. And, on that reasoning, the fact she had just kicked a guard, who presumably wanted the pillowcase to give to a favourite lag, didn't seem to matter much.

Hope gathered the rest of her belongings that were still scattered outside the cell quickly before chucking them up onto the top bunk, and then she pushed the door closed.

She stepped over what was left lying on the floor inside

the cell, and sat beside Charity again and said, 'What's happened? I saw Mummy yesterday, and she said you and Little Danny were getting on better and she was really happy about it.'

'Yes, we were. But after she'd left to see you, me and Little Danny had a belter of a row, as he suggested that perhaps we'd do better if we didn't live so close to everyone, and I said I couldn't live anywhere else. And he asked if that meant even if he wasn't there in Cadogan Terrace? I said yes, and he went out, slamming the door. So I went hoisting to make me feel better, but I didn't go up west, I tried Hatton Garden instead. And I got caught—'

'Oh, Charity, what the hell were you doing? Gold's never been your thing to thieve.'

'I was so angry with Little Danny that I couldn't think. But they wouldn't let me leave the jewellers, and they locked the door and the security metal came down, and I felt really strange and I can't remember much. And the police came, and there was a bit of a rumpus as I was so furious. And I was charged with affray and theft, and then contempt of court when I was before the magistrate this morning, as I just couldn't stop myself shouting, and bail was refused. And look—' Charity lifted her fringe to show her twin that she'd skinned her forehead, and it was swollen and weepy '—I was calling for you, and I think I banged my head a couple of times against this side of the door and

Hope

I might have been screaming, and the guards came in and pushed me onto the bed. And then it all goes a bit dark until you got here, and I suppose they fetched you . . .'

'Oh, I don't know what to say, Charity,' said Hope.

'I'm tired and my head hurts,' Charity whispered. 'If I lie down, will you lie with me?'

'Of course, sweet thing.'

They made themselves comfortable and Charity's breathing immediately slowed and she fell asleep.

Hope couldn't square in her mind what to make of it, as out of the three Wills sisters, in many ways Charity had seemed the calmest and least outrageous, and what she had just said she'd felt like earlier in the day was the first time Hope had heard anything like this.

But her twin was the one person in the world she didn't mind lying close to, and so Hope concentrated on holding Charity closely, and making sure Charity felt safe and loved should she wake up through the long night.

Over the next few days, Charity calmed down, although her face became very bruised and puffy. She was lethargic and nauseous, and sweaty too, but although her eyes swivelled oddly from side to side when she was tired, and now and again Hope thought that one of Charity's pupils was slightly larger than the other, she didn't seem out of control in the way she'd described she'd been in Hatton

Garden or in court. She was taken to the prison doctor twice as she'd become very anxious in the minutes Hope would be away to fetch their food, but the doctor seemed at a loss.

Hope was worried about her and thought she may have had a severe concussion as Charity's memory definitely seemed affected, and several times she screamed in the night and sleepwalked, things Hope had never seen her do before.

She tried not to show how concerned she felt to Charity, and so she encouraged her sister to focus on the good times and the things she liked. And so Hope heard a lot about Little Danny but she made sure never to look in the least bit bored.

Slowly Charity began to rally, and after a while the sisters even began to have a little fun, as they resuscitated the daft games they'd used to play as kids, back when they'd shared a bedroom in Senrab Street.

Little Danny was diligent in coming to the prison to see Charity, and a solicitor too, and Maria came on other occasions, as did Faith. Charity perked up after these visits, although there were days when she only wanted to lie on her bed and not eat or talk to Hope.

One day Charity returned to the cell after Little Danny had visited her to find Hope had received a letter that she'd been waiting for.

Hope

'What are you looking so pleased about?' she asked.

'I knew I'd be able to get out of here,' said Hope.

Charity's brow crinkled. 'Wait, how?'

'Two of my regulars at Chantal's were high court judges, although not together. And this letter tells me I've been granted my leave to appeal,' Hope explained. 'All I need now is the roster that puts these two old boys together with a member of the Court of Appeal, who will also be a judge, and that will then make up the panel of three judges I need.

'And so the day my case goes back to the Court of Appeal Criminal Division before them, these two subs will make sure the appeal is allowed and declare what happened at the Old Bailey a mistrial or else an unsafe conviction, and I'll be home free.'

'You jammy thing, you!' squealed Charity, almost as happy about it as Hope was. 'Good on you. Such great news. Who says there's not a silver lining in every cloud – it seems your work at Chantal's did have an upside after all as how else could you have met two high court judges?'

There was a silence, and then Charity asked, 'What did they like you to do to them?'

Hope spent the rest of the day grinning like a loon, to the point her cheeks ached when it was lights out and she was trying to get to sleep.

CHAPTER TWENTY-FIVE

'Between you, me and the gatepost—' Maria dropped her voice low to make sure that only Hope could hear her as there were other prisoners having their visits at nearby tables '—Tom tells me that there's been a shocking technology glitch, and it seems that a lot of what the police had regarding Charity's case has mysteriously been corrupted and is irretrievable from the system. And she's not the only one affected.'

'Cheeky bugger.' Hope understood without Maria having to say that Tom had done some manoeuvring behind the scenes.

'Isn't he?' Maria couldn't help but smile, even though usually she didn't like any idea of police corruption, but in the case of Charity, she was very grateful Tom had stepped in to help. 'Big Danny's had to promise a car to the person who did it, as it had to be dealt with across all the backup systems too and it was quite complicated to fudge it everywhere, and that was why the files to other cases had to go too, so it looked like a big data outage and not specific to Charity.'

Hope thought that there'd be some offenders who would see this as a piece of good luck if it made their cases collapse too.

Maria added, 'Big Danny also has sorted it at the Hatton Garden end, and paid them recompense, and so although the police have been in touch with them, they've said they are refusing to give evidence. And Charity's representation has told the CPS that she will be putting forward a not-guilty plea, and so as it was obvious they wouldn't be able to get a conviction without the police documents or the jeweller's evidence in court, it looked like Charity wouldn't have to stand trial for anything that happened inside the shop.

'Outside, it's a different matter. Originally there was her affray charge, but as this was only more or less a scuffle with the police as they pulled her from the shop to the police car, the indications are that this is going to be reduced to criminal damage as it was more a planter and a waste bin that got affected, rather than any officers being injured. It helps that apparently nobody saw anything, so they're having to keep it as a magistrates' court case as the judge will come down on them if it goes to the crown court,' said Maria.

Hope laughed, and said, 'Lucky nobody saw anything,

Hope

on a busy street in London in broad daylight, and all those jewellers in that street must have security CCTV – seems that Big Danny will have pulled a few more strings to get all those films out of the picture.'

'Yes, he's said it was hassle he could have done without. He's going to tell Charity she's got to behave herself from now on, or else Little Danny will have to deal with it next time,' Maria agreed. 'How is she?'

'She's in quite good spirits at the moment, as far as I can see, although I don't think she quite knows what tipped her to the space that started everything. Anyway, although she and Little Danny had had an argument, to me it didn't sound a deal-breaker. And although she's done a term inside before, this time I think Holloway has scared her, so she's saying she is keen to keep her nose clean from here and make sure it doesn't happen again,' said Hope.

'So if she gets into court this week, I think she'll go free, as they'll give her three months' imprisonment, and this is her sixth week here, and so that will be her done and dusted, with the time off for good behaviour. Holloway won't take into account how nuts she acted on the first day as she injured herself quite badly during that, and so they won't want that coming up in court when the screws should have prevented it.'

*

Sure enough, Charity went to the magistrates' court, and was given the three-month sentence and the good behaviour allowance exactly as Hope had predicted.

'Good luck, missus,' said Hope, as she hugged Charity before she left to go to attend her hearing. 'I'll see you soon back in Hackney, and we'll share a bottle of bubbly.'

'Thank you for looking after me, Hope. I couldn't have got through this stretch here without you.' A tear threatened to roll down Charity's cheek.

'Don't cry,' said Hope, as she hugged her sister. 'This is a happy day, remember.'

'Everything makes me cry at the moment.'

'Well, not today, as before you know it you'll be on your way home with Little Danny. And if you do, you'll ruin your make-up,' said Hope, knowing Charity would hate that, and Hope then more or less pushed her out of the cell, where a screw was waiting to escort her off the wing for the prison-to-court transport.

Not long after that, Hope was back in court herself, this time at the cathedral-like Royal Courts of Justice, with its soaring arches and stained-glass windows, which was on London's busy Strand thoroughfare that had a constant stream of red double-deckers and black cabs going by.

Her barrister presented the case for the appeal to the judges, and there was a response on behalf of the prosecution. The judges left the court and returned in two hours.

Hope

It could not have gone more smoothly, one of her subs on the dais before her even risking a daring lightning-quick wink at Hope as he and the other two judges came back following their deliberations.

Sure enough, Hope's conviction had been overturned, and she could walk out of court that day a free woman.

Hope and her barrister, followed by everyone else who lived at Cadogan Terrace who had been watching the proceedings from the public gallery, walked across the dramatic mosaic marble floor in the reception area, Hope's stilettos making a satisfying clatter on the tiles, and out through the wooden doors.

Outside the press was waiting, and at the kerb beyond Hope could see Bud standing beside a taxi, ready to take her away.

'I have a few words for you,' said Hope, looking straight at the cameras of the TV crews as she spoke without notes.

'This case was never really about me, but was more about the establishment's disapproval of women who service men's sexuality. You, the press, were biased in this way, and so were the judiciary and the police, and in turn this biased the jury. But an establishment like Chantal's wouldn't exist if men didn't want and need to act out their deepest desires, and I saw precious little attention paid to *that* from commentators and the press during and following my trial at the Old Bailey. The assumption seemed to be that I should feel ashamed of how I spent my time, and that although I hadn't been involved in the actual crime, still that I needed to pay, and moreover pay with a lengthy sentence, and frankly I deserved what I got. But I am not in any way ashamed of anything that I did for money, and neither should any woman be who is involved in sex work.

'Moreover, the lurid details of how the establishment Chantal's operated was used to obliterate the memory of the wonderful person that Alice Smith, known as Chantal, was. I miss her every day, and I feel privileged to have known her. And I have sympathy for a man like Harry Stewart, her killer – his story is not a warning to other people over how things can escalate at a BDSM parlour, but more an indictment over the way society does its best to ignore those with mental health problems in our midst. I would like to think lessons have been learned through Harry's case, but I suspect they have not been.

'Thank you – that is all I have to say. I will not answer further questions or make any subsequent comment.'

Hope strode right through the middle of the journalists with her head high, ignoring the clamour of their calls to her, and climbed into the taxi where Bud was holding the door open for her.

'Good going, Hope,' he said. 'Where to?'

Hope

'Yours for a bit, so I can decompress. And then I'll go home later, as I don't want this rabble following me to Hackney. Is that OK?'

Bud nodded and told the taxi driver to drive on, and the cab did a U-turn to head to west London, and Hope leaned back in her seat and closed her eyes. It felt good to be outside of prison and a courtroom again.

CHAPTER TWENTY-SIX

The next evening there was a party at the house in Cadogan Terrace to celebrate Hope's release. It was held in Charity and Little Danny's flat, as that had the biggest entertaining space.

'What now, gal?' Big Danny asked Hope at the time in the party when everyone was starting to become relaxed and just a little well oiled.

'A rest – I feel I could sleep for ever, and then Charity and Little Danny have asked me to go to the timeshare with them,' answered Hope. 'After that, I'm not so sure, other than my days of being a mistress are well and truly over. I don't want to rush a decision.'

Big Danny's wife Lisa came over and said, 'I'm liking the new look, Hope. It suits you.'

Hope was wearing a drapey and boxy petrol-blue silk shirt, and palazzo trousers the same colour but in wool, with Gucci loafers made from a suede soft as butter. She had ended up sleeping over at Bud's, and even made it to a bed this time, although not with him. It had been an expensive visit to Harvey Nichols on the way home, but Hope felt pleased that she had paid for every item herself.

She looked down, and said, 'Yeah, thanks, Lisa. You know – new times, new life, new me. Well, it might not last, but it's fine for now. Feels odd though not to be full goth when at home.'

'Well, you look much more than fine,' said Lisa, and she pulled Hope to her for a hug.

Bud arrived at the same time as Father O'Reilly and Shamus, and clearly he liked what he saw when he caught sight of Hope, especially when up close he noticed that Hope was wearing the jet-stone pendant he'd given her.

But before he could say anything, Big Danny came over and greeted Bud, and it wasn't long before they were standing in a corner deep in conversation.

At the other end of the room Little Danny and Charity were overseeing some food coming out of the oven, and Maria went over, saying to them, 'I can do that. You two go and enjoy yourselves.'

'Thank you, Mummy, that would be good,' Charity said. She turned to Little Danny, 'Come on, you, let's grab that sofa while we can. And you can choose some music.'

Maria watched them head towards the sound system, Little Danny following obediently. He still appeared to be

Hope

a bit cautious of Charity, but things between them were looking reasonably hopeful, Maria thought.

She turned around to lift the quiche from the oven, and found Shamus with a folded tea towel as he reached down to lift it out.

Maria smiled. 'Let me get a board for you to put that on.'

She was never quite sure what happened next, but as she put down the board on the worktop, somehow her and Shamus's hands touched, and she felt a jolt of electricity right to her very core. It was so intense that it verged on the painful. Maria jumped, and then she froze. She didn't know what to do. Or what it meant.

Shamus's eyes found hers for what may have been the very first time, and she noticed they were sea-green.

She heard him take a breath as if to muster his courage, and as silently she implored him not to say anything, Shamus stuttered, 'I'm sorry, Maria, I didn't mean to startle you. But you must know how I feel about you. I'd—'

'No, I don't know. And I don't want to!' she cried and she saw Shamus's face fold in on itself instantly, and brusquely she pushed past him to get to the French doors to the garden terrace, her hand fumbling with the handle.

Outside, there was nobody in the garden although Maria could hear Tom telling a risqué joke from the other side of the door as she stood with her back against the cool bricks of the wall, making sure she was out of sight of the partygoers, breathing deeply as she tried to calm the racing of her blood.

Eventually Hope came outside and said, 'Is everything OK? I saw Shamus say something to you, and you push him out of the way, and then he left immediately. Did he say something rude to you?'

'He's gone?' Maria asked as her heart dipped unexpectedly.

'Um, yes, he has. Is there something going on I should know? Do I need to get Father O'Reilly?'

'No, Hope, absolutely not. Nothing happened, nothing at all. I just needed some fresh air, that's all.'

Hope's face told her mother that she didn't believe a word of what she had said.

While Maria and Hope were speaking, Faith stood in Charity and Little Danny's bedroom, taking a telephone call from Ted's solicitor.

'Miss Wills, I'm afraid I have some very bad news for you. Early this afternoon Mr Edward Walton had a cardiac arrest at his house. His cleaner found him and called an ambulance, but he was pronounced dead on his arrival at hospital,' the solicitor told a dumbstruck Faith.

'Oh . . .' Faith felt the loss of Ted as a punch in her guts.

Hope

'The thing is, Miss Wills, I need to message you a document tonight. In it will be instructions to be followed first thing tomorrow. Would that be possible? Mr Walton was very insistent I ask you to do this, and that I contact you as soon as possible upon his death.'

'Um, yes, I'm not at home right now, but I have a fax so send it there.' And Faith gave the solicitor her personal facsimile number.

She sat down on the bed and gathered her thoughts. Ted's death felt a real loss to her and she realised that even though he'd only been in her life a short time, and even though he was the father of the monstrous Fred, Ted had in many ways become the father figure in life that she'd always wanted. She was so glad that she had got to know him and Martina before they had died.

Faith got up and left the bedroom. The party was now in full swing, and so she decided not to break the mood and announce what had happened to Ted, not even to Maria. She couldn't actually see her mother, which was probably just as well.

'Tom, we need to go,' she told him.

'Really?' he said. 'It's just kicking off.'

She stared at him.

'OK, OK, I get it,' he said.

And as they left, what they didn't know was that Maria was staring out of the window from her own flat upstairs.

After that moment with Shamus, whatever that was, she hadn't wanted to be at the party any longer either.

But up in her room, as she watched Faith and Tom get into the Peugeot, Maria hoped they were sneaking off to have some wild sex, not that she thought Faith was the type for abandonment really. But Tom might be, and Maria hoped that Faith wouldn't exclude that side of things from her life as she seemed to have up to now.

For what that single brush against Shamus's hand told Maria was that despite the hundreds of men she'd had sex with, she had never countenanced that a nice man might find her attractive, or she him, and this made her realise how much she had been missing out on over all those years.

Faith and Tom didn't go to her flat and have wild sex.

Instead they sat up for hours talking through what the fax from Ted's solicitor might mean.

It told her to go to the bank where she had dropped Ted off on Piccadilly. Faith must take with her three forms of identification, and if the bank agreed that she was who she claimed to be, she would then be given a safe deposit box key. The box would be in the vaults at the bank, and in a private room someone at the bank would take her to, she must open the box immediately, and she must take somebody she trusted along with her for protection in case

Hope

she wanted to remove any items. The bank had already been faxed and should be expecting her. She should take a zip-up bag with her in case she decided to take away any of the items she found.

It was all very cloak and dagger, and Tom thought the zip-up bag was to deter any random pickpockets and so there might be things of value in the box.

First thing the next morning Faith and Tom both called in sick for work, saying they couldn't come in, and they were therefore waiting outside the bank when it opened.

Faith made it through the bank's security checks although it took a long while, and she could see Tom on the point of dozing off as he sat in a squishy leather chair to wait for her. Then she was handed an envelope that contained the promised key, and after Tom had provided evidence of his own identity, which he did with his driving licence and police warrant card, the second causing a raised eyebrow from the person checking the documents, and they had both been photographed for the bank's peace of mind, a man in a burgundy blazer led them downstairs to a small room.

'I shall get the security box and bring it back to this room. You will watch me unlock the first lock, after which I will leave the room, and you can then unlock the second lock, and this will open the box and enable you to see the contents,' the man explained.

He left them for a few minutes, and then returned with the safe deposit box and put it on the table, which had a top of green baize. 'You can take the contents of the box with you, or leave them in the box. This box is yours now, Miss Wills, and only you can open it in the future. You can spend as long as you need to in this room. When you are finished, you may press this buzzer and I will come back to you,' he said.

After she had said thank you and the man had left, Faith realised that she felt nervous. She looked at the ring on the ring finger of her right hand that Martina had given her, and Ted had wanted her to keep. The diamonds sparkled, and Faith thought Ted wouldn't have left anything unpleasant in the box for her to find.

Would he?

Tom kissed her cheek, and said, 'I'm here, so go on, Faith.'

The key turned easily in the lock, and she lifted the lid.

Inside was a letter and various packages wrapped in brown paper, one uneven in shape and another squarer, and one that was soft. There was also a black velvet bag with a drawstring, and another envelope. The letter said:

Hope

My dear Faith,

Now that Martina has died, it is important to me that I make sure that you have some security against Fred. If you are reading this, it means I am dead too, and in turn this means he will be a free agent, and who knows how he will react to that. As one can never predict how or when or where death arrives, I felt strongly that you should read this letter and have these things quickly, in case Fred is with me when I die, as he may go immediately rogue.

I hope sincerely he has no idea of who you are or any details about you. Martina and I have tried very hard to make sure of this.

But in case not, in one of the parcels, there is a gun.

It was used by Fred in a murder that is still unsolved in Wakefield of a man called Bill Perkins, which happened eight years ago – it has Fred's prints on it, and some of Fred's blood, and also the blood and prints of the victim, as there was a fight with a knife and then a scuffle over the gun. I know this because I was there, and I took away the gun when I left, along with a bloody T-shirt of Fred's that he wore during the crime (also in the safe deposit box for you) that would have gun residue and other forensic evidence.

I have stored the gun and the T-shirt in a safe in a lock-up ever since in a manner a forensic scientist told me was best for preserving evidence. In the safe in the lock-up also are some other weapons. The other envelope in the box has instructions of how to find the lock-up should you want to, as well as the keys to it and the combination of the safe.

But this gun and T-shirt give you decent leverage against Fred, as at heart he is a coward, as most bullies are. He is also quite stupid, but he does have the odd flash of intelligence, so take care not to underestimate him. I hope you never need to use this leverage, of course.

The other envelope contains cash, which I would like you to give to Maria – it is one hundred thousand pounds, and came honestly from customers to my bookies. I know she will not be expecting it after the money she had for the women's refuge, but I would very much like her to have it, so she can do something with it that's just for her and that hopefully will make her happy. It will be up to your discretion when to give it to her.

The bag of jewellery is for you – it is extremely valuable and does not come from any crimes (by this, I mean that it was all acquired perfectly legally by me, and none of it was ever stolen goods). I would have liked to leave you some property, but I think Fred might

Hope

get wind of that, so the house and business properties have been left to him, mostly. It is safer for everyone therefore if he never knows if you were even born after Maria left Wakefield. The jewellery has never been insured and I long ago destroyed all paper records of it – I felt it sensible to have assets I could liquify if I needed to, assets that Fred didn't know about, and jewellery seemed the most sensible way of funnelling this money, as Martina could just wear it out of the country without questions being asked if we needed to leave.

I hope this all makes sense, and I am not placing you in any sort of difficult or awkward situation, but you feel more, as the Bible says, that to be forewarned is to be forearmed.

Yours, in gratitude for the sunlight
you've brought to our lives,
Ted Walton

Faith had to read the letter through twice before she could take on board all its implications.

It, and the contents of the box, made Ted's death seem real to Faith in a way that it hadn't the night before when the solicitor had telephoned her.

It also made Faith realise that now Ted was no longer alive, there was absolutely nothing and no one to stand in her way of her going after Fred. She'd understood that in a remote, almost academic sense from the call with the solicitor, but now she knew and embraced it from her heart.

Every time Faith saw Maria's face she always thought that she would make Fred pay for what he had done. And Maria had told Faith about Fred's current girlfriend Anna, and her being the first woman in the refuge, even though it was still yet to open, while Ted had described how despicable Fred had been on the last visit he made to Wakefield while Martina was alive.

A man like that, well, he deserved whatever he got, was Faith's reasoning.

She didn't know where Fred was, and she had to make sure that Maria never got wind of what she was thinking.

She needed time to plan things carefully.

Faith looked at Tom, who was gently chucking the package of Maria's money from hand to hand as if to see how much one hundred thousand pounds in used notes weighed.

'Fuck me, Faith,' he said softly, shaking his head in amazement at what he was looking at.

'Perhaps that can happen later, Tom. But for now, I'm going to leave everything here, as I need to think seriously about the implications and what needs to be done,' she told him.

Hope

Carefully she put everything back in the box, including Ted's letter. And then she closed the lid and locked it.

At a press on the buzzer, the man in the burgundy jacket came back in, and she watched him turn his lock, and then she went with him and observed him slide the box into a huge bank of boxes on the other side of a security door.

As she and Tom walked down the corridor towards the bank itself, Tom looked at Faith and nudged his shoulder against hers as he asked, 'Did you mean it about the "later" bit?'

'Maybe.'

'The Ritz is nearby and I bet they have a room,' he said. 'Just saying.'

CHAPTER TWENTY-SEVEN

Ten days later Hope was in Marbella with Little Danny and Charity. Although it wasn't yet Easter, it was a warm night, and they were on the terrace of a nice restaurant, with a large gas heater nearby they could ask the waiter to light for them if they felt cold.

Since those six weeks of sharing a cell together in Holloway, Hope and Charity felt the closest they had been to each other since they were teenagers. They, and Little Danny, were enjoying their break at Big Danny's timeshare.

As they relaxed, Hope reflected quite often on Ted Walton.

She had been sorry to see Faith, and to some extent her mother too, upset at the news of Ted's passing. She'd never met him. His son sounded a twat, and he had been happy to let Annie service his illegal gamblers. But the fact Faith and, oddly, Maria were sorry he wasn't around any longer suggested he probably had more to him than might be assumed with a thumbnail sketch, Hope thought. And Big Danny was used to reading people, and he'd seemed impressed by Ted. When he heard what had happened, he said it was a shocker, but on the upside, Ted had had the good timing to put something big his – Big Danny's – way before he'd passed.

As they waited for their food in the restaurant, Charity said she was really pleased Hope had decided to lay aside for good her whip and paddle, and Hope teased her by saying that Charity shouldn't get too excited as she might think up something even more outrageous to do with her time.

'If Bud divorces his wife and marries you, then that would be quite wild,' Little Danny said, his face a picture of innocence that was spoilt by a twinkle in his eye.

'That is not the sort of relationship we have,' Hope muttered through slightly gritted teeth as it wasn't the first time she'd heard him make this sort of insinuation.

'That's what they all say.' And Little Danny dodged her swipe as he got up and went to the balustrade, where he lit a cigarette as Charity couldn't abide the smell of it so close to her at the supper table.

The sisters listened in as a middle-aged man on the table next to them tried to impress a much younger date by bragging about a make of car she'd clearly never heard of.

Hope

Hope whispered in Charity's ear, 'Clearly a Brit. And punching above his weight.'

'I suppose he's rich,' Charity murmured back, 'but she couldn't look more bored if she tried.'

'Not everyone is love's young dream like you and Little Danny.'

Charity pushed herself back a little from Hope and firmly changed the subject. 'What do you reckon on that guy Shamus? Father O'Reilly asked if he could bring him, but I doubt he was there more than a quarter of an hour. And then the father was looking for him everywhere.'

'I thought he looked all right. But I think Mummy and he disagreed over something, although she wouldn't tell me what,' said Hope.

'You don't think . . .'

'No! Not our Maria. Never . . .'

They watched the waiter place the Carabinero shrimp starters in front of them. They looked delicious, oozing with butter and with garlic wafting upwards through the sprinkled fresh parsley. A large bowl of lemon quarters was put in the middle of the table, and some bowls of water to rinse their fingers in as they took the shells off the shrimps.

Charity looked at hers, and wrinkled her nose, saying, 'I'll be back in a minute.'

Hope watched her head to the Servicio de Señoras. Whatever bug Charity had picked up in Holloway was still making its presence felt.

An overly tanned man in a loud shirt and lots of gold rings stopped at the table next door and said in a Liverpool accent to the man who'd been talking about the car, 'Fred, what the fuck are you doing here? My dad is in Yorkshire for Ted's funeral tomorrow. Out of anyone, you should be there, no?'

Fred shrugged. 'Didn't fancy it.'

As Little Danny returned to the table, Hope stood up.

'Something I said?' he asked looking at her and Charity's empty chair.

'I won't be a min, Dan. Charity's in the ladies'.'

'Ach, not again.'

At the podium of the maître d', Hope asked where there was a telephone as she had an urgent call to make to the UK. She'd left her mobile phone back at the timeshare.

'We don't have one expressly for the public. But as your companions are regulars, you can use the one in the office,' she was told.

That gave Hope an idea.

'I don't suppose you could tell me if that man on the table next to us is a regular too?'

She knew she was pushing her luck asking this, as

exclusive restaurants like this one were all about the privacy of their clients.

Even here it seemed that Big Danny had tendrils of power, for then the maître d' added, 'But, señora, I'm not telling you he's *not* a regular.'

With two negatives making a positive, this was enough for Hope. She said, 'He should have tipped you better, shouldn't he?' And as she walked off, she heard the maître d' chuckle.

The office was empty, and Hope made sure to shut the door, just in case any flappy ears were nearby.

She rang Faith's mobile.

'Well, Faith, it's a waste of time you being up in Wakefield, hoping Fred Walton is there for his father's funeral. There can't be too many men of the right age called Fred, with a father called Ted, who is having a funeral in Yorkshire tomorrow,' Hope told her sister. 'And one of them is sitting right now at the table next to us in Marbella . . .'

To be continued . . .

ACKNOWLEDGEMENTS

Firstly, a big thank you to Jenny Parrot. Jenny has allowed me to explore this amazing new world of drama on the page, and my journey is all the better for it. I started these books with the help and guidance of my literary agent, Kerr MacRae, and we have watched together as my thoughts and ideas have come to life on the page. He keeps me on the straight and narrow and makes sure we make every right move along the way. To my publishers, Mountain Leopard Press at Headline, a massive thank-you for all your hard work behind and in front of the scenes. To my editor Beth Wickington for her advice and enthusiasm, and to Jenni Edgecombe for editorial support. To Marta Juncosa, Phoebe Khalid and Isabelle Wilson for marketing and publicising my books to get them in to readers' hands. Thanks too to Dominic Gribben for creating the wonderful audiobook. Finally, a big thank-you to you, the readers. Your response to my new-found life has been amazing. The incredible reviews for my stories make it all worthwhile.

RAISING READERS
Books Build Bright Futures

Dear Reader,

We'd love your attention for one more page to tell you about the crisis in children's reading, and what we can all do.

Studies have shown that reading for fun is the **single biggest predictor of a child's future success** – more than family circumstance, parents' educational background or income. It improves academic results, mental health, wealth, communication skills and ambition.

The number of children reading for fun is in rapid decline. Young people have a lot of competition for their time, and a worryingly high number do not have a single book at home.

Our business works extensively with schools, libraries and literacy charities, but here are some ways we can all raise more readers:

- Reading to children for just 10 minutes a day makes a difference
- Don't give up if your children aren't regular readers – there will be books for them!
- Visit bookshops and libraries to get recommendations
- Encourage them to listen to audiobooks
- Support school libraries
- Give books as gifts

Thank you for reading.
www.JoinRaisingReaders.com